EYE AND EAR

For *King* or *P*
in their own day, and i

On the eve of the Battle of Edgehill both sides thought the war would be over by Christmas, followed by a negotiated settlement. Nobody foresaw two successive civil wars, the execution of Charles I, the rise of the Levellers, a Commonwealth government or a third civil war.

Army intelligence was sparse, maps unreliable, newsletters biased and the political and religious situation fluid. Communications relied on bad roads but good horses, and despatches from London could reach York in 20 hours and Edinburgh in three days.

Quotations are taken from letters, despatches, diaries, memoirs and 'true relations', written at the time or shortly after. Joshua Sprigge's *Anglia Rediviva* appeared in 1647, Clarendon's *History* finished in 1671 was not published until 1702, Aubrey's *Brief Lives* in 1696 and the *Memoires of the Reigne of King Charles I* by Philip Warwick in 1701. The *Memoirs of Colonel Hutchinson - written by his Widow Lucy* appeared in 1806, Henry Slingsby's *Diary* in 1836 and Nehemiah Wharton's *Letters* in 1853. The *Thomason Tracts* were purchased by the British Museum in 1866.

by the same author

Ring the Bells of London Town   Terence Dalton Ltd
Lord Mayors of London - 800 years   Comerford & Miller
Slay Us a Dragon   AnnaBooks

-i-

Published by **Partizan Press**
26 Cliffsea Grove, Leigh on Sea,
Essex SS9 INQ

Copyright © Anna Milford 1992
Kent Edge, Crockham Hill, Edenbridge, Kent TN8 6TA

Cover design and map artwork
Central Print Design, Westerham, Kent TN16 1AL

crc. illustrations & colour cover film positive
The Advertising Designers, Fircroft Way, Edenbridge TN8 6EJ

Printed and bound in Great Britain by
Hobbs the Printers Ltd, Millbrook, Southampton SO9 2UZ

ISBN 0-946525-95-1

EYE AND EAR WITNESSES

350th Anniversary of the English Civil War

Anna Milford

'... an unparallel'd violation acted upon the Parliament on Monday last by a Multitude from your City ... I am assur'd from Eye and Ear-Witnesses, that divers of the Common Council greatly encouraged it.'   1647 July.
Sir Thomas Fairfax to the Lord Mayor.

THE CIVIL WAR

1642-1651
350th
ANNIVERSARY

Partizan Press

ACKNOWLEDGEMENTS

Alfred, who nobly trudged round castles and battlefields, and Simon and Paul who have already seen and heard more than enough about the English Civil War.

Magnus Magnusson for masterminding the Foreword.

The Marquis of Northampton and the trustees of the Tabley House Collection, Manchester, for the splendid portraits of Sir William Compton and John, Lord Byron. James Morton of Sotheby's and Peter Clayton of Seabys for providing information and photographs of Charles I coinage, and John Ryan of the Royal Mail.

Sarah Kemp, National Portrait Gallery; Cathy McDermott, Royal Armouries; Julian Humphrys, National Army Museum; Michael Barrett, National Maritime Museum for their help and interest with pictures and information.

Clare Lyall, the Commandery, Worcester; Peter Dix, Edgehill Battle Museum; Jonathon Taylor, the English Civil War Society; the English Tourist Board; English Heritage.

The London Library for the extended loan of rare books no other library would let out of their sight; Westerham and Oxted Libraries; Jane Tweedy; Claire Berg; Helen Long; Darenth Writers; John Dawes, STAG, Society of Authors.

Michael Wortley, Central Print Design; Colin Harrington, Advertising Designers. Dave Ryan, Partizan Press; Peter Radburn, Hobbs the Printer.

CONTENTS

ILLUSTRATIONS

ILLUSTRATIONS -2-

ILLUSTRATIONS -3-

Grateful acknowledgement is made for permission to reproduce
many interesting and unusual portraits and other pictures to
enhance the text, and these are credited in italics. Those marked
AM were taken by the author. (EH) = *English Heritage* properties

Thanks also to the *English Tourist Board* for permission
to use the Civil War logo on the title page.

FOREWORD

MAGNUS MAGNUSSON KBE

"You have two minutes, starting now - what is a 'swine's feather'?"

What indeed! Seventeen years after taking part in **Mastermind**, the English Civil War is still Anna Milford's 'special subject'; and she vividly remembers my first question and, after a time-wasting pause, her correct answer: "A sharpened stake used by infantry to repel cavalry."

The 350th anniversary of the battle of Edgehill falls this year, but if the Black Chair would fit into a time capsule we would transport it back to 1644, a time when the outcome of the conflict was still in the balance:

"Tonight beneath the Rubens ceiling of the Banqueting House in London we welcome not four, but six contenders in this year's final. Who will carry off the title - indeed, the crown - in this life and death struggle almost within the shadow of Parliament and the Palace of Whitehall?"

The six contenders would be: King Charles I on 'Van Dyck's Portraits'; Sir John Gell on 'Plunder and Pillage', Lady Sussex on 'English Spelling'; Prince Rupert of the Rhine on 'Historic Cavalry Charges'; Sergeant Nehemiah Wharton on 'The Life of a London Apprentice'; Sir Thomas Fairfax on 'Blood Lines in Horse Breeding'; and Mr Oliver Cromwell, of Huntingdon, on 'Political Leaders'.

"But what's the use of **Mastermind**?" the critics cry.

An unusual book such as *Eye and Ear Witnesses* is one good answer. But anybody who dips into its pages and has cherished views on the rights and wrongs of King and Parliament, Cavaliers and Roundheads, had best be warned. They might find them overturned by the testimony of those who saw and heard it all.

Glasgow
May 1992

Magnus Magnusson

-ix-

THE CIVIL WAR 1642-51
fought between the forces of KING
& PARLIAMENT: *Pikeman*

THE CIVIL WAR 1642-51
fought between the forces of KING
& PARLIAMENT: *Drummer*

THE CIVIL WAR 1642-51
fought between the forces of KING
& PARLIAMENT: *Musketeer*

THE CIVIL WAR 1642-51
fought between the forces of KING
& PARLIAMENT: *Standard Bearer*

350th Anniversary

1

OVERTURE TO WAR

On 23 October 1642 two English armies confronted each other in the very heart of the kingdom in the first pitched battle since the Wars of the Roses ended on the bloody field of Bosworth in 1485.

The quarrel between King and Parliament had flared into open hostility when the Commons met in 1640 after the 'Eleven Years Tyranny'. It had been no such thing, but the country gentlemen, prosperous merchants and ambitious lawyers now back in the House were determined to remain there until their legitimate grievances were redressed.

Since the dissolution of 1629 the King had ruled through his counsellors, Lords and bishops. Money was raised by taxes, customs dues, cuts from monopolies on anything from wine to starch, and forced loans, benevolences was the 17th century weasel word. These were frequently demanded of the City of London, but seldom repaid.

Unparliamentary government might have long continued had the King not appointed William Laud, Archbishop of Canterbury in 1636, and the pair of them not 'inter-meddled' with religion. Between them they alienated both Puritans and moderate Anglicans by their innovations and leniency to Catholic priests, the latter in marked contrast to the harsh penalties inflicted on Protestant preachers and Puritan lecturers.

The terror of the Spanish Armada and Gunpowder Plot were within living memory, and papal urgings to English catholics to murder their sovereigns had lost nothing in the telling to the next generation. Few now expected a continental invasion, but the influence of the Vatican, a foreign power, and the tactless behaviour of the French Catholic Queen, fuelled the already simmering fear and suspicion of the papist Irish.

The folly of King and Archbishop led to two humiliating 'Bishops' Wars', a Scots army of occupation encamped around Newcastle and the inevitable calling of a Parliament to buy it off.

Early legislation by the Long Parliament proved a watershed in English constitutional government, and broke for ever the absolute power of the monarchy. Several major Acts were passed, among them no taxation without lawful consent, no arbitrary dissolution of the Houses and any armed forces raised to be under Parliamentary control.

In November 1641 the Grand Remonstrance was passed after fiery debate, and by the narrowest of majorities. It was an immensely long catalogue of grievances, many genuine if exaggerated, that the nation had endured under the King's arbitrary rule, and calling for radical reform.

The Remonstrance was followed by a second momentous event in January 1642. With armed guards at his back, the King breached the age-old privilege of Parliament by entering the Commons to arrest the 'Five Members', John Pym, John Hampden, Arthur Haselrig, William Strode and Denzil Holles, men he regarded as ringleaders of the House. Had he succeeded triumph would have obliterated the outrage, but, forewarned, the five escaped to the City by river minutes before his arrival.

It was a turning point. Those who felt opposition politicians had gone too far and should be curbed before stability and the social order were overturned, reverted to unswerving allegiance to the King, headed by Edward Hyde and Lord Falkland. Others battled on, headed by Pym and Hampden, convinced that Charles Stuart was untrustworthy and would revoke all Parliament's constitutional changes once the Scots crisis, and the brewing Irish revolt, were over.

Men holding identical views on bishops, papists, and the 'King's evil counsellors' would be sharply divided on the key issue of the King's good faith, and fight on opposing sides. Others, antagonistic in rank and religion, would become uncongenial allies under the same banner.

Despite a fanciful theory that 1642 heralded the last fling of the medieval barons, the Civil War no more a class war, a social uprising, than had been the wresting of Magna Carta from King John by the overmighty barons four hundred years earlier. Nor was it primarily a religious one.

At the outset it was essentially a contest for political power within the broad acres of the ruling class. Later the Levellers and the Diggers sprouted from the ranks of the New Model Army, causing acute disquiet to both sides with their unwelcome creed of social equality, extension of the male suffrage, and a primitive agrarian communism.

The majority of the House of Lords sided with the King through loyalty or self-interest; two thirds of the peerage owed their titles to the Stuart monarchy, and the price of baronetcies had sunk to a mere £400.

The austere Sir Marmaduke Langdale is a death's head at the Cavalier feast while the dashing Earl of Warwick commanded the Parliamentary fleet. Lord Goring's troops were as notorious for indiscipline as the Roundheads of Sir John Gell, his equal as drunkard and lecher.

The London merchants and burgesses of provincial towns who had the vote, were for Parliament. So too most tradesmen, craftsmen, and shopkeepers, and many small farmers. The Anglican clergy mainly supported their anointed sovereign while many Roman Catholics, grateful for his toleration, officered his army. Some local gentry drew up agreements to avoid the conflict, but servants, retainers and tenant farmers had no choice but to follow their landlords and countless simple folk fought and died for their King, brave but bewildered.

Stuart women did not swoon at the first sound of trumpets. With besiegers at their gates neither the husband of the Countess of Derby at Lathom House or of Lady Brilliana Harley at Bampford Castle hastened home in arms. Derby spent most of the War on his hereditary island of Man and Sir Robert Harley fought his wordy battles at Westminster.

John Milton, although for Parliament, wrote a tactful poem on martial valour, 'Captain, or Colonel or Knight in arms', and nailed it to his London door to appease looters. The more practical John Evelyn locked up his Deptford home and went abroad 'for the duration where he spent much time in Paris enjoying the hospitality of his father-in-law, Charles's I's ambassador. 'A plague on both your houses' summed up many people's frustrations, among them Dr Plumtre of Nottingham, for 'what is the Cause to me if my goods be lost?'

As in any long war the objectives, and the commanders, at the outset were not those as its conclusion.

At Edgehill the Cavaliers under the King and Lord Forth faced the army of Parliament led by the Earl of Essex. At Marston Moor Prince Rupert and the Earl of Newcastle were opposed by Lord Manchester, Lord

Fairfax and the Scots, Lord Leven and David Leslie. By 1645 the King and Prince Rupert were defeated by the New Model Army under the Lord General Thomas Fairfax at Naseby,

The Parliamentarians believed their opponents fairly beaten in the field by 1646, and when all hopes of peace foundered and Royalist uprisings in 1648 led to the Second Civil War it was fought, in the perceptive words of a modern historian, by 'tired and angry men' with less chivalry and greater ruthlessness.

At Preston in 1648 the Duke of Hamilton and Sir Marmaduke Langdale were routed by Cromwell, Maidstone and Colchester fell to fairfax, and in January 1649 Charles I was beheaded in Whitehall.

There were two major battles in the Third Civil War. At Dunbar in September 1650 Cromwell's out-numbered army defeated the Scots led by David Leslie, and at Worcester in 1651 he destroyed the last Royalist army under Charles II and the second Duke of Hamilton. The duke died of his wounds, but the young King escaped eventually to France.

Dunbar and Worcester were fought on 3 September, and on that same day in 1658 died Oliver Cromwell, Lord Protector of England.

Charles II had been crowned in Scotland in 1651, and on his birthday in May 1660 he rode into the London he had last seen as a child in 1642. England welcomed his return as a practical, peaceful and popular solution to twenty years of conflict, but he entered the capital as a constitutional monarch, not as a conqueror. His Restoration left no-one unaware, least of all Charles, that it was due to men who had first drawn their swords against his father in the name of 'King and Parliament.'

He had returned from Holland aboard the *Royal Charles*, the repainting scarcely dry over *Naseby*, and there were equally sharp reminders of the past at his English coronation. Prominent in the procession was the Earl of Manchester, Parliamentary commander at Marston Moor, while the King's mount came from Thomas Fairfax's Yorkshire stud, bred from the chestnut mare the Lord General had ridden at Naseby.

14

2

BACKGROUND TO BATTLE

Cavaliers & Roundheads

'Caballeros', corrupted to cavaliers, were the despised but fearsome Spanish cavalry, and 'roundheads' were the riotous crop-haired apprentices of the City of London.

At the outset both these epithets were terms of abuse but the former was soon proudly adopted by the Royalist troops. The King himself remarked that 'the valour of Cavaliers hath honoured that name ... it signifying no more than a gentleman serving his King on horseback.'

'When puritanism grew into a faction the zealots distinguished themselves, by affectations of habit, looks and words ... few of the puritans what degree soever, wore their hair long enough to cover their ears, and cut it close round their heads with so many little peaks as was something ridiculous to behold ... from this custom that name of round-head became the scornful term given to the whole parliament party, whose army indeed marched out as if they had only been sent out till their hair was grown.'

Lucy Hutchinson's description applied only to the trained band recruits of 1642, because few officers of Parliament at any stage referred to themselves as Roundheads. 'Two or three years after any stranger would have inquired the reason of that name,' she continued. 'It was very ill applied to Mr Hutchinson, who, having naturally a very fine thickset head of hair kept it clean and handsome, so that it was a great ornament to him, although the godly of those days, would not allow him to be religious because his hair was not in their cut.'

Denzil Holles' jibe that most Parliamentary 'colonels are tradesmen, brewers, tailors, goldsmiths, shoemakers and the like' was also wide of the mark. Nine of the thirty seven commanders of the New Model were of the nobility, twenty one were gentlemen and only seven of humble birth, Men like Hewson, Pride and Okey could rise from ranks on merit in the 1640s, but after the Restoration promotion by purchase became customary and continued on into the armies of Marlborough and Wellington.

Ship Money

The Civil War was almost a case of 'for want of a nail', or rather, for want of 31s.6d' the kingdom was lost.'

An annual Ship Money tax was levied on maritime counties to pay for the upkeep of the Fleet. In 1635 the King extended the tax nationwide, ordering Sheriffs and Justices to deliver the moneys to the Admiralty. Under threat of invasion this was acceptable 'for if we lose the dominion of the seas, we lie open to all dangers ... {and} to preserve our trade which enriched inland as well as maritime places, by the vent {sale} of wool, lead and other commodities.' But there was no threat, the tax was levied without the consent of Parliament, so where would it end, men demanded? Even so, most of them did pay up, if slowly and reluctantly.

However, in 1636 John Hampden MP refused on principle to pay his assessment of 31s.6d. Lord Saye and Sele also refused, but the King's advisers recommended the prosecution of the commoner. The case was followed avidly, and final judgement for the crown by only seven of the twelve judges proved a hollow triumph for the royal authority.

'No taxation without representation' cast a long shadow before it, one that stretched across the Atlantic to the American colonies.

Commissions of Array & the Militia Ordinances

Charles I's sister had married the Elector Palatine, and in 1618 the misguided couple had accepted, and been swiftly ejected from, the disputed throne of Bohemia, losing at the same time their Rhineland principality. Prince Rupert was born in Prague, but Prince Maurice in exile in The Hague where their father died in 1632.

English and Scottish soldiers fought and died to regain the Palatinate for their brother, Charles Louis, with no military or financial encouragement from Charles I, his uncle. 'How lives the Lady Elizabeth?' stormed the Earl of Bristol. 'We have been like the broken staff of Egypt to all that have relied upon us. The distress of our friends lies before us.'

Two of Thomas Fairfax's uncles died fighting for the Princes's cause, and when Rupert occupied his Yorkshire home at Denton before Marston Moor and saw their portraits, he forbad all plundering.

By 1625 the Anglo-Scots brigade in Holland was reckoned at over 17,000 men. The Swedish army alone contained three Scottish generals, eight colonels, eleven majors and thirty captains.

When the King called for volunteers to fight in the 'First Bishops War' in 1639 the response was lamentable. Few of his English subjects supported any cause promoted by Laud, and even fewer returned from abroad to fight their neighbours. Meanwhile hundreds of experienced men poured across the North Sea to Edinburgh, and the Pacification of Berwick concluded Charles I's first inglorious martial episode.

By 1640, when the Scots advanced over the Tweed and the Tyne, a number of veteran English officers had joined the King's colours. Among them were Jacob Astley, Thomas Fairfax, George Goring and George Monk, but their ill-trained levies were routed at Newburn. The Ripon Treaty proved even more humiliating than Berwick, with the Scots encamped in Northumberland at a cost in English gold of £850 a day.

Only a Parliament could raise such funds by lawfully voted taxation, but the 'Short Parliament' of May 1640 and was dissolved after a bare three weeks. The body that assembled at Westminster in November lasted for twenty years, to go down in history as the 'Long Parliament'.

The Tower, together with several major ports and cities, was a garrison and an arsenal, but apart from the Londoners the trained bands of the counties were a standing joke, rather than a standing army. They mustered once a month to fire off a volley or two before adjourning to the nearest tavern, but both sides aimed to gain control of this unpromising manpower and transform it into fighting soldiers. Parliament issued its Militia Ordinance and the King his Commissions of Array, and both condemned defaulters as traitors.

A gentleman could be served with conflicting commands on the same day as the perplexed Sir Thomas Knyvett MP wrote to his wife in May 1642: 'Oh sweete harte, I am now in a great strait what to do ... at

17

Westminster Sir John Potts, with commissary Maltford saluted me with a commission from the Lord Warwick to take upon me, by Ordinance of Parliament, my Company ... I had not received this many hours but I met with a declaration point blank against it by the King.'

The Navy fought no pitched battles during the War being mainly engaged in blockading, victualling besieged ports and transporting *materiel*. Thanks to the royal tax gathering of Ship Money it was in excellent shape, but declared for Parliament under the Lord High Admiral, the Earl of Northumberland, and the swashbuckling Earl of Warwick.

Self-Denying Ordinances - Dec. 1644 & April 1645

An Act was passed 'on a sudden, in one session, with great unanimity', by which no individual could exercise command in the Army and also hold a seat in Parliament and all commissions to be resigned within forty days.

Elected MPs had a choice, but the peers unable to bring themselves 'to beat the King' too thoroughly, Essex and Manchester, had no such option. A Scots observer dourly wrote that the Ordinance was 'admired by some as the most wise, necessary and heroic action. By others as the most rash, hazardous and unjust action as ever Parliament did ... a wonderfully troublesome affair, the bottom of it is not understood.'

It was understood all too clearly when, on Fairfax's insistence, Oliver Cromwell MP's military commission was extended yet again and he was appointed Lieutenant-General of Horse on the eve of Naseby.

Relationships

Blood proved thicker than water, and there is little evidence of hostility or rancour between opposing kith and kin but many instances of financial and practical help. Nor did many families torn by conflicting loyalties actually face each other on the battlefield; it was not the sword that divided Ralph Verney from his father and brother, but politics. Some of ancient lineage and large estates prudently maintained a son in each camp while others endeavoured to keep their neutral heads below the parapet.

Family trees are complicated by many marriages in one generation since wives so frequently died in childbirth. Lady Sussex, and earlier Bess of Hardwick, were unusual in each having four husbands. Three direct generations of Montagus had ten wives between them, and when in 1656 Sir Gervase Clifton, 'seventy years old at least', married again he took a seventh bride, Lady Alice Hastings, along with her dowry of £,4000.

There was much interlocking and overlapping kinship:

Robert, Earl of Warwick and Henry, Earl of Holland were sons of Penelope Devereux and Robert Rich. The Earl of Newport, was their bastard half-brother by Penelope and the Earl of Devonshire. Robert Devereux, Earl of Essex, was their first cousin, whose sister married William Seymour, Earl of Hertford. All were for the King, except Essex.

Sir Thomas Fairfax was related by blood and marriage to half the gentlemen of Yorkshire, among them Bellasis, Slingsby and Cholmley. He married Anne Vere, and their daughter Mary, married the second Duke of Buckingham, son of Charles I's murdered favourite. Anne's aunt, Lady Vere's sister, was the mother of Brilliana, third wife of Sir Robert Harley.

Oliver Cromwell's connections spread even wider. He had eighteen relatives in the Long Parliament, and the 'Great Cousinage' ranged from the Earl of Manchester, to John Hampden, Valentine Walton, Edward Whalley, Henry Ireton, Charles Fleetwood, John Desborough and Oliver St John, who married Catharine, Anne Fairfax' sister. When he was Lord Protector, his daughter Mary married Henry Bellasis, Lord Fauconberg.

The Verneys of Claydon were related to Speaker Lenthall, John Hampden and the Temples of Stowe.

Lady Sussex, born Eleanor Wortley of Yorkshire, and tireless correspondent of the Verneys, was affectionately referred to them as the 'Old Men's Wife'. She married in succession Sir Henry Lee of Ditchley, and the Earls of Sussex, Warwick and Manchester; with this last marriage the couple notched up nine spouses between them.

3

THE 'PRINCIPALLE PAYNTER' to the KING

"The picture is very ill favoured and makes me quite out of love with myself, it pleases me not at all - but truly I think it is very like the original. If ever I come to London before Sir Vandyck go, I will get him to mend my picture, for though I be ill favoured, that makes me worse than I am."

The dismay of *Lady Sussex* gives the lie to this court painter always flattering his sitters.

Van Dyck's career was short and brilliant. The seventh of an Antwerp silk merchant's dozen children, he was apprenticed to a local painter at the age of ten. He first came to England in 1620 in the suite of Peter Paul Rubens, and was soon hailed as to 'appear as much a master'. He moved to Italy, then back to Antwerp, and finally in 1632 took up his appointment in London as 'principalle paynter to the King'.

Charles I's image to posterity owes much to Sir Anthony, for in Dame Veronica Wedgwood's words 'the inhibited adenoidal face of King Charles, unflatteringly depicted by Mytens, was transfigured by Van Dyck's hand with indefinable spiritual grandeur'; without it the cult of the doomed, martyred monarch could never have taken root.

The King was a slight, fastidious man, delighted Henrietta Maria stood no higher than his shoulder, and any hint that the royal couple were doomed to tragedy would have astounded both artist and sitters alike. Bernini is said to have found the King's 'countenance so full of foreboding and unhappiness', but there is no confirmation of this from Cardinal Barbarini, Bernini's patron, who had commissioned a marble bust from Van Dyck's triple portrait. As papal envoy in Paris the Cardinal, later Pope Urban VIII, had known *Henrietta Maria* as a child, and continued to corresponded with her at the English court when she became Queen.

Charles I was a noted connoisseur, and his agents acquired the finest works from the Gonzaga Collection - twelve Mantegnas, ten Breughels, two Raphaels and nineteen Titians were shipped from Mantua with other paintings for £30,000. It was a price the King could ill afford, and it might be said that Mantegnas *Triumph of Caesar* canvases, now at Hampton Court, were purchased at the cost of his throne.

Parliament brought down both King and courtiers like a pack of cards, court cards depicted by Van Dyck in the years of peace, although the Queen endured twenty years of widowhood as a resentful pensioner, rather than a Daughter, of France. Once she had taxed Van Dyck with flattering her hands even more than her face, and with startling candour he replied 'the reason is that I expect my reward from them.'

He also painted the *Five Eldest Children of Charles I*. James succeeded his brother Charles as king, smallpox killed Henry in the year of the Restoration, the baby Anne died young, and Elizabeth in captivity at Carisbrooke; Henriette was born during the war. Both Elizabeth and Henry were taken to bid their father a last farewell at Whitehall.

The *Earl of Northumberland* weathered the storm, but of the King's Stuart cousins only the *Duke of Richmond* survived the War. *Lord George* was killed at Edgehill, *Lord John* fell at Cheriton and *Lord Bernard* died at Chester. Like other gallant youths on both sides there had been steel and courage beneath the satin doublets and beribboned lovelocks.

The dapper Colonel *Arthur Goodwin* was a staunch Parliamentarian, and his portrait nails another lie - that they were all killjoy, crop-haired Puritans. His Buckinghamshire Horse formed the guard of honour at John Hampden's funeral in 1643, for which he had begged a friend for 'a broad black ribbon to hang about my standard'.

The artist was spared the misfortune of seeing the flesh and blood of his canvases destroyed in the carnage, but his own brief life was scarred by tragedy. His mistress, Margaret Lemon, the voluptuous model in *Cupid and Psyche*, proved a virago, and his Czech friend, Wenceslaus Hollar, recoiled from this 'demon of jealousy' who caused 'horrible scenes' and tried to 'bite off Van Dyck's thumb to prevent him ever painting again".

He married one of the Queen's maids of honour in 1640, a fine match for a 'mere paynter', but he died shortly before the birth of their daughter Mary. Though a victim of the plague, he was buried in St Paul's.

Within a year the first golden Stuart youths fell at Edgehill.

The 'SERGEANT PAINTER' to the KING

William Dobson's years of fame were equally brief, overshadowed first by Van Dyck, and then by war. As 'Sergeant-Painter to the King' he worked from a cramped studio in Oxford with the trumpets calling away many of his sitters almost before the paint was dry on the canvas.

As an apprentice Dobson had copied Tintorettos and Titians, and Van Dyck is said to have seen him skilfully reproducing one of his own portraits and taken him to court as his protege.

William had the pleasing manners and ready wit of a Stuart gentleman, but he was as unbusinesslike as his spendthrift father and his debts increased as the fortunes of his noble sitters declined.   A s with most Cavaliers, the disaster of Naseby spelled utter ruin and he was thrown into a debtors' prison. A kindly benefactor bought him out but he died shortly afterwards aged only thirty six.

During the Oxford years Dobson's loyalty must have lain with the King, but several earlier portraits depict men soon to be Charles' bitterest opponents: *William Strode*, a fiery, intemperate man, and one of the 'Five Members'; *John Thurloe*, later one of Cromwell's Secretaries of State, and *Sir Harry Vane*, former Governor of Massachusetts and a key figure in the Commons after the death of John Pym.

Sir William Compton, son of the Earl of Northampton of Compton Wynyates, is Dobson's masterpiece and the epitome of the gallant cavalier. Buff-coated and sashed with scarlet the handsome young governor of Banbury stands before angry clouds tinged with pink, the firm mouth, prominent nose and hooded eyes lending him a gravity beyond his years.

Van Dyck and Dobson both painted Prince Rupert, and Dobson's portrait of the twelve year-old Prince of Wales shows him bravely clad for steel cuirass and buff coat. The two men also depicted that 'Renaissance Man', *Intgo Jones*, himself a skilled artist, architect, sculptor and theatrical designer of 'wondrous machines to enliven Masques'.

The War dragged on. By 1648 both Van Dyck and Dobson, 'the most excellent painter that England hath yet bred', were dead and most of the Royalists who had not fallen in battle had fled abroad to a longer and harsher exile than the past years at Oxford.

Anthony Van Dyck had been born at the close of Elizabeth's reign, as had *Oliver Cromwell*, but when the Lord Protector had his portrait painted he ordered 'Mr Lely ... to remark all these roughness, pimples, warts and everything ... otherwise I will never pay a farthing for it."

An attitude as incomprehensible to Van Dyck as to Lady Sussex.

The moment the axe fell on Charles I, his eldest son succeeded to the throne, but it was to be twelve years before he regained it and the *Charles II* who returned in 1660 was far removed from the gallant portraits of his youth. The bread of exile had been bitter, and to retain his crown he became the most hardened and cynical politician of them all, vowing 'never to go upon his travels again.

Sir Peter Lely's portrait tells it all.

* * *

In 1972 the Tate presented the *Age of Charles*, and in 1982/83 the National Portrait Gallery staged both *Van Dyck in England*, and *William Dobson - The Royalists at War*, all of which displayed the wide range of personalities involved in the Civil War. Many portraits were loaned by the Queen, and the illustrated catalogues give the locations of every picture.

Britain's stately homes and ancient castles contain fascinating family portraits and historic pictures, some by indifferent artists, and most are open to the public, as are all the nation's galleries and museums.

A few pictures in private hands are never on show, but the most extensive collections of 17th century portraits by Van Dyck, Dobson, Mytens, Honthorst and Lely are in the Stuart Galleries of the **National Portrait Gallery** and the refurbished glory of the **Queen's House, Greenwich**, part of the National Maritime Museum.

Van Dyck painted several *Charles I on Horseback*. One is in the National Gallery, and another 'in Armoure upon a White Horse, in a great large Carved frame' is in the royal collection.

4

FOR KING OR PARLIAMENT?

'In troubled Water you can scarce see your Face, or see it very little, till the Water be quiet and stand still. So in troubled times you can see little Truth; when times are quiet and settled, then Truth appears.' John Selden.

'I shall not lead any man farther back in this journey, for the entrance into these dark ways, than the beginning of this king's {Charles I} reign. For I am not so sharp-sighted as those who have discerned this rebellion contriving from, if not before, the death of Queen Elizabeth.' Clarendon.

'The King raised a Parliament he could not rule, and the Parliament raised an Army it cannot rule, and the Army has raised Agitators they cannot rule, and the Agitators are setting up the People whom they will be unable to rule.' c.1647. Mr Secretary Nicholas.

* * *

'All were Englishmen and the pity of it was that such courage should be spent in the blood of each other.' Bulstrode Whitelocke.

'Brother, what I feared is proved too true, which is your being against the King; give me leave to tell you in my opinion 'tis most unhandsomely done, and it grieves my heart to think that my father already and I, who so dearly love and esteem you, should be bound to be your enemy. I hear 'tis a great grief to my father.' Edmund to his elder brother, Ralph Verney MP.

'... I see he {sir Edmund} is infinitely melancholy, for many other things I believe besides the difference betwixt you ... but in going the way your conscience tells you to be right, I hope he hath more goodness and religion than to continue in displeasure with you for it.' 1642. Lady Sussex to Ralph Verney.

'Thou wouldest think it strange if I should tell thee there was a time in England when brothers killed brothers, cousins, and friends their friends ... when thou wentest to bed at night , thou knewest not whether thou shouldest be murdered afore day.' 1642. Sir John Oglander.

'Not against the King I fight, but for the King and Commons' right.' Device on Hampden's banner.

'When he {Hampden} first drew the sword, he threw away the scabbard ... he had a head to contrive, a tongue to persuade, and a hand to execute any mischief.' Clarendon.

'I hope the Parliament will lay no more taxes on for rents are paid no where ... I wish all were well, for things stand in so ill a condition here as we can make no money of our coalpits. If rents fail, and those fail too, we shall be a hard case.' 1642. Yorkshire.

Charles I's gilt parade armour c.1612 &
harquebusier's equipment of Colonel Alexander Popham

Charles I & Henrietta Maria c.1630s

Sir Thomas Fairfax and Anne Vere c.1637

Charles, Prince of Wales   James, Duke of York

Sir Arthur Capel & Family c.1640

The Earl of Newcastle   General George Monk

Sir Henry Kingsmill's tomb, Radway, Edgehill

'... {gentlemen} well affected to the King, yet there were people of inferior charges who by good husbandry, clothing and other thriving had gotten very great fortunes and by degrees getting themselves into gentlemen's estates were angry they found not themselves in the same esteem and reputations with those whose estates they had.' Clarendon

'... {seeking to condemn the King} upon less evidence than would serve to hang a fellow for stealing a horse.' 1641. Ralph Hopton in the Commons.

'Beacons are new made, seamarks set up, and great posting up and down with packets; all symptoms of the ensuing war.' Whitelocke.

'The sea coasts of the West, the great trading towns of Bristol, Lyme, Falmouth, Plymouth and Exeter, (the King's Navy being now under the command of the two Houses), their interest as well as their inclinations made them Parliamentarians. Only the Cornishmen, as old bold Britains, were eminently loyall and Royalist ...'
'The most eminent Noblemen and Gentry thro' the country were firmly loyall to their Prince; and those eminent Members of the Parliament such as Greenvill, Slanning, Hopton, Stowel, Strangewaies, Rogers, Windham etc., and many more joyning themselves to the Marquis of Hertford.' Warwick.

'With a Spanish blade at his side and a Welsh heart in his bosom.' Volunteer.

'No man knew for what reason he {Sir John Gell} chose the {Parliament's} side; for he had not understanding enough to judge the equity of the cause or piety or holiness being a foul adulterer all the time he served the Parliament, and so unjust that without remorse he suffered his men indifferently to plunder both honest men and cavaliers.' Lucy Hutchinson.

'This may be said of a Fairfax and a Sheffield, that there is not one of either of those names in England but was {other than} engaged for the services of Parliament.' *Weekly Intelligencer*

'When I found a preparation of arms against the King under a shadow of loyalty I rather resolved to obey a good conscience than particular ends, and am now on my way to His Majesty, where I will throw myself down at his feet and die a loyal subject.' 1642. Lord Paget.

'Now there is so much declared as makes all officers in the Kingdom traitors of one side or the other ... neither are standers by in any better condition'. 1642. Sir Thomas Knyvet.

'I hope though we differ in opinion concerning King and Parliament, yet I hope, we have one Lord, one Faith, one Baptism, and if we have so it is more than many brothers ... I am afraid they will shortly find out a new God, but enough of that subject.' 1642 July. Thomas Barrow.

'... {those for Parliament} in so doing stand for the King, and consequently both for King and Commonwealth.' 1642. Sir John Oxinden.

'When the Standard was set up at Nottingham Sir Edmund Verney, Knight Marshall, as Standard Bearer with whom he {Clarendon} had great Familiarity ... told him ...

'You have satisfaction in your conscience that you are in the right, that the King ought not to grant what is required of him, and so you do your duty and your business together. But for my part I do not like the quarrel, and do heartily wish that the King would yield and consent to what they {Parliament} desire; so that my conscience is only concerned in honour and in gratitude to follow my master.

'I have eaten his bread and served him near thirty years, and will not do so base a thing as to forsake him, and chose rather to lose my life, which I am sure to do, to preserve and defend those things which are against my conscience to preserve and defend; for ... I have no reverence for the bishops for whom the quarrel subsists.'
Life of Clarendon

'I cannot contain myself within my doors when the King of England's standard waves in the field upon so just occasion ... I desire to acquire an honest name or an honourable grave. I never loved my life or ease so much as to shun such an occasion, which if I should I were unworthy of the profession I have held as to succeed those ancestors of mine who has so many of them sacrificed their life for their country.' 1643. Sir Bevil Grenvile.

'When I put my hand to the Lord's work I did it not rashly, but had many an hour and night to seek God, to know my way.' Captain John Hodgson, Fairfax's Yorkshire Horse.

'Unless a man were resolved to fight on the Parliament side, which for my part I had rather be hanged, it will be said without doubt that a man is afraid to fight. If there could be an expedient found to solve the punctilio of honour, I would not continue here an hour.' 1642. Lord Spencer, letter to his wife.

'Here {London} is great preparation for war, but not against the King, happily not against his person, but Crown; yet ... had you but heard the discourses I heard from a Parliament man this day, you would persist from being so strong a Parliamentarian.' To Henry Oxinden.

'I am forced to draw my sword {for Parliament} not only against my countrymen but many near friends and allies, some of which I know both to be well-affected in religion and lovers of their liberties.' 1643. Hugh Cholmley.

'Gentlemen then kept good horses, and many horses for a man-at-arms, and men that could ride them, hunting horses.' Aubrey *Lives*

'... that your Worship will not {think} us ill-affected or false-hearted tenants in refusing to venture our lives ... we would not for the world harbour a disloyal thought against his Majesty, yet we dare not lift up our hands against the honourable assembly of Parliament whom we are confidently assured do labour both the happiness of his Majesty and all his kingdom.' c.1642. To a Cheshire landowner.

'One extravagant word spoken but by one man is enough to confiscate the goods of a whole family to the Parliament soldiers. Sir Thomas Gardiner.

'The Earl of Rutland was so modest as to think himself not sufficiently qualified for such a trust {power under the Great Seal}, and therefore excused himself on a point of conscience.' 1644 Jan. Westminster.

'I must needs say that my judgement was for the Parliament, as the King's and Kingdom's great and safest council.' Sir Thomas Fairfax.

'The Cavaliers are extremely outrageous in plundering, putting no difference at all between friends and supposed enemies ... these malignants ripped up feather beds and throw the feathers in the wind to be blown away for sport, and scanned all the barrels of beer and wine and spilt it in their cellars.' Complaint to the Mayor of Sandwich.

'Under pretence of defending our laws and religion ... but a new way to deprive us of laws, liberty and property.' Contemp. comment.

'He {Lord Falkland} would with a shrill and sad accent, ingeminate the word Peace, Peace.' Clarendon.

'12th Nov {1642}. The Battle of Brentford surprisingly fought, and to the great consternation of the City ... came in with my horse and arms just at the retreat, but ... the Army's marching to Gloucester, would have left both me and my brothers exposed to ruin, without any advantage to his Majesty. ...
    '23 July {1643} ... finding it impossible to evade doing very unhandsome things, and which had been a great cause of my perpetual motions hitherto between Wotton and London I obtained a licence of his Majesty dated at Oxford and signed by the King, to travel again ... I went by post to Dover, having reasonable good passage we came before Calais.' Evelyn *Diary*

'Walter Baskervile, first for the Parliament, then for the King, then theirs, then taken prisoner by us, and with much adoe gott his pardon and now, *pro rege*, God wott.'
Diary of a Royalist officer.

'The Earl of Kingston, a man of vast estate and no less covetous, who divided his sons between both parties and concealed himself till at length his fate drew him to declare himself absolutely on the King's side, where in behaved himself honourable and died remarkably ... The Earl of Clare was very often of both parties, and never advantaged either.' Lucy Hutchinson.

5

THE ROYAL FAMILY
Charles I

'Sweet, sweet brother, I will give anything I have to you; both my horse and
my books and my crossbow or anything that you would have.   Good
brother, love me and I shall ever love
and serve you.'   Prince Charles to
Prince Henry, who died in 1612 leaving
Charles heir to the throne.

'Charles Stuart I am, Love guides me
afar. To the heaven of Spain
And Maria my star.' 1624. Trans. from
Lope de Vega, on the Spanish wooing.'

'Steenie, {Buckingham} I command
you to send all the French away tomorrow out of the town. If you can, by fair
means, but stick not long in disputing,
otherwise force them away, driving
them like so many wild beasts - and so
the devil go with them. Let me hear no
answer, but of the performance of my
command.   So I rest your faithful,
constant, loving friend, C.R.' Ejection
of Henrietta Maria's protesting attendants from Somerset House.

'They {Parliaments} are of the nature
of cats; they ever grow curst with age
... cut them off handsomely when they
come to any age, for young ones are
ever more tractable ... nothing can
more conduce to the beginning of the
new than the well ending of the former
Parliament.' c.1632. To Strafford.

'... always an immoderate lover of the
Scottish nation, having not only been
born there but educated by that people,
having few English about him till he
was king ... His treasure was gone, his
subjects were irritated and his ministry
all frightened ... so that he had brought
himself into great straits, but had not
the dexterity to extricate himself out of
them.' 1639. Clarendon *History*

'A skilful watchmaker, to clean his
watch, will take it asunder, and when
it is put together it will go the better, so
that he leave not out one pin of it.'
1641.   Charles I to Parliament

'He was forced with his Queen, of
whose person he was always more
chary than of his business, to remove
to Hampton Court, and from thence to
Dover. 1642 Jan, after the 'Arrest of
the Five Members'. Warwick *Memoirs*

'His Majesty accompanied his wife as
far as the shore, and did not know how
to tear himself away from her, nor
would they restrain their tears, moving
all who were present.'   1642 Feb.
Venetian envoy's despatch.

'... that the King would leave every
officer respectively to look to his own
proper charge, and that his Majesty
would content himself to overlook all
men to see that they did their duties in
their proper places, which would give
abundant satisfaction, and quiet those
that are jealous to see some men
meddle, who have nothing to do with
affairs.' 1643. Secretary Nicholas.

'There are three things I will not part with: the Church, the Crown and my Friends.' 1644, Nov. Oxford. Reply to Parliament's Peace Commissioners.

'Arrant rebels, and that their end must be damnation, ruin and infamy.' 1644 Nov. King to Secretary Nicholas

'King Charles was temperate, chaste and serious ... he was a most excellent judge and a great lover of painting, carvings, gravings and other ingenuities ... but it was not in his power, though a great prince, to control destiny.' Lucy Hutchinson.

'Their own party are most weary of the war, and likewise great distractions amongst themselves, as Presbyterians against Independents in religion, and General against General in point of command ... be confident that in making peace I shall ever show my constancy to the Bishops and all our friends and not forget to put an end to this perpetual Parliament ... I will neither quit Episcopacy nor that sword which God hath given into my hands ... the unreasonable stubbornness of the rebels gives daily less and less hopes of an accommodation this way.' 1645 Spring. To the Queen, from the *King's Cabinet Opened*, captured at Naseby.

'I am not without hope that I shall be able so to draw the Presbyterians or the Independents to side with me for extirpating one another, that I shall really be King again.' 1646. Oxford. To George Digby.

'So as in April 1646 the King puts himself into a disguise and only with Mr Hudson, a minister as his guide, and Mr John Ashburnham ... he quits Oxford and comes on a sudden into the Scotch army ... The Scots seemed surprised at his coming among them ... for tho' he was seemingly free, yet his person was under guard ...

'But Newark being surrendered by the King's command, the Scots march away with the King to Newcastle, and to please their brethren in England they got his Majesty's directions for the surrendering the few remaining garrisons in England, Oxford, Worcester, Wallingford, Litchfield, Ragland etc.' Warwick.

'I never knew what it was to be barbarously treated before.' 1646 April. Charles I to the Queen, on his treatment by the Scots Presbyterians.

'The Scots knew so well how to value him ... they parted with him for a good price; for they are paid £20,000 upon their marching from Newcastle, and delivering up of that town, as likewise Berwick and Carlisle ... the King is left in the hands of the English Commissioners who carry him to Holmby-House, rather as their Prisoner, than their Prince.' Warwick.

'It is as fair a commission and as well written as I have seen a commission in my life - a company of handsome, proper gentlemen.' 1647 June. Charles to Cornet Joyce, on his troop of horse at Holdenby.

'This may be truly said, that he valued the Reformation of his own Church before any in the world.' Warwick

'If we tarry long, the King will come and say who will be hanged.' 1647 Oct. Captain Audley, Putney Debates.

'They who had not seen the King for near two years found his countenance extremely altered ... he would never suffer his hair to be cut, nor cared to have any new clothes, so that his aspect and appearance was very different ... otherwise his health was good, and he was much more cheerful in his discourses toward all men ... He was not at all dejected in his spirits, but carried himself with the same majesty he had used to do ...
    'His hair was all gray, which making all others very sad, made it thought that he had sorrow in his countenance which appeared only by that shadow.' 1648. Clarendon.

'One honest soldier said but "God bless you, Sir", and his Captain caned him". The King told the Captain "the punish-ment exceeded the offence".
    'About the bar a numerous rabble cry out for justice against him, and in the Court he is saucily treated by all the Officers.' 1649 Jan. Westminster Hall. Warwick.

'He had such an ungracious way of showing favour, that the manner of bestowing it was almost as mortifying as the favour was obliging.'
Gilbert Burnet *History*

'Nothing lay so heavily on his con-science as his consenting to the death of the Earl of Strafford.'
1649, January. Whitehall. Charles I on the scaffold to Bishop Juxon

Queen Henrietta Maria

'You are rather the ambassador of your brother the King of France, than Queen of England.' 1626 Charles to his wife.

'... every day she concentrates in herself the favour and love that were previously divided {by the King} between herself and the duke.'
1628 Sept. Venetian envoy, after the murder of the Duke of Buckingham.

'The only dispute that now exists between us is that of conquering each other by affection, both of us esteeming ourselves victorious in following the will of each other.' 1630. Charles to Marie de Medici, his mother-in-law.

'I was the happiest and most fortunate of Queens. Not only had I every pleasure which heart could desire, but above all, I had the love of my husband who adored me.' During the 1630s.

'... to seduce with Pictures, Antiquities, & Vanities brought from Rome ... Plays, the very pomps of the devil, sinful, heathenish, lewd, ungody spec-tacles, and most pernicious corrup-tions ... notorious whores.' 1634. William Prynne's pamphlets libelled the Queen by implication since she loved dancing and performing in masques.

'... chase the Pope and the Devil from St James's, where is lodged the Queen, Mother of the Queene.' 1640. Henrietta Maria's chapel in Somerset House was also a target of anti-catholic abuse.

'You must provide some bodie sure for my lettre must not be lost, and I would not trust to an ordinaire poste. I am ill provided witt personnes that I dare truste, pray do whatt you can to helpe me, if little Will Murray can not go, to send this letter, and so I trust, your assured friend, Henriette Marie R.' 1641 Nov. To Secretary Nicholas.

'Delays have always ruined you, you are beginning again your old game of yielding everything ... My whole hope lies in your firmness and constancy, and when I hear anything to the contrary, I am mad ... If you had not delayed this going to Hull so long as you did, I think that you would not have lost your magazine.' 1642. Letter to the King from Holland.

'Priests, Jesuits and Papists have powerful influence upon the Queen who is permitted to intermeddle with great affairs of state.' 1642 Feb. Parliamentary Grievance.

'As an angel and mediatrix of peace I suppose she may be most happily welcome {at Bridlington with arms}; there is no other way for her, either of honour or safety, nor for this poor kingdom to hope of quenching a consuming fire.' 1643 Feb. Sir Thomas Roe to Elizabeth of Bohemia.

'Her She-Majesty Generalissima.'

'The woefullest spectacle my eyes yet ever looked on; the most worn and weak pitiful creature in the world, the poor Queen, shifting for one hour's life longer.' Exeter. A Cornish Cavalier.

'... from Oxford unto Exeter, where she was delivered of the Princess Henriette, soon after embarks for France, for the two Houses impeach her of treason.' 1644 June. Newsletter.

'The Queen's colours {taken} richly embroidered with the Crown in the midst, flower-de-luces wrought about in gold, with a golden cross on top.'

'{Thanks} for the arms and munitions of war sent, and the promise that new assistance and money will be sent to me.' 1645, Sept. Letter to the Pope.

*

'God grant that it {baby} belongs to him. A woman who gives herself to a prince will just as readily give herself to another.' 1660 Paris. James, Duke of York had secretly married his mistress, Clarendon's daughter Anne.

'Arrived the Queene Mother in England, whence she had been banished almost 20 years.' 1660 Nov. Evelyn.

'A great queen, daughter, wife, mother of kings, and sovereign of three realms ... in a single life all the extremities of things human, happiness without bound as well as misery.' 1669, Paris. Bishop Bossuet's funeral sermon.

Elizabeth of Bohemia

'Your Majesty's Sister, when she was younger, adorned her head with some single Eglantine Roses with jewels and pearls ... and her habit adorned all over with Carnations and White Ribbons.' c.1610. Isaac Oliver's miniature.

'Would to God, that we had a little corner of the world in which we could live quietly and contentedly together.' 1632. The exiled Elector Frederick to his wife, shortly before he died.

'Her Majesty had her family brought up apart from herself, greatly preferring the sight of her monkeys and dogs.' Princess Sophie, Rupert's sister.

'You meaner beauties of the night
That poorly satisfy our eyes,
More by your number, than your light,
You common people of the skies,
What are you when the moon shall rise.' 1620. Sir Henry Wotton.

'The crowning of his {Rupert's} mother while she bore him in her womb seemed not to be the presage of an ordinary fate.
'No rejoicings, as usual, at the birth of the Bohemian prince {in Prague}; the King is said to be a strange father who will neither fight for his children, nor pray for them.
'The little Rupert is very learned to understand so many languages.' Contemp. comments.

'{A member} began a health to the distressed Lady Elizabeth, and having drunk, kissed the sword.' 1622. Inns of Court.

'The Prince Elector coming to see the King ... dined with the general {Fairfax}, showing great respect unto him, and the general answered it with discharging {22} pieces of cannon at his going away.' 1647 July. Rushworth.

'I should rather have lived upon bread and water than have complied with the Parliament, which he, the King, said I did, to have only one chicken more in my dish, and that he would have thought it a design more worthy his nephew, if he had gone about to have taken his crown from his head.'
1647. The Elector to his mother; it was suspected that Charles Louis hoped to be offered his uncle's crown.

'... send your letters that are for the Queen of Bohemia's family under a cover to Sir Charles Cotterell, who may be paid for them, and not stuff your letters every week with others' epistles.' 1653. An exile in The Hague.

'... I am extreme glad to hear that the King is satisfied with Rupert's letter and that he has answered him so kindly.' 1654. To Secretary Nicholas.

'The Elector {restored} behaves so unhandsomely ... I hope now you will not blame me for not desiring to live with him ... I could tell you more, but will not out of charity, because he is my son.' 1655. To Secretary Nicholas.

Charles II

'When the news came of the Prince's birth there was great Joy shown by all the rest of the Parish, in causing Bonfires to be made and Bells to be rung ... from the rest of the Houses being of Presbyterian or Puritan Party, there came neither Man, nor Child nor Wood nor Victuals, their doors being shut close all the evening, as in a time of general mourning and disconsolations.' 1630. A town near Gloucester. *Cyprianus Anglicus*

'He is so fat and so tall, that he is taken for a year old, and he is only four months ... at present he is so dark I am ashamed of him ... I wish you could see the gentleman, for he has no ordinary mien. He is so serious in all he does that I cannot help fancying him far wiser than myself.' 1630. Henrietta Maria, letters to Mme St Georges.

'... a wooden billet, without which in his arms he would never go abroad or lie down in his bed.' c.1632

'Le Prince Carles avecq le duc de Jarq ... in a carved guilded frame. £200.' 1637. Van Dyck's bill was later halved.

'Thinking to unboy him by putting him into some action and acquaintance with business out of his sight.' 1644, Oxford. Charles I appointed the prince to high command.

'He was governed by his Mother with such strictness, that though his highness was above the age of seventeen he never put his hat on before the Queen, or had above ten pistoles {money} in his pocket.' 1647. Paris. Clarendon.

'Almighty God, who dost establish thrones of princes, and the succession in those thrones, by giving Thy judgments to the King, and thy righteousness to the King's son.' 1648. Prayer for the Prince of Wales.

'If God would send him among us, without some of his present counsellors, I think he would make, by God's blessing, as good a king as Britain saw these hundred years.' 1649. Paris. A Scots commissioner.

'If the King take the Covenant God will never prosper him, nor the world value him.' 1650. Secretary Nicholas.

'I, Charles, King of Great Britain, France and Ireland, do assure and declare by my solemn oath, in the presence of Almighty God, the searcher of all hearts, my allowance and approbation of the National Covenant and Solemn League and Covenant above written ...

'I shall observe these {imposition of Presbyterian government} in my own practice and family, and shall never make proposition to any of these, nor endeavour any alteration therein.'

1650 July.

Signing the Covenant was the price of a Scottish coronation, and 'caught in the snare of the Kirk' the new King was crowned at Scone on 1 January

'... to St Germain's to kiss his Majesty's hand; in the coach which was my Lord Wilmot's, went Mrs Barlow {Lucy Walter}, the King's mistress, and mother to the Duke of Monmouth; a brown, beautiful, bold, but insipid creature.' 1649, Paris. Evelyn.

'Hath not resolution enough to discountenance those he {Charles II} knows to be false, and to cherish those he believes to he honest and faithful; ... an unhappy infirmity, but I doubt past cure in him,' 1650. Nicholas.

'{One Douglas}, informed the King that great scandal had been given to the godly {by his dalliance with females}, enlarged on the heinous nature of the sin, and concluded with exhorting his Majesty, whenever he was disposed to amuse himself, to be more careful for the future in shutting the windows.' 1650 Edinburgh. Contemp. report.

'If that rogue {himself} were taken he deserved to be hanged, more than all the rest for bringing in the Scots. Upon which he said, I spoke like an honest man, and so we parted.' 1651. In disguise, to a countryman.

'{We hid} in a great oak, in a pretty plain place, where we might see around us ... carried up with us some victuals for the whole day, namely bread, cheese, small beer ... here we stayed all the day {and} slumbered away some part of the time.' Charles II and Colonel Carlis in Boscobel Wood after Worcester.'

'A tall, black man, above two yards high, with dark brown hair scarcely to be distinguished from black.'

'... his immediate delight in empty, effeminate and vulgar conversations is become an irresistible part of his nature, and will never suffer him to animate his own designs and others' actions with that spirit which is requisite for his quality, and much more to his fortunes.' c.1655. Ormonde.

'I was very well pleased with the account of the activity you have lately used for the promoting my interest, in which so many have followed the good example you gave, that I hope I and you and the whole nation shall shortly receive the fruite of it, and that I may give you my thankes in your own country: in the meane time, you may be confident I am, Your affectionate friend CHARLES R.' 1660. Breda. To John Rous of Henham Hall, Suffolk.

'He doubted it had been his own fault that he had been absent so long, for he saw no one that did not protest that he had ever wished for his return.' 1660. Clarendon reporting Charles' ironic comment on his loyal reception.

'The City with a present of £10,000 to his Majesty, £1000 to the Duke of York, another to the Duke of Gloucester ... the Journals fetched, and those Acts and Orders razed out which {were} inconsistent with the Kingly government ... York is declared Lord High Admiral.' 1660 May. Warwick.

6

THE TRIAL OF STRAFFORD

'The opinion by the judges declaring the lawfulness of the assignment {Ship Money} is the greatest service that profession has done the Crown in my time. But unless His Majesty hath the like power declared to raise a land army upon the same exigent state, the Crown seems to me to stand but upon one leg.' 1637. Earl of Strafford.

'I am for Thorough, my lord, less that Thorough will not do.'
Strafford to Archbishop Laud.'

'When the House was in consultation how to frame the particular charge against the great Duke {Buckingham}, he {Strafford} advised to make a generall one, and to accuse him of treason, and to let him afterwards get off, as he could; which befell himselfe at last.' Warwick *Memoirs*

'Pity me, for never came any man to so lost a business. The army altogether un-exercised and unprovided of necessities ... our horse all cowardly ... an universal affright in all a general disaffection to the King's service.' 1640. Strafford, on taking command in the Second Bishops' War.

'His understanding, aided by a good phansy, made him quick in discerning the nature of any business, and thro' a cold brain he became deliberate and sound of judgment. His memory was great, and he made it greater by confiding in it. His elocution very fluent, readily to reply, or freely to harangue upon any subject. All lodged in a sour and haughty temper ... expected to have more observance paid to him than he was willing to pay to others ... not like {willing} to conciliate goodwill of men of lesser station.

'Many of his Confidents ... were wont to swear he endeavoured to be just to all, but was resolv'd to be gracious to none but to those whom he thought inwardly affected him ...' Warwick

'Go on with a vigorous war as you first designed ... {being} loosed and absolved from all rules of government. Being reduced to extreme necessity, everything is to be done that power might admit ... They {Scots} refusing, you are acquitted towards God and man.' 1640 May. To Charles I.

'That great engine the Lord Strafford hath battered down their laws and liberties, and levelled them with the most servile nations.'
1640. Thomas Stockdale.

'In his person he was of a tall stature, but stooped much in the neck. His countenance was cloudy, whilst he moved, or sat thinking; but when he spake, either seriously or facetiously, he had a lightsome and very pleasant ayre ... The greatness of the envy that attended him, made many in their prognosticks to bode him an ill end'. Warwick.

'... He should not be able to do his Majesty any service {in Parliament}, but should rather be a means to hinder his affairs, in regards to the great envy and ill-will of Parliament and of the Scots bent against him ... being provoked by his coming amongst them, would presently fall upon him, and prosecute his destruction.'
1640. Strafford to Charles I.

'You have an army here {in Ireland} to reduce this kingdom.' Strafford to Charles I. Did the ambiguous word *kingdom* refer to Scotland or England?

'I {Strafford} am tomorrow for London with more danger beset, I believe, than any man went with out of Yorkshire, yet my heart is good and I find nothing cold within me.' 1640 Nov.

'... {as} King of England, he was able to secure him from any danger; and that the Parliament should not touch on a hair of his head.'
1640. Charles I's promise to Strafford.

'I repaired to London to hear and see the famous trial of the Earl of Strafford, Lord-Deputy of Ireland who had been summoned before both Houses and now appeared in Westminster-hall which was prepared with scaffolds {platforms} for the Lords and Commons who, together with the King, Queen, Prince and flowers of the noblesse, were spectators and auditors of the greatest malice and greatest innocency that ever met before so illustrious an assembly.' Evelyn.

'I did ever hold that the happiness of a kingdom consists of a just poise of the King's prerogative and the subject's liberty; and that things would never go well till they went hand in hand together ...
'I will go and look my accusers in the face ... These gentlemen {judges} tell me they speak in defence of the Commonweal against my arbitrary laws. Give me leave to say that I speak in defence of the Commonweal against their arbitrary treason.'
Strafford's defence.

'Upon the word of a King, you shall not suffer in life, honour or fortune'.
1641. Charles I to Strafford.

'... be it therefore enacted by the King's Most Excellent Majesty, and by the Lords and Commons in this present Parliament assembled ... that the Earl of Strafford, for the heinous crimes and offences aforesaid be adjudged and attainted of high treason, and shall suffer such pains of death, and incur the forfeitures of his goods and chattels, lands ...'
1641 May. *Bill of Attainder*

'... I thought, very unjustifiable prosecution, made me one of the fifty six, who gave a negative to that fatall Bill, which cut the thread of his life.'
Warwick.

'Sir, if your conscience is against it {signing the death warrant}, do not consent.' Bishop Ussher, Primate of Ireland.

'The King has two consciences, a public one and a private one.'
Bishop Williams of Lincoln.

'To set your Majesty's conscience at liberty ... to a willing man there is no injury done ... only beg that in your goodness you would vouchsafe to cast your gracious regard upon my poor son and his three sisters ... God long preserve your Majesty. Your Majesty's most faithful and humble subject and servant, Strafford.' From the Tower

'If my own person only were in danger I would gladly venture it to save Lord Strafford's life, but seeing my wife, children and all my kingdom are concerned in it, I am forced to give way unto it ... if he must die, it were charity to reprieve him till Saturday.'
Charles I to the Privy Council.

'Put not your trust in Princes, nor in the sons of men, for in them there is no salvation.'
1641, Strafford's reputed comment on being shown the King's signature on his death warrant.

'In all honour I had to serve his Majesty, I had not any intention in my heart but what did aim at the joint and individual prosperity of the King and his people ...
'I dare look death in the face ... I care not how I die, whether by the hand of the executioner or by the madness and fury of the people. If that may give them better content, it is all one to me.'
1641 12 May. Tower Hill.

'More like a general at the head of an army than like a condemned man to undergo death.' Contemp. report.

'Brought from the Tower of London to the scaffold on Tower Hill, where with undaunted courage he told the people he was come thither to satisfy them with his head, but that he much feared the reformation which begun in blood would not prove so fortunate to the Kingdom as they expected ... with marvellous tranquillity of mind he delivered his head to the block, where it was severed from his body at a blow.'
Clarendon.

'I beheld on Tower-hill the fatal stroke which severed the wisest head in England from the shoulders of the Earl of Strafford; whose crime, coming under the cognizance of no human law, a new one was made, not to be a precedent, but his destruction, to such exorbitancy were things arrived.'
Evelyn.

'His head is off! His head is off!.'
London mob.

'The English are so mad that they have killed their wisest man.' 1641 May, Paris. Cardinal Richelieu.

'I am glad that justice is executed on my Lord Strafford, who I think died like a Seneca, but not like one that had tasted the mystery of godliness. My dear Ned, let these examples make you wise in God's word.'
1641. Lady Brilliana Harley.

7

IN PARLIAMENT ASSEMBLED

'God will not prosper us. I think the Duke of Buckingham is the cause of all our Miseries; and until the King be informed thereof, we shall never go out with Honour, or sit with Honour, that Man is the Grievance of Grievances.' 1628. Sir Edward Coke.

'They were summoned and again dissolved {Parliaments of 1628} ... and that there should be no more assemblies of that nature, and all men inhibited on penalty of censure so much as to speak of a parliament ... no man show me a source from whence these waters of bitterness we now taste have more probably flowed, than from these unseasonable, unskilful and precipitate dissolutions of Parliament.' Clarendon.

'The Parliament is now absolutely dissolved and nothing done all this while. It is like to be a fearful, heavy time for this land when as the King and people agrees not to the other ... divers of the Commons are committed to the Tower and other prisons about the town. I am persuaded you shall hear more of this business.' 1628, Huntingdon. Dr John Symcotts

'Sir, Your Judges have committed me to prison here in your Tower of London, where by reason of the quality of the air I am fallen into a dangerous disease ... I am heartily sorry I have displeased your Majesty, and ... do humbly beseech you once again, to set me at liberty, that when I have recovered my health, I may return back to my prison, there to undergo such punishment as God hath allotted unto me.' 1631. Sir John Eliot MP to Charles I.

'Let Sir John Eliot's body be buried in the Church of that Parish {the Tower} where he died.' 1631. The King rejected Eliot's family's request for his burial in Cornwall. John Hampden became guardian of Eliot's children.

'But we {Huntingdon} do lend the King 6 or 7 thousand pounds which we never look for again. It cost me for my part fifty pounds, but we must not speak of it for fear we fare the worse for it.' 1634. Dr John Symcotts.

'As an old servant of the Crown he could no longer refrain from representing to him {Charles I} the universal discontent of his subjects. The new levies of money were repugnant to the fundamental laws of England and those privileges which their ancestors and themselves had till the present time enjoyed.' 1636. Earl of Danby.

'By the same right the King upon like pretence {Ship Money} might gather the same sum ten, twelve or a hundred times redoubled ... when and as often as he pleased; and no man was in conclusion worth anything.' 1637. Contemp. diarist.

'I agree Parliament to be a most ancient and supreme court where the King and Peers, as judges, are in person, and the whole of the Commons representatively ... but the former fancied policy I utterly deny. The law knows no such king-yoking policy.

'There are two maxims of the law of England which plainly disprove {Hampden's lawyer's } supposed policy ... 'that the King is a person trusted with the state of the commonwealth' ... and 'that the King can do no wrong'.' Ship Money Judgement, Sir John Berkeley.

'... Mr Hampden ... the very genius of that nation of people leads them always to oppose, both civilly and ecclesiastically, all that ever authority ordains for them ... in truth I still wish Mr Hampden, and others to his likeness, were well whipped into their right senses. And if the rod be so used that it smart not, I am the more sorry.' 1637. Strafford to Laud.

'Your letters by the carrier I have received, and I thank you for them and the King's speech and the verses. I hope the Parliament will, by God's mercy, have as happy proceedings and endings as it has a hopeful beginning.' 1640, Nov. Lady Brilliana Harley.

'{Pym} that great stickler against the King and his Prerogative, the Speech-Maker of the Commons that could wiredraw money with every word he uttered to the City.' *Chronicle of the Late Intestine War*

'It was not the intention of the House to abolish either Episcopacy or the Book of Common Prayer, but to reform both ... with the concurrence of the King and Lords, they should do a very acceptable work ... such as had not been since the Reformation.' 1640. John Pym, the 'Root & Branch' Bill.

'.... that for the future your Majesty will vouchsafe to employ such persons in your great and public affairs ... as your Parliament may have cause to confide in.' Petition to Charles I.

'The Gentry were not so precise and strict against an oath or gaming, or plays or drinking, nor troubled themselves so much about the matters of God and the world to come ... {happy} to hear a sermon which lashed the Puritans ... the main body were against the Parliament.' Richard Baxter.

'It is here said that we shall shortly before His Majesty's departure have a great change and addition of officers ... Lord Saye shall be made Lord Treasurer, John Hampden Chancellor of the Duchy, Mr Pym Chancellor of the Exchequer, Denzil Holles, Principal Secretary of State, and that the Earl of Bath and Lord Brook shall be sworn of His Majesty's Privy Council.' Secretary Nicholas.

' ... be it declared and enacted by the King ... that this present Parliament now assembled shall not be dissolved unless it be by Act of Parliament to be passed for that purpose.' 1641 Nov.

'Arrest' of the Five Members
4th January 1642

'Go, pull those rogues out by the ears.'
Alleged challenge by the Queen.

'Mr Speaker, I must for a moment make bold with your chair ... Is Mr Pym here? ... I must have them. Where are they?' Charles I in the Commons.

'May it please your Majesty, I have neither eyes to see nor tongue to speak in this place but as this House is pleased to direct me, whose servant I am here; and I humbly beg your Majesty's pardon that I cannot give any other answer than this to what your Majesty is pleased to demand of it.'
Speaker Lenthall's reply.

'No matter, I think my eyes are as good as another's ... I see my birds are flown ... send them unto me as soon as they return hither. If not, I will seek them myself, for their treason is foul ... I assure you, on the word of a King, I never did intend any force, but shall proceed against them in a legal and fair way, for I never meant any other.'

'To you tents, oh, Israel! ... privilege!' Londoners mobbing the King's coach on his way to demand the 'Five Members' from Lord Mayor Pennington.

'... I hope we shall not be killed ... your Parliament flies high, they have so much courage to stand to maintain their right, truly they are to be commended, the King's party will be too weak that he must yield to the Parliament ... a blessed thing those gentlemen were from the Parliament when the King came, he had ill counsel surely to come in such a way.'
Lady Sussex to Ralph Verney.

'Every countryman's mouth almost is full of breach of privilege of Parliament.' 1642 Jan. Contemp. letter.
*
'How is it I have lost the heart of these water rats.' Charles I of the Navy

'Neptunes of the Sea ... having the greatest trust and honour imaginable put into his {Northumberland's} hands, he thought it no irreligion, rather to deliver into the hands of the enemies of the King, than into the hands of the King himself who directed him to deliver up the Navy unto Sir John Pennington.' Philip Warwick.

'{Earl of Warwick} foremost in fight, capable of climbing mast and yard.'

'... those persons who are most powerful with the King do endeavour to bring Parliament to such a condition that they shall only be made instruments to execute the command of the King, who were established for his most supreme council.' 1642. Letter from the Earl of Northumberland.

'Saye is the principal firebrand and nothing will satisfy him unless he may be advanced ... to render the church and kingdom independent and bring all to confusion.' 1643. Letter to Ormonde.

'Pardon to those that will withdraw from the King except Richmond, Cumberland, Newcastle, Rivers, Caernarvon, Newark, Falkland, Nicholas, Porter, Hyde.' 1642. The Commons.

'A Solemn League and Covenant for Reformation and defence of Religion, the Honour and happiness of the King and the Peace and Safety of the three Kingdoms of England, Scotland and Ireland. We Noblemen, Barons, Knights, Gentlemen, Citizens, Burgesses, Ministers of the Gospel and Commons of all sort in the Kingdoms ... by the Providence of God living under one King, and being of one reformed Religion, having before our eyes the Glory of God and the advancement of the Kingdome of our Lord ...
'After mature deliberation, resolved and determined to enter into a mutuall and solemn League and Covenant. Wherein we all subscribe, and each one of us for himself, with out hands lifted up to the most high God, do swear...'
1643 March. Reformation on the lines of the Kirk was the price of the Scots alliance but Sir Harry Vane managed to add the ambiguous phrase 'according to the word of God.'

'Let us not trouble ourselves to send an answer; but rather answer them with scorn as being unworthy of our further regard.' 1643. Henry Marten MP, of peace proposals from Oxford.

'This, I cannot say famous, notorious man {Pym}, loaded with various diseases, died this very day of the Herodean visitation, so as he was a most loathsome and foule carkasse.' 1643 Dec. *Mercurius Aulicus*

'A pint pot could not hold a pottle of liquor, nor could they {Committee of Safety} be capable to despatch so much business as was committed to them ... did not think one man {Charles I} wise enough to govern all ... it were better one family should be destroyed than many.' Henry Marten.

'A godly member made a Motion to have all profane persons expelled the Houses. Henry Marten moved that all Fooles might be putt out likewise, then there would be a thin House ... wont to sleepe much in the House, Alderman Atkins made a Motion that such a scandalous members as slept and minded not the businesse should be putt out. Marten starts up 'Mr Speaker, a motion has been to turne out the Nodders, I desire the Noddees may also be turned out.' Aubrey.

'Unnatural, irrational, sinful, wicked, unjust, devilish and tyrannical it is for any man whatsoever, spiritual or temporal, clergyman or layman, to appropriate and assume unto himself a power, authority, and jurisdiction to rule, govern or reign over and sort of man in the world without their free consent ... to appropriate and assume unto themselves the office and sovereignty of God, and to be like the Creator, which was the sin of devils...' 1646. Lilburne, *The Free-man's Freedom Vindicated*, Leveller pamphlet.

'The authority of Parliament is a thing which most here would give their life for, but the Parliament to which we would loyally subject ourselves has still to be called ... Consider what we soldiers have to propose and if you {Council of the Army} find it reasonable join with us. So may the kingdom have peace; so may your fellow soldiers be quieted in spirit.' 1647. Putney Debates. Edward Sexby.

'... the earth, a common treasury of relief to all, both beasts and men, was hedged into enclosures by the teachers and rulers, and the others were made servants and slaves ... And that earth that is within this creation made a common storehouse for all, is bought and sold and kept in the hands of a few ... from the beginning it was not so ... the work we {Diggers} are going about is this: to dig up George's Hill {Weybridge} and the waste ground thereabouts, and to sow corn and to eat our bread together by the sweat of our brows.' 1649. *The True Levellers' Standard Advanced*

'The power of the sword'. 1648. Hugh Peter's 'authority' for Pride's Purge.

'These are the men who have cozened the State of our money, and kept back our pay.' A soldier arresting MPs.

'He {Cromwell} declared that he had not been acquainted with their design {Pride's Purge}, yet since it was done, he was glad of it, and would endeavour to maintain it.' Edmund Ludlow.

'Un-kingship was proclaimed {by Parliament}, and his Majesty's statues thrown down at St Paul's portico and Exchange ... this night was buried with great pomp Dorislaus, slain at the Hague, the villain who managed the trial against his sacred Majesty ... I got a pass from the rebell Bradshaw, then in great power.' 1649. Evelyn.

'I do declare and promise that I will be true and faithful to the Commonwealth of England, as the same is now established, without a King or House of Lords.' 1650s

'Upon this dispute betwixt the army and the Parliament, Cromwell, Lambert and Harrison enter the House of Commons and declare a necessity of their dissolution, and the sword men determined the question. Harrison pulling the speaker out of the chair, and Cromwell commanding the Mace to be carried away, and the doors of the House to be shut up, and the House to be guarded by soldiers to prevent any further meetings.' 1653 Dec. Warwick.

'High time to put an end to your sitting. I do dissolve this Parliament, let God judge between you and me.' Cromwell.

'What do you here?' asked a colonel. 'We are called of God to this place, we seek the Lord,' claimed defiant MPs. 'Come out of this place then' replied the colonel, 'for to my knowledge the Lord hath not been here these twelve years passed.' Contemp. account.

8

THE CHURCH MILITANT

'... the sad condition of the Church, if God should at any time determine the days of the King {James}; the Prince {Charles} then being only conversant with Scotchmen, which made up the greatest part of his family, and were ill-affected to the government and worship of the Church of England.' 1620s. Bishop Lancelot Andrewes of Ely.

'Kneeling ne'er spoiled silk stocking; quit thy state;
All equal are within the Church's gate.'
George Herbert

The Church 'too mean an employment and too much below his {George Herbert's} birth, and the excellent abilities and endowments of his mind.' Friends of the ex-courtier.

'It hath been formerly judged that the domestic servants of the King of Heaven should be of the noblest families on earth, and though the iniquity of the late times have made Clergymen meanly valued, and the sacred name of priest contemptible, yet I will labour to make it honourable, by consecrating all my learning and all my poor abilities to advance the glory of that God.'
George Herbert's response.

'... criticism to cease, but if we shall be deceived in this our expectation and that by reading, preaching and making books ... these differences men begin anew to dispute, we shall take such order with them and those books that they shall wish that they had never thought upon these needless controversies.' 1629. Charles I's warning to the Puritans.

'... {would leave the Church of England} tomorrow if it obliged him to believe that any other Christians should be damned; and that nobody would conclude another man to be damned who did not wish him so.' 1630s. John Hales, Canon of Windsor.

'That little low red-faced man.'
'The meddling hocus-pocus'
Contemp. comment on William Laud.

'... never failed before he {Charles I} sat down to dinner to have part of the Liturgy read unto him and his menial servants, came he never so hungry or so late in ... and on Sundays and Tuesdays he came to the Chapel.' Philip Warwick *Memoirs*

'The Bible, I say, the Bible only, is the religion of Protestants.'
1637. Rev. William Chillingworth. *The Religion of Protestants*

'Fie upon the doctrine {Calvinism} that the greatest part of the world shall be damned.' 1640. A Surrey clergyman.

'Never heretic yet rent the Church of Christ but he pretends some great abuses which his integrity would remedy.' Archbishop Laud.

'Cardinals, Patriarchs, Primates, Metropolitans, Archbishops, Bishops, Deans and innumerable such vermin ... not known in sacred writ, nor never come from God, rather from the Pope and the Devil.' John Bastwick.

'Thus did Lodowick Muggleton, by sliding out of one religion into another so dissatisfy his judgment himself from the solid basis of his first principles; first degenerating from the orthodox tenets of the Church of England to Presbytery, from thence to Independency, thence to Anabaptism, thence to Quakerism and lastly to no religion at all ... a poor, silly despicable creature, yet had the confidence to wheedle a company of silly, credulous proselytes out of their souls and estates ... as has often been told him, since the first day of his standing in the pillory.' On the founder of the Muggletonian Sect.

'Our manifold griefs to fill a mighty and vast circumference yet so that from every point our lines of sorrow do lead unto him {Laud} and point at him, the centre from whence our miseries do flow. ' 1640s. John Colepeper MP.

'Whensoever there was anything proposed in the House of Commons, which it was thought the Lords would stick at, or the King not grant, by and by the rabble came about the House, and called for this and that justice, as they were prompted.' Laud.

'{Cromwell} did not understand that there was any necessity for the great revenues of Bishops ... more convinced than ever before ... they would not endure to have their condition come to trial.' An MP's comment.

'New presbyter is but old Priest writ large.' Milton *On New Forces of Conscience under the Long Parliament*

'I hear it is reported that I am resolved at my return to alter the form of the Church Government in England to this here {Scotland}. Therefore I command you to assure all my servants there, that I am constant for the doctrine and discipline of the Church of England as it was established by Queen Elizabeth and my father, and resolve by the Grace of God to live and die in the maintenance of it.' 1641 Oct. Charles I to Secretary Nicholas.

'... had {Charles I} commanded him to have withdrawn his affection and reverence for the {Anglican} Church, he would not have obeyed him.' 1641. Clarendon, then Edward Hyde MP

' ... those who were of the Calvinian faction, which was then very powerful and who according to their useful maxim and practice call every man they do not love, Papist.' Clarendon.

' ... those malignant parties, whose proceedings appear to be mainly for the advantage and increase of Popery, is composed, set up and acted by the subtle practice of the Jesuits and other engineers and factors for Rome, to the great danger of this kingdom ... have so far prevailed as to corrupt divers of your Bishops and other in prime places of the church ... and other about your Majesty, the Prince and the rest of your royal children.

'Depriving the Bishops of their votes in Parliament and abridging their immoderate power usurped over the Clergy, and other your good subjects, which they have perniciously abused to the hazard of religion and great prejudice and oppression to the laws of the kingdom and just liberty of your people.' 1641 Dec. Religious clauses from the *Grand Remonstrance*

'... this good Archbishop {Laud} ... failed in those prudences which belong unto a great Minister of State, who like a wise physician is to consider times and seasons as well as persons and diseases.' Warwick.

'I can honour and esteem a virtuous or learned Papist, who being educated in that religion, supposeth it to be truth. But for men to call themselves Protestants, as Bishop Laud, Bishop Wren {of Norwich} ... to inveigh against Popery in word only, and in the main to project and plot the ruin of the truth and the Gospel ... this my soul abhors.' c.1642. Sir Simon D'Ewes MP.

'I much rejoice the Parliament goes on so well ... and I hope it will be with them {the bishops} as it was with Haman; when he began to fall, he fell indeed ... my brother was one of the six and thirty lords that voted against the bishops.' 1642. Lady Brilliana Harley.

'He {Laud} never studied the best ways to those ends ... persons of the Court were every day cited into the High Commission Court, upon the fame of their incontinence or other scandal and prosecuted to their shame and punishment, and was never forgotten, but watched for revenge.' Clarendon.

'{Selden} of the Assembly of Divines was like a Thorne in their sides ... wont to mock their little gilt Bibles and would baffle and vexe them sadly; 'I doe consider the original'; for he was able to runne them all downe with his Greeke and antiquities.' Aubrey.

'There shall be no banding, mincing and carving by halves in God's cause.' Robert Baillie, Scots Covenanter.

'O God, when wilt thou take a chair and sit among the House of Peers. O Lord, when I say, wilt Thou vote among the Honourable Commons?' Pamphlet.

'Fears and tears, cries and prayers, night and day ... though I was afraid to be killed, yet was I weary of so much fasting and praying.' A Bradford youth.

'A Sect, the 'Family of Love' ... Mrs Susanna Snow led away through their base Allurements at length fell mad ... the poet courted her, till time and opportunity both favoured him ... and indeed, she said Nay, and yet he took it ... sustained great wrong, consenting to the lust of the poetical brother ... till by a great Miracle was delivered of her distemperature.' Contemp pamphlet.

'... the very best harmonical musick that ever I heard was in the stately cathedral of the loyal city of York ... the occasion was the great and close siege strictly maintained by three very notable and considerable great armies.' 1644 York. Thomas Mace.

'That he hath expressed his disaffection to the Parliament and their proceedings in the exercise of his ministry and preaching that Schismatics and Heretics did raise an amy against the King, and hath prayed that God would prosper him in all his undertakings, as in his private conference in saying the Parliament have done no good.' c.1644. Accusations against a Surrey rector.

'We played there with our granadoes from our mortar pieces, cut off a commissioner of theirs {Cavaliers} by the thighs ... The Lord's Day we spent in preaching and prayer, whilst our gunners were battering,' 1645. Winchester. Hugh Peter, chaplain.

'A Great fight in the Church at Thaxted, Essex between the Sequestrators and the minister, and the Mayor being present; the men and women in this fight fell all together by the ears on the Lord's Day ... divers of the chief actors were brought before the House of Lords in Parliament assembled, this present Friday, September 24th 1647, with the manner of the tryall and the several charges brought in against them at the Lord's Barre. London. Printed for Henry Becke in Aldersgate Street. Anno Domini 1647.' Pamphlet.

Parish Registers

'By the authority of the most excellent Prince Henry, by the Grace of God Kynge of Englande and of France, defensor of the faithe, Lorde of Irelande, and in the erthe supreme hedd under Christ of the Church of England. '... that every parson, vicar or curate within this diocese for every churche kepe one boke or register wherein ye shall write the day and yere of every weddyng, christenyng and buryeng ...' 1538, Sept.' Injunction of Henry VIII for the keeping of Parish Registers.

Christenings

'Remember-death, the son of Roger Parker.' 1617. Kent.

James, son of Ambrose Bell, was the last Baptism with the Book of Common Prayer in this Parish.' 1645. Whitworth, Durham.

'John, son of Joseph Lloyd and Elnor baptised. The infant was the first baptized after the new forme of the Directory, and not the Common Prayer Book.' 1647. Salop.

'Mary Lane, a child found in the Lane, whose father and mother we know not, was baptized.' c.1640. Bucks.

Marriages

'Richard Clinkadagger & Elizabeth Harris were married.' 1630. Cranford, Middlesex.

'James Herriot Esq and Elizabeth Josey were married Jan 4. This James Herriott was one of the 40 children of his father, a Scotchman.' 1625. Bermondsey.

Burials

'Lawrence Wilcox and John Carter that were killed in the Colepitt with the earth damp {firedamp}.' 1604. Walsall, Staffs.

'Emme Wilbey was buried, slaine by a brick falling down the chimney.' 1627. Ipswich.

'Everest, a creeple ... Faint-Not, sonne of Abel Willsons wife ... a poore wretch dying in Mr Johnson's Barne ... Thomas Holmes senior, yeoman of the guard ... John Battie, a Blackamore or Indian ... Mr Walter Leigh, ye sword bearer of London ... Jone Gadson, an old mayd ... Mr Turner, ancient gent.' 1614-1649, Sevenoaks, Kent.

'A prisoner brought unto ye goal leaped over into the water and drownde himself, was buried by the highway at the foote of the bridge.' 1620. Derby.

'John Colcott, aged 108 years was buried.' 1627. Dorking, Surrey.

'Prothasia Sheen buried, in the night, but not by a minister.' 1631. Methley, Yorks.

'Mr Richard Napier, rector, renowned physician both of body and soul.'1634.

'Buried Symon Wilkes, gentleman, executed upon presumption of murder, but he denied it to death.' 1631. Reading.

'Frances, wife of Robert Haslowe was buried, perished with colde on ye moor.' 1638. Derbyshire.

'A man that was shot by the Scottish in the meadows, as he was coming up the water in a boat.' 1644. Durham.

'Rose, ye wife of Robert Lunford was buried, she was a recusant papist, she was buried in the night without the church ceremonies.' 1642. North Elmham, Norfolk

'Mr Thorntone, a quarter-master of the Kinges Majesties armie was buried.' 1643. Helmdon, Northants.

'Nine soldiers in a skirmish in the field of Reby buried. Charles Skelton, a soldier wounded in the same skirmish, was buried.' 1645, June. Reby, Lincs.

'Thomas Boivell, a wounded souldier, dyed and was buried.' 1645. Collyweston, Northants.

'John Harrington, Lieutenant Colonel, slain at the fight at Reby Gapp, was buried. John Pugson, a Cavileere, wounded at the fight, buried.' 1645, June. Stallingborough, Lincs.

'James Store, being 122 years of age.' 1647. Newcastle.

'A Lieutenant shot by William Parr, his name not known.'
1648. Kensington.

'William Joplin, a soldier slain at the siege of Raby Castle buried in the church. Many soldiers slain before Raby Castle, which were buried in the park and not registered.'
1648, Aug. Staindrop, Durham.

*

'This year was the Communion table railed in, by the appointment of the chancellor to the Archbishop of Canterbury {Laud}, who commanded this uniformity to be general throughout the kingdom.'
1637. East Peckham, Kent.

'When Advent comes do thou refraine
Till Hilary sett ye free again.
Next Septuagesima saith thee nay,
Yet at Rogation thou must tarrie
Till Trinitie shall bid thee marry.'
1641. Beverley, Yorks.
'Rules for Marriage'

'This year the Scotts entered this kingdome; the first Parliament {Short} broke, and a second one {Long} was assembled, in which were various consultations about the affairs of the kingdome.' 1641. Wadhurst, Sussex.

'The 22nd of this August ... *errectum fuit Nottinghamie Vexillum Regale*, {was raised the royal standard at Nottingham} Matt.xii.25.'
1642. All Saints, Derby.

'Prince Rupert besieged the Close at Lichfield which was valiantly maintained till ye 21, and took full quarter and with great honour marched away. The Hon. Lord Brooke slain at the Siege.' 1643, March. All Saints, Derby.

'By His great power wee put to flight,
Our rageing foes that Thursday night,
Who came to Plunder, Burne and Slay,
And quite consume us ere the day.
Serve God with fear, on him depend,
As then, soe ever, he will defend.'
1643. Bruton, Somerset.
Repulse of a Roundhead attack.

'All men were warned to go against the Scotts, and that day was the heavens set on fire {by beacons} to warn all the Country.' 1644. Whorlton, Durham.

'Order of Penance ...
'Mary T shall upon Sunday next after divine service stand in a white sheet from head to foot and in the presence of the congregation make her confession: Good people, I have grievously offended Almighty God by falling into ye foul sin of fornication, thereby giving an evil example to my neighbours.
'Elizabeth S for the foul sin of adultery with Thomas H ....
'Anne H falling in to the foul sin of fornication ...'

'To the ringers when the King came through the town   8s.0d'
1647 June. St Albans. Escorted by men of the New Model, the King was greeted with enthusiasm and respect throughout his journey to London.

'Thirteen slain men on the King's party was buried.
York besieged by the Scots. We waite for York.
York yielded, b.g.p.h {blessing, glory, praise, honour}.
Nazeby victory b.p.g.h.t. {blessing, praise, glory, honour, truth) be given.
Kingdome now quite doubtful of the treaty broken up, the King and Prince {Rupert} threaten sore, the Lord prevent it.
Debate betwixt Parliament and Army - Lord cease it.' 1643-1647. Register of St Mary's, Beverley, Yorks.

'Our great Scrimmage in Beverley, and God gave us the victory at that tyme, ever blessed be God.

'... grossly particularising in his sermons, and for suffering his poultry to roost and his hogs to lodge in the chancel.' Episcopal Visitation to a country parish.

'The Lord goeth out against us in the season, which was wonderful wet ... We never had the like in my memory, and that for the greatest part of the summer. Commonly we had one or two floods weekly, or indeed in the meadows there was as it were a continual flood.' 1648. Essex.

'This day by the wonderful goodness of God, his sacred Majesty King Charles II was peacefully restored to his martyred father's throne ... from this day ancient orders began to be observed. Laus Deo. 1660, May. Maids Moreton.

'{a Puritan} declared in public congregation he would rather hear a plain countryman speak in the church, that came from the plough than the best orthodox minister ... upon Christmas day last one Bunyan, a tinker, was countenanced and suffered to speak in his pulpit.' c.1665 contemp. report.

'Here lieth expecting the Second Coming of our blessed Lord and Saviour, Sir Henry Kingsmill, Knight, who serving as a Captain of foot under His Majesty King Charles I of blessed memory was at the Battle of Edgehill in the year of our Lord 1642 as he was manfully fighting on behalf of his King and Country unhappily slaine by a cannon bullett - in memory of whom his mother, the Lady Bridget Kingsmill, did in the 46th year of her widowhood 1670 erect this monument.'
Radway Church, Edgehill, Warwicks.

Bells

'Lord, quench this furious flame,
Arise, run, help, put out the same.'
1652 bell inscription Sherborne Abbey.

'1507. Coronation of Henry VIII 1.0d
'1586. Paid for ringing at the beheading
of the Queen of Scots 1.0d
'1588. Paid bellringers at the Defeat
of the King of Spayne 1.0d
'1605. Paid for ringing at the time
the Parliament House should
have been blown up 2.0d
'1660. Paid to the ringers on the
Day the King returned 10.0d
Accounts from various registers.

53

9

SCOTLAND & IRELAND
The Bishops' Wars

'In 1637 there was as little curiosity either in the court or the country to know anything of Scotland, or what was done there, that when the whole nation was solicitous to know what passed weekly in Germany and Poland, no man ever inquired what was doing in Scotland.' Clarendon *History*.

'No sooner had the Dean of Edinburgh opened the Book {of Common Prayer}, but there were among the meaner sort, especially the women, clapping of hands and hideous execrations and outcries. The Bishop of Edinburgh {David Lindsay}, went into the pulpit, thinking to appease the tumult and presently a stool was thrown at his head ... outcries, rapping at the doors and throwing in stones at the windows, crying "A Pope, A Pope, Antichrist, pull him down", that the bailiffs were forced to come again ... Service and sermon ended, the Bishop repairing home, was near trodden to death but rescued by some who observed his danger.' 1637 July. St Giles Cathedral. Rushworth.

'Wilt thou say Mass in my lug?'. Jenny Geddes. 'The brood of the bowels of the whore of Babylon.' Montrose.

'The whole people think Popery at the doors. I think our people possessed with a bloody devil ... I may be killed and my home burnt over my head. 'I am affrighted with a bloody civil war.' 1637. Minister Robert Baillie.

'Covenant for Religion according to the Word of God, Crown and Kingdoms' 1638. Standard of the Covenanters.

'If the Scots chose another king, the whole power of England could not subdue them.' 1638, London. Francesco Zonca, Venetian envoy.

'His Majesty's royal pleasure is that all occasions sett apart you be in readiness ...at Yorke as a curassier in russett armes, with guilded studds or nayles and befittingly horsed. 1639 Feb. Lord Pembroke's summons to Sir Edmund Verney, Knight Marshall.

'For the earl of Holland, the ill-chosen Generall of the English horse, was appointed ... to face the Scotch army, whose horse were inconsiderable, and whose foot were ill-appointed and very numerous .. without trying the metall of either makes a retreat ... Thus the English credit sunk down, and the Scotch rose.' Warwick *Memoirs*.

'I have not yet seen my armour for it is at Newcastle ... it will kill a man to serve in a whole cuirass, I am resolved to use nothing but back, breast and gauntlet ... if I had a pot for the head that were pistol proof it may be that I would use it ... ships coming daily to Newcastle for coals, send it with an extraordinary charge to deliver it with all speed.' Sir Edmund Verney.

Sir William Compton, son of the Earl of Northampton
'the sober young man and godly Cavalier'

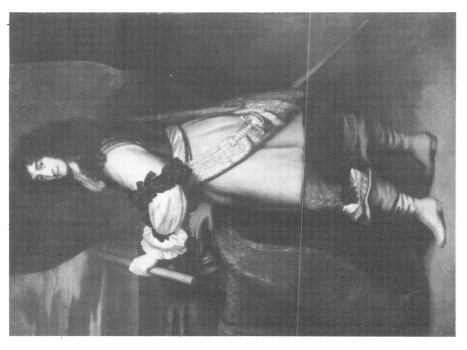

Prince Rupert - before the Civil War & after the Restoration

Sir Thomas Fairfax

Bilborough Church, near York

John, Lord Byron
'tended to engage the enemy when he needed not'

'The dishonourable Pacification soon ensued ... attended by my lord Say, Brook, Wharton ... that they might do no mischief at home in his {king's} absence, they did much more here ... the actions of the Scots, they took the liberty of justifying them by not censuring them.' Warwick.

'... this day English and Scotch nobility meet, in great hope of an honourable peace ... the King has promised them {Scots} a new assembly, and to ratify in Parliament anything that shall be agreed on in their assembly.' Verney.

'I think as you do, Scotland is the veriest devil that is out of Hell.' 1640. Laud to Strafford.

'... the Earl of Northumberland's either casual sickness or resolved deserting {refusal} of his command.' Warwick.

'The infamous, irreparable rout of Newburn ... never so many ran from so few.' 1640 Aug. Contemp. reports.

'The Parliament is observed to be more forward to pay the Scotch, than the English Army.' 1641. Warwick

'The Scots bringing in lice and presbytery.' Contemp. comment.

'Go on with a vigorous war... reduced to extreme necessity everything is to be done that power might admit ... They {Short Parliament} refusing, you {Charles I} are acquitted towards God and man.' 1641 5 May. Strafford.

Irish Rebellion 1641

'Ireland is universally revolted.' A Catholic priest

'We are now at our last gasp, if England do not speedily help us, we are buried alive.' 1641. Earl of Cork

'The frights and terrors we here live in cannot well be expressed ... by the great personages going away, our danger ... by gaining the king or some great man's letters to procure for me a Company of foot, I shall have them garrisoned at Youghal when we leave the field.' 1641 Dec. Sir John Leeke.

'... barbarous rebels who delight in cruelty and take pleasure in insolency, above and beyond the worst of infidels ... though I have never been much in love with Papists, yet I believed them to be christians, but if they offer violence to you or yours I shall change my opinion.' 1641 Nov. Ralph Verney.

'... from my brother now at Chester; by general reports and by the calculation of judicious and knowing men, the papists have murdered and destroyed in Ulster fifty thousand Protestants, men, women and children ... it concerns us all to endeavour the prevention of the like in this Kingdom. 1641. Thomas Stockdale.

'I hope these ill news from Ireland may hinder some of these follies in England.' 1641 Charles I to Secretary Nicholas.

'Ormund cannot come from Dublin either to succour his wife, his country or chastise his brainsick brother, his country is more infested than any of our parts, three lords of the Butlers {Ormonde's family} are in action.' 1641. Letter from Ireland.

'Whilst the King was in Scotland broke forth that dismal, inhumane and bloody rebellion of the Irish; for it was not unlikely that Popery would be projecting her advantages when Presbytery was making such a harvest by her disloyalty both in England and in Scotland ... For these men carried their plot with that Jesuitical secrecy and cruelty ... it has been thought that in one week they massacred very near one hundred thousand persons, men, women and children.' Warwick.

'While the King was in Scotland that cursed rebellion in Ireland broke out, above 200,000 were massacred in two months' space, being surprised and many of them inhumanly butchered and tormented; and besides the slain, abundance of poor families stripped and sent naked away out of all their possessions ... the providence of God miraculously prevented the surprise of Dublin Castle.' Lucy Hutchinson.

'A company of naked rogues {rebels}.' Sir William St Leger, Lord President of Munster.

'Like swarms of bees,{the rebels in Kildare} in the woods, bogs and other places of advantage.'

'Bloody Irish butchers, no tomb or continent enough to hide the slain.'

'... neither sparing the rebel because he is my kinsman or was my friend, nor yet will I one jot the more sharpen my sword to satisfy anybody but myself in the faithful performance of my charge ... if they {his wife and children} shall receive injury by men, I shall never revenge it on women and children, which, as it would be base and unChristian would be extremely below the price I value my wife and children at.' 1641. Earl of Ormonde.

'... In a most pitiful and lamentable case. We have and hear of nothing but fire and sword and pitiful sights of poor people stripped naked as ever they were born, and we can expect nothing but famine for they destroy all - they which at Michaelmas last were worth three or four thousand pounds now begs at our door ... Lord {Barrymore} behaves himself gallantly ... every day and look to be besieged and our town fired, the enemy takes our cows and cattle to our very door, God help us we know not what to do.' 1642 March. Magdalen Faulkner.

'Irishmen unanimous for God, King and Country'. 1642 Sept. Kilkenny. Declaration of the Irish Confederation.

'He left a distressed lady and four children, with an encumbered and disjointed estate and all his country wasted.' 1642. Death of Lord Barrymore after a skirmish at Liscarrol.

'The cruelty of one enemy cannot excuse the unhumanity of another.' 1642 protestant soldier.

'... ill news that there is peace betwixt Spain and France, sure they will come upon us and help Ireland. I pray God keep us from the miseries that other nations have suffered by war.' 1642 Lady Sussex to Ralph Verney.

'Your distractions in England keep us so poor in Ireland that we scarce know how to put bread in our mouths.' 1643 Oct. Letter from the Royalist army.

'Cromwell, freed from the fear of his Levellers, little regards ... his dear brethren the Scots, who now bewayle the King's murder, the Kirk's little reformation, and the Covenant's dying condition; but he casts his eye rather upon Ireland, where he knew, there was in chief command an eminent person, the Marquis of Ormond, at the heart of a stout and loyall army. Which he conceived fittest for to grapple with, and to me made an occasion to divert the fury of his own army, which he saw would be too busy in England if they were not employed abroad. 1649 Feb. Warwick.

'If Cromwell come over, we shall more dread his money than his face.' 1649. Ormonde.

'Drogheda, was lately reinforc'd by five and twenty thousand men, and a good soldier Governor thereof, Sir Arthur Aston, yet he takes it by storm, and puts both the Governor and all the Officers and the soldiers, and very many of the inhabitants to the sword .. the Parliament army in the north of Ireland likewise under Sir Charles Coot, freeing themselves from the siege of London-derry, so that in less than a year he subdued the whole force of Ireland.' 1649. Warwick *Memoirs*

'... ordered by me to put them all to the sword ... in the heart of action I forbad them to spare any that were in arms in the town, and I think that night they put to the sword about two thousand men ... about a hundred of them possessed St Peter's Church ... being summoned to yield to mercy, refused, whereupon I ordered the steeple to be fired ... one of them was heard in the midst of the flames 'God damn me, God confound me, I burn, I burn.' 1649. Cromwell's despatch. Like Colchester, the storm of Drogheda was according to the Articles of War.

Scotland - Civil War

'Your affairs will at any rate be in no worse case than they are at present, even if I should not succeed.' 1643 Oxford. Montrose's offer to raise the Highlands was rejected by the King.

'If your Majesty beat the Scots, your game is absolutely won.' 1644 Feb. Lord Newcastle, before Marston Moor.

'Give me a thousand of your Horse, and I will cut my way into the heart of Scotland.' 1644. Montrose to Rupert.

'King Campbell - Gruamach the Sullen The Campbells ... worthy of a better chief and a juster cause - He wanted nothing but honesty and courage to be a very extraordinary man.' Contemp. comments on the Marquis of Argyll.

'I was willing to let the world see Argyll was not the man his Highlanders believed him to be, and to beat him in his own Highlands.' Montrose.

'Jesus, and no quarter.' 1644 Sept. Perth. Lord Elcho's Covenanting army.

'Montrose {at Tippermuir} makes his files only three deep ... the ranks all to discharge at once, those in the first ranks kneeling, in the second stooping and in the hindmost where he had the tallest men, upright.' 1648.
'The King's Affairs in Scotland.'

'A man could have walked to Perth on the dead.' After victory at Tippermuir.

'The riches of that town hath made all our soldiers Cavaliers.' 1644 Sept. Sack of Aberdeen by Montrose's Irish Macdonalds.

'Left neither house no hold unburned, corn nor cattle that belonged to the name of Campbell.' The Macdonalds.

'Have you not once gotten your fill of blood?' 1646, Philiphaugh. Covenanting army turned on its own ravening ministers after Montrose's defeat.

'Good sermons and prayers, morning and even, under the roof of heaven, the drums did call for bells.' Baillie.

'{Capture of Newcastle by Leslie} ... the common Souldier betook himself to what he could, and the Officer almost to what he would ... the Scots are more orderly than the English ... a Scots souldier will very orderly stand sentinel at the door ... so that the Town was not spoiled in specie, but only purged by a composition ... some good bargains, some ill.' 1646. *Manifest Truths*

'We {Scots} had no cannon, nay, not one field piece, very little ammunition, and not one officer to direct it. Dear Sandy {Leslie} being grown old and doted, and given no fitting orders.' 1648, Preston. Sir James Turner.

'Give assurance that you will not admit or suffer any that have been active in or consenting to the Engagement against England to be employed in any public place or trust whatsoever.' 1648 Oct, Edinburgh. Cromwell dictating terms to Argyll.

'But when the Stork Cromwell was sent to subdue and govern this disloyall people {Scots}, his ships were lighter, but his arms heavier ... runs up with his ships unto Inverness, or those parts, and cuts off all communication betwixt the north and south of Scotland, insomuch as he forced our present King Charles the second, afterwards defeated at Worcester, rather to march into England upon necessity than choice.' 1651. Warwick.

10

THE HIGH COMMAND

Robert Devereux, Earl of Essex

'The Earl of Essex searched for
his wife
And where do you think he found her?
Upon the bed of Robert Ker,
As flat as any flounder'.
Contemp. ballad. c.1612.

'On Tuesday last the Earl of Essex,
now Lord Chamberlain, was by His
Majesty declared at the Council Board
to be General of all the forces on this
side Trent.' 1641 July.
Secretary Nicholas.

'Impotent Essex, is it not a shame,
Our Commonwealth, like to a
Turkish dame, should have a eunuch
guardian. May she be ravished by
Charles, rather than saved by thee,
a gelding earl.'
1642. John Cleveland.

'The Lawes and Ordinances of Warre,
Established for the better conduct of
the Army by his Excellency the Earle of
Essex, Lord Generall of the Forces
raised by the Authority of Parliament,
for the defence of the King and
Kingdom.' 1642 Sept.

'... the whole Parliament cause had
been often hazarded, how many opportunities of finishing the war had been
overslipped by the Earl of Essex; and
it was believed that he himself, with his
commanders, rather endeavoured to
become arbiters of war and peace,
than conquerors for the Parliament.'
Lucy Hutchinson *Memoirs*

'{Essex} wished only to be kindly
looked upon, kindly spoken to, and
kindly to enjoy his own fortune.'
Clarendon *History*

'Hurrah, hurrah for Old Robin.'
1643. The army at Hounslow Heath.

'I shall desire ... that you avoid cruelty,
for it is my desire rather to save the life
of thousands, than to kill one.'
Essex to his troops.

'... summer in Devonshire, summer in
Yorkshire and cold winter at Windsor.'
1643. Henry Marten, on Essex taking
up his winter quarters too early.

'I thought it fit to look to myself, it
being a greater terror to me to be a
slave {prisoner} to their contempts
than a thousand deaths.'
1644 Sept. Essex excusing his escape
by sea, and abandonment of the army,
after his defeat at Lostwithiel.

'... {why should the Roundheads
swear} to live and die with the Earl of
Essex, since the Earl hath declared
that he will not live and die with them.'
1644 Sept. Royalist pamphlet.

'There is but a step between us and
death, and what is worse, Slavery.'
1644. Essex in the Lords.

'Rather than they {Essex, Manchester etc.} would consent to make the King a prisoner, they would all die.' Clarendon.

'... {had he lived} he might have been able to have undone much of the mischief he had formerly wrought; to which he had great inclinations, and had indignation enough for the indignities himself had received from the ingrateful Parliament, and wonderful apprehension and detestation of the ruin he saw like to befall the King and kingdom ... ' Clarendon.

Edward Montagu, Earl of Manchester

'... by his natural civility, good manners and good nature which flowed towards all men, he was universally acceptable and beloved.
'Of a soft, obliging temper, of no great depth but universally beloved, being both a virtuous and a generous man.
'A sweet meek man.'
Contemp. comments.

'We find our men never so cheerful as when there is work to do ... we have some {Manchester} amongst us much slow in action.' Cromwell.

'Thou are a bloody fellow. God give us peace, for God does never prosper us in our victories to make them clear victories.' 1644. To Haselrig.

'So long as the enemy continues in the field we cannot advise that you should go to your winter quarters, but are very desirous that, keeping your forces together, you will use your best endeavours to recover the advantage the enemy hath lately gained.'
1644 Autumn. Orders from the Committee of Both Kingdoms.

'His backwardness was not merely from dullness or indisposedness to engagement, but withal from some principle of unwillingness in his Lordship to have this war prosecuted unto a full victory and a design to have it ended by accommodation on some such terms to which it might be disadvantageous to bring the King too low.'
1644 Nov. Cromwell to the Commons.

'If we beat the King ninety-nine times yet he is King still, and his posterity, and we subjects still; but if the King beat us once we should be hanged and our posterity undone.'
1644. Manchester to Cromwell.

'If that be so, my lord, why did we take up arms at first. This is against fighting ever hereafter.' Cromwell.

'The Earl is become the owl of the Commonwealth wherein every bird hath a peck at him, if he escape with the loss of his feathers only, his condition will be very much above the expectation of his friends. He is set upon the falconer's stall to let the people see there's such a creature and of no use, or else the better to set their new high flying hawk of the North {Fairfax}.' 1645 Feb. Royalist letter.

Prince Rupert

'I know my cause is so just that I need not fear; for what I do is agreeable both to the laws of God and man, in the defence of true religion, a King's prerogative, an uncle's right and a kingdom's safety.' 1642 Sept. Rupert's challenge to Essex of single combat.

'The old General {Forth} was set aside and Prince Rupert put into the command, which was no popular change, for the other was known to be an officer of great experience ... the Prince was rough and passionate, and loved not debate, liked what was proposed as he liked the person who proposed it, and was so great an enemy to Digby and Culpepper, who were only present in debates of the War with the officers, that he crossed all they proposed.' Clarendon.

'My fear is most of Prince Rupert, for they say he has little mercy when he comes ... such grievous fears that if they see but a gentleman riding they think it is to rob them.'
1643. Lady Sussex to Ralph Verney.

'The King is much troubled to see your Highness discontented, and I could wish that some busy-bodies would not meddle as they do with other men's offices ... There is speech as if there had been discovered by Prince Maurice a design to have betrayed Worcester, but I have not any certainty of this; but since I see treachery, though not in request, yet not punished, I am apt to believe that traitors will multiply.'
1643 May. Nicholas to Rupert.

'How many towns hast thou fired? How many virgins hast thou ruined? How many godly ministers hast thou killed? How many innocents hast thou slain? How many oaths hast though belched out against God and his people? ... the Robber Prince ... the flying dragon prince ... Prince Robber of Plunderland ... the ungrateful viper.'
1643/44. Parliamentary pamphlets

'I {Charles I} must profess to you upon the faith of a Christian ... that concerning your generosity and particular fidelity and friendship to me, I have implicit faith in you.' 1644, Oxford.

'I shall not trouble you with any great business, supposing that Secretary Nicholas hath orders to acquaint you with all particulars ... we are in much better condition since you have brought off so many gallant men and among them yourself. Your faithful friend to serve you, Rupert.' 1644 Oct. Cirencester. To George Goring.

'At Oxford a lamentable fire, which hath burnt near two hundred houses ... the enemy press upon the King; Prince Rupert is so much given to his ease and pleasures that every man is disheartened that sees it. This city of Bristol is but a great house of bawdry, and will ruin the King, and by all I see, Prince Rupert is resolved to lie by it.'
1644 Oct, Oxford. Secretary Nicholas tc Ormond in Ireland.

'Nephew, I am not half so troubled with Sir John Winter's ill luck as I am glad you will be able so soon to march from Bristol and that you will bring more Foot with you, at your being last with me you promised. As for my reasons for my quick marching this way, ... there was great necessity for it ...
Your loving and most faithfull friend, Charles R.' 1644 Oct. Whitchurch.

'For God's sake, sire, prevent accidents {quarrels} that may make us less at unity among ourselves, and then I am confident the enemy will not prevail.' 1645 June. Clarendon to Rupert.

'...{the King} had no way left to preserve his posterity, kingdom and nobility but by treaty. I believe it a more prudent way to retain something than to lose all.' 1645. Rupert to friends in Oxford after Naseby.

'The Prince clad in scarlet, very richly laid in silver lace, mounted upon a very gallant black barbary horse the General {Fairfax} and the Prince rode together, the General giving the Prince the right hand all the way.' 1645 Sept. Report of surrender of Bristol.

'Though the loss of Bristol be a great blow to me yet your {Rupert's} surrendering it as you did is ... the greatest trial of my constancy that hath yet befallen me ... one that is so near to me as you are both in blood and friendship, submits himself to so mean an action, (I give it the easiest term) ... you assured me that, if no mutiny

happened, you would keep Bristol four months. Did you keep it four days? was there anything like a mutiny? ... my conclusion is to desire you to seek your subsistence somewhere beyond the seas, to which I send you herewith a pass.' Oxford. Charles I to Rupert.

'... I am sorry to understand that Your Majesty hath not that satisfaction which I endeavoured to give in my last letter {surrender of Bristol} ... I shall once again freely acknowledge my errors and humbly entreat Your Majesty to consider me by the better and more lastinge expressions of my Zeal and affection, and to pardon what is done amiss ...
  'My humble duty and service to Your Majesty in which way be pleased to command and dispose as you shall think fit.' 1645 Oct. Prince Rupert's apology was accepted, but he was not restored to favour or command, and he prepared to leave England with his brother Maurice.

'At Walton, within two miles of Belvoir, I met with Prince Rupert and Prince Maurice, with three or four hundred horse, and within a short time after engagement, their forlorn hope ran away ... we took in the pursuit one major, three captains, sixty gentlemen, and several other prisoners, many slain, about one hundred and fifty horse taken; and the two princes, the Lord Mullineux and the Lord Hawley, and eight other great persons, escaped narrowly with the rest.'
1645 Oct. Colonel Rossiter.

'... he {Rupert} suffered two or three mutinies, in one of which he had been compelled to throw two or three seamen overboard by the strength of his own arms.' 1648. Clarendon.

'This day, or yesterday, I hear, Prince Rupert is come to Court; but welcome to nobody.' 1660 Sept. Pepys.

'It is a life of honour {a soldier's}, but a dog would not lead it.' Rupert.

William Cavendish, Marquis of Newcastle

'My Lord, I would not have you take too much Phisick for it doth alwaies make me worse and I think will do the like with you ... I ride every day, and am ready to follow any other directions from you. Make hast to returne to him that love you. Charles P.' 1638. Prince of Wales to his governor.

'He would put off his hat to the merest artisans.' Contemp. comment.

'Her Majesty, having some present occasion for money, My Lord presented her with £3,000 sterling.' 1643.

'Farewell, great soul, the glory of thy fall, outweighs the cause.' 1641. tribute to his friend, Strafford.

'... which generosity gained more than any reputation he could have gotten in detaining a lady prisoner upon such terms.' 1643 June. Return of Lady Fairfax to Hull in his own coach.

'... his Majesty forbears to agree to any cessation until he shall be, from the Earl of Newcastle fully informed of the state of his army ... Prince Rupert to keep himself to his instructions ...' 1643 April, Oxford. Secretary Nicholas.

'Redeemer of the North and Saviour of the Crown ... I am made of nothing but thankfulness and obedience to Your Highness.' 1644 July, York. Rupert took these words literally, but Newcastle was slow to act upon his peremptory orders before Marston Moor.

'I will not endure the laughter of the court.' 1644, 3 July, Scarborough. Newcastle taking ship for Holland after the Royalist defeat in the North,

'{creditors} shewed themselves very civil to My Lord, yet they grew weary at length ... I must of necessity pawn my clothes to make so much money as would procure dinner.' 1645, Paris.

'Sir, I am not ignorant that many believe I am discontented, and 'tis probable they'll say I retire through discontent {but} I am in no kind of ways displeased ... I have no other will but your Majesty's pleasure.' 1660. Letter to Charles II, quitting the court.

'I observe your gracious master does not love you, as well as you love him.' Margaret, his second wife. Newcastle retired to Welbeck as Lord-Lieutenant of Nottinghamshire and was made a duke 1665. His duchess took up her pen in 'My Lord's' defence.

SENIOR OFFICERS

'If he {Lindsey} was not fit to be a general he would rather die a colonel at the head of his regiment.' 1642. Edgehill. Lord Lindsey at the Royalist council of war, later killed leading his Foot into battle.

*

'He {Astley} could not give any assurance against His Majesty being taken out of his bed if the rebels should make a brisk attempt to that purpose.' 1642 Aug. Nottingham.

'As fit for the office of Major General of Foot as Christendom yielded.' Contemp. report.

'Lord, I shall be very busy this day, if I forget thee, do not thou, forget me.' 1642, Edgehill. Astley to his troops before the battle.

'You may now go play, unless you fall out among yourselves.' 1646. Stow-on-the-Wold. Astley to his captors after the last battle of the First Civil War.

*

'Come, my brave boys, pray heartily and fight heartily and God will bless us ... I will run the same hazards and fortunes as you.' 1642 Edgehill. Sergeant Major General Philip Skippon, to the London trained bands.

'The Christian Centurion'. Skippon's book of soldierly devotions.

'That by the grace of God they that would wrest that standard from his hand, must first wrest his soul from his body.' 1642 April, Nottingham. Sir Edmund Verney, Knight Marshall.

'There is no absolute certainty of his Death {though} I have sent three messengers to both armies ... {one} tells me that there is no possibility of finding my dear Father's body {at Edgehill}... and twenty others of my acquaintance assured him he was never taken prisoner, neither were any of them ever possessed of his body, but that he was slain by an ordinary trooper.' 1642. Ralph Verney.

*

'... I received a declaration of Parliament with a commission from his excellency the Earl of Essex, to command in chief over the forces of the North and other adjacent counties ...
'The Earl of Newcastle is come to York, about 8000 men, horse and foot - a strength far too potent to be resisted by the small power which I have here.' 1642 Dec. Yorkshire. Lord Fairfax.

'Sir Thomas Fairfax's troops killed his {Bellassis} horse under him and ... he had certainly been slain but for the goodness of his arms ... though he asked it not, they gave him quarter and carried him to the Lord Fairfax, their General, my Lord's kinsman, who treated him civilly and sent his chirugeon to dress his wounds.'
1644 April, Selby. J Moone.

'A body torn & mangl'd with shott.'

68

'{Colonel Hutchinson} understood well the military art ... he never disdained the meanest person nor flattered the greatest ... he ever himself in his rank, neither being proud so as to despise any inferior, nor letting fall that just decorum which honour obliged him to keep up.' Lucy Hutchinson *Memoirs*

*

'We were plainly enjoined to draw the train bands to Selby & to oppose the King. All things were for the Parliament's service and this I refused to accept, saying it were to begin the war, which I intended not.' 1642 May. Hugh Cholmley. *Thomason Tracts*

'{Sir Hugh Cholmley} governor of Scarborough, revolted from the Parliament, whereof he was a member and came to the Queen, with three hundred men. Browne Bushell also, who was left in charge of the town, yielded it up.' Lucy Hutchinson.

'I quitted the Parliament without any diminution to my honour either as a gentleman or a soldier.' Hugh Cholmley

*

'If you think fit ... be pleased to make him general {Waller} and me the major general of some brigade.' 1643 June. Essex to Committee of Both Kingdoms.

'The Lords Essex, Northumberland, Pembroke, Holland, Saye & Sele; {MPs}, Pym, Hampden, Holles, Marten, Fiennes, Pierrepoint, Glynne, Waller, Stapleton, Meyrick.' The Committee.

'All the ends I had were but to bring things to a fair and peaceable issue ... That God might had have had his fear; the King his honour; the Houses of Parliament their privileges; the people of the kingdom their liberties and properties; and nothing might have remained upon the score between us, but ... love.' Waller *Memoirs*

'Our reasons are, we believe the war can never end if the King be in any part of the land and not at the Parliament, for break his army never so often, his person will raise another; all the histories of England will manifest that.' 1644. Waller.

*

'The loss of Colonel Hampden goeth near the heart of every man that loves the good of his king and country ... little content to be at the army now that he is gone ... the memory of this deceased colonel is such that in no age to come but it will more and more be had in honour and esteem.' 1643 June. *The Weekly Intelligencer*

*

'To command the Regiment of the train bands of the City of York ... received an order from the King to do the duty of a soulgier, & to be a guard to the King's person ... perceiv'd a great backwardness in {many} ... Sir John Hotham & his Son who refus'd him ...' Sir Henry Slingsby *Diary*

'... met at Huworth moore {Heyworth Moor} but produc'd nothing else but a confus'd murmur & noise ... some crying the King, some the Parliament.' 1642 Aug, Yorkshire. Slingsby.

'I beseech you, think whether it be fit to put Imployment into the hands of Sir John Hotham , now that he denies to pay the ship Money.' 1638. Strafford.

*

One loss we have sustained that is un-valluable, to wit Sidney Godolphin is slain in the attempt {Chagford}, who was as gallant a gent as the world had.' 1643, Feb. Bevil Grenvile to his wife.

'{Godolphin} ... put himself into the first troops raised in the West for the King, and bore uneasiness and fatigue of winter marches with an exemplary courage and alacrity; until by too brave pursuit of the enemy, in an obscure village in Devonshire, he was shot with a musket.' Contemp. report.

'Gone the four wheels of Charles' wain, 'Godolphin, Grenvile, Slanning and Trevanion slain.' By late 1643 all four Cornish leaders had been killed

*

'Had Sir Arthur been victualled as well as fortified he might have endured a siege of seven years.' A rare joke of Charles I on Haselrig's regiment of 'Lobsters', heavily-armed cuirassiers.

'An absurd, bold man.' Clarendon.

'Of disobliging carriage, sower and morose of temper, liable to be trans-ported with passion and to whom liberality seemed a vice.' Ludlow.

*

'As for Sir Marmaduke Langdale, I always took him to be a Person of ill affections ... that gentleman carries an itch about him that will never let him take rest till at one time or another he happen to be thoroughly clawed indeed ... for the love of Christ counsel them out of their madness {refusal to pay Ship Money}.' c.1638. Strafford *Correspondence*

'A lean, mortified man {called} the Ghost ... being the father of many children {his son}, a man of high spirit, regarded him {Sir Marmaduke Langdale} with childish awe.'

'Gentlemen, you are all gallant men, and have done bravely, but there are some that seek to scandalise your gallantry for the loss of Naseby field. But I {Langdale} hope you will redeem your reputation and maintain that gallant report which you ever had.' 1645 Oct. Sherburn, Yorks. Before the last stand of the Northern Horse.

'The Northern Horse ... to march North to joyn with my Lord Mount-ross {Montrose} ... being receiv'd by Coll. {Robert} Lilburne they were quite rout'd leaving dead upon the spot about 40, Sir Richard Hutton was one & Coll. Carnaby & others.' ... My Lord Digby, my Lord Carnwath, Sir Marma-duke Langdale & the better sort, got a boat which wafted them into the Isle of Man, the rest endur'd a great deal of misery.' 1645 Oct. Slingsby.

*

'{Goring} would have broken any trust or done any act of treachery to satisfy an ordinary passion or appetite ... {yet}in truth he had wit and courage and understanding and ambition ... to have been as eminent and successful in the highest attempt in wickedness of any man in the age he lived in, or before.' Clarendon.

*

'Of mean calling ... a drayman and afterwards a stoker in a brewhouse in Islington, and then a chandler in Thames Street ... the low extraction of {Colonel} Okey is buried in obscurity being a tallow-chandler in London.' Royalist pamphlet.

'A cheerful and generous nature and confessedly valiant {Falkland} ... of the strictness and piety of a Puritan, of the charity of a Papist, of the civility of an Englishman ... he was called the only courtier that was not complained of.' Contemp. account.

'... his House was a University in a less Volume, whither they {friends} came not so much for Repose as Study; and to examine and refine those grosser Propositions which laziness and consent made current in vulgar Conversation.' Clarendon of Great Tew, home of Lord Falkland, c.1635.

*

'A prisoner {Lord Kingston} in a pinnace sent down the river to Hull, when my Lord Newcastle's army marching along the shore shot at the pinnace, and the Earl went up on deck to prevail with them to forebear shooting, but a cannon-bullet flew from the King's army and divided him in the middle ... and thus he perished.' Lucy Hutchinson.

'... my window blowndown so that a cart might have entered at the breach. My pistols being wheel-locks and wound up all night I could not get to fire, so that I was forced to trust to my sword for keeping down of the enemy {Royalist attackers}, being alone in the chamber and all relief excluded from me, except such as came in by my windows that looked into the court of the castle.' 1644, Wardour Castle. Governor Edmund Ludlow.

*

'Let the old Drum (Sir John Meldrum) be beaten early on the morrow.' 1644. Newark. Rupert's coded message to the governor, Sir Richard Byron.

*

Sir John Danvers MP, a Roundhead Colonel '... was wont in fair mornings in the Summer to brush his Beaver-hatt on the hyssop and thyme, which did perfume it with its naturall spirit.' John Aubrey *Lives*

*

'{Ormonde} was in every way fitted for a Court; of graceful appearance, a lively wit, and a cheerful temper; a man of great expense, but decent even in his vices.' Burnet 'History'

*

'I {Charles I} have lost one of the best commanders in this kingdom.' 1644. Sir Richard Bolle killed at Alton.

*

'I think that the poorest he that is in England hath a life to lead as the greatest he ... every man that is to live under a government ought first by his own consent to put himself under that government; I do think that the poorest man in England is not at all bound in a strict sense to that government that he hath not had a voice to put himself under.' 1647. Putney Debates. Colonel Thomas Rainsborough.

'Give me leave to tell you that if you make this the rule I think you must fly for refuge to an absolute natural right, and you must deny all civil right.' 1647. Putney Debates. Commissary General Henry Ireton.

'Posterity, we doubt not, shall reap the benefit of our endeavours, whatever shall become of us'. John Lilburne.

'All you intended when you set us a-fighting was merely to unhorse and dismount our old riders and tyrants that you might get up and ride in their stead.' 1648. Lilburne to Parliament.

'If left alone on earth John would quarrel with Lilburne, and Lilburne with John.' Contemp. comment.

'To the Council {of Officers} came the General Cromwell, and the whole gang of creature-colonels and other officers, ... there Ireton showed himself an absolute king, if not an emperor, against whose will no man must dispute ... I took my leave of them for a pack of dissembling, juggling knaves amongst whom in consultation ever thereafter I should scorn to come, as I told some of them, for there was neither faith, truth nor common honesty amongst them.' 1649. John Lilburne. *Legal Fundamental Liberties*

'He either fears his fate too much, Or his deserts are small. Who dares not put it to the touch To gain or lose it all.' Montrose.

'It is spoken of me that I would blame the King {Charles II}. God forbid ... never any people, I believe might be more happy in a King. His commands to me were most just and I obeyed them. He deals justly with all men. I pray he be so dealt withal.' 1650 May, Edinburgh. Montrose on the scaffold.

*

'Without my Lord Fairfax engaging in Yorkshire, Lambert's army had never quitted him, nor {Monk} marched out of Scotland.' Duke of Buckingham.

'He {Lambert} was taken by Colonel Ingoldsby at the head of a party, by which means their whole design is broke, and things now very open and safe ... every man begins to be merry and full of hopes.' 1659 April. Pepys.

*

'I have learned a proverb, that he who follows Truth too close upon the heels will, one time or another, have his brains knocked out.' George Monk.

'This Monk will bring in Charles Stuart ... He is a Black Monk, and I cannot see through him'. Contemp. comment.

*

'Hide the outcasts; betray not him that wandereth.' 1661 New Haven, Conn. Rev. John Davenport to his congregation. Col. Whalley and Maj-Gen Goffe had escaped to New England, and later moved to Milford, Massachusetts.

11

THOMAS FAIRFAX

'...tall, yet not above just proportion, yet taller, as some say, when he is in the Field ... as if victory were in his spirit beforehand ... his body is not without its infirmities, as of rheums and distillations ... and an impediment in his speech.' Joshua Sprigge.

'... exceedingly long for and desire your appearance here; which I am confident were enough to clear these parts if the opportunity be not slipped.' 1644 March. John Lambert to Fairfax.

'... taking along with them a young child {Moll} of Sir Thomas Fairfax, (his Lady fell into my Lord Newcastle's hands who us'd her with all civility) ... Sir Tho. Fairfax having got a shot in his arm ... a goodwife brings him as he sat on horseback a cup of ale, and desired him to go to York. You say well, saith he, but I must not go thither yet.' 1643. Slingsby.

'The man best beloved and relied upon by the rebels in the north.' Pamphlet

'Though there were various opinions about his intellect, there was no doubt about his courage, and that he was a man of his word.' 1644, Lathom House. Countess of Derby

'There is a design to have the Militia new moulded ... I hope that no stranger, but one or our own nation, have the command in chief. It is probable Sir Thomas Fairfax will be called up to be general of the horse.' 1645. James Chaloner to Lord Fairfax.

'... the Army was New Modelled, and a new General was proposed to command it. For which, by the votes of the two Houses of Parliament, myself was nominated though most unfit and so far from desiring it ... I was induced to receive the command.' Fairfax.

'Their new high-flying hawk of the North.' 1645 April. Arthur Trevor to Ormonde in Ireland.

'... for General they chose Sir Thomas Fairfax, who had been in the wars beyond sea and had fought valiantly in Yorkshire for the Parliament ... he was acceptable to sober men because he was religious, faithful, valiant and of a grave, sober, resolved disposition very fit for execution and neither too great nor too cunning to be commanded by the Parliament.' Richard Baxter.

'I have observed him at councils of war, that he hath said little, but hath ordered things expressly contrary to the judgement of all his council.' Whitelocke *Memoirs*

'... if you knew how well I was known to your noble grandfather, I am sure I should receive favour at your hands.' 1646 The Marquis of Worcester seeking terms for surrender of 'my poor cottage at Ragland', Raglan Castle.

'It was the custom of the Ancient Romans, after a glorious and successful prince, to derive his name to posterity in memory of his virtues, as after Julius Caesar his successors retained the name of Caesar, as Augustus Caesar, Tiberius Caesar ... hereafter famous and victorious succeeding generals in this kingdom ... will desire the addition of the name of Fairfax.' 1646, Nov. Speaker Lenthall.

'It is very well known how long now the soldiers have been without pay; and how can it be expected that either I or my officers should have that influence upon them that is meet, considering the straits they are put into for want of pay? 'The private soldier is not ignorant that you have money by you, and the knowledge, and the sense of their own wants, doth not a little heighten them in their discontents.' 1647, Summer. Fairfax to Parliament.

'... 'tis strange that Sir Thomas Fairfax could be so abused by Cromwell, as to believe that Cornet Joyce could go out of the Army with a thousand Soldiers to fetch the King {from Holdenby}, and neither the General {Fairfax}, nor the Lieutenant-General {Cromwell}, nor the Body of the Army, take Notice of it.' Thomas Hobbes *Behemoth*

'For the General, who was but too innocent, I am clearly of the opinion that he was a stranger to this design.' William Waller *Vindication*

'I called for a Court of War to proceed against Joyce for this high Offence and Breach of the Articles, but the Officers, whether for fear of the distempered Soldiers, or rather as I fear a secret Allowance of what was done, made all my Endeavours in this ineffectual.' Fairfax *Memorials*

'As the Honour of these Actions, under God Yours ... when this Generation have exhausted themselves, and done their part, they must commend it to their Posterity, to pay the Remainder to your Name.' 1647. Joshua Sprigge's dedication of *Anglia Rediviva*

'When he hath come upon action, or been near an engagement, it hath been observed, another spirit hath come upon him, another soul hath looked out at his eyes; I mean he hath been so raised, elevated, and transported, as that he hath been not only unlike himselfe at other times, but indeed more like an Angell than a man ...
'He was still for action in Field and Fortification ... for man to do in God's strength, if they would be up and be doing ... he hath done all so soon, because he was ever doing.' Sprigge.

'... to afford all kind usage to his Majesty's person is the most Christian, honourable and prudent course. I further think that tender, equitable and moderate dealing, both towards his Majesty, his royal family and his late party, is the most hopeful course to take away future feuds amongst ourselves and our posterity, and to procure a lasting peace and agreement in this now distracted nation.

'I find this to be the clear sense of the generality, or at least of the most considerable part of the army.'
1647 July. Fairfax to the Speaker.

'This is what we fought for, and by God's help, must maintain.'
1647 Aug. Fairfax, called for a copy of *Magna Carta* when taking over as Constable of the Tower.

'It hath pleased the Lord of Hosts, who was called upon to decide the controversy of this nation, to write His name upon your sword in very legible characters.' 1648. Petition of Colonel Pride's Foot Regiment to the Lord General.

'Fairfax whose name in arms through Europe rings,
Filling each mouth with envy or with praise.' 1648. Milton.

'Not without love, clemency and meekness, by which {Fairfax} kept his Army less stained in the Blood of his Enemy, but not less Victorious.' Sprigge.

'... baited with fresh dogs all Tuesday night to bring him into the Hall on the morrow ... Cromwell put a guard upon Fairfax accusing him of an intention to deliver the King.' 1649. Pamphlet.
*

'I bless God that the noble Lord, having received so many wounds, is here on my right hand.' 1659 Jan. Haselrig, on Fairfax taking his seat for Yorkshire in Richard Cromwell's Parliament.

'If General Monk had any other design than to restore Parliaments to their ancient freedom, and settle the nation upon its ancient government, I {Fairfax} will oppose him ; but otherwise I will heartily join with him.'
1659 Dec. Contemp. report.

'The Lord Fairfax on that subject said that if any man must be excepted {from pardon} he knew no man that deserved it more than himself, who being General of the army at that time, and having power sufficient to prevent the proceedings against the King, had not thought fit to make use of it to that end.' 1660. Ludlow *Memoirs*

'I hope that God will one day clear this Cause we undertook, so far as concerns His honour and the integrity of such as faithfully served Him. For I cannot believe that such wonderful successes have been given in vain, and though cunning and deceitful men must take shame to themselves, the purposes and determinations of God shall have happy effect, to His glory and the comfort of His people. Amen.'
Conclusion of the Fairfax *Memorials*

'He sat like an old Roman, his manly countenance striking awe and reference into all that beheld him, and yet mixed with so much modesty and meekness as no figure of a mortal man ever represented more ... in reading good books, in all modern languages, as appears by those he hath writ and translated.' c.1660s. Nunappleton, Yorkshire. Brian Fairfax.

OLIVER CROMWELL

'I was by birth a gentleman, living neither in any considerable height, nor yet in obscurity.' Cromwell.

'... throwing the stone, tennis, wrestling, running, swimming, handling weapons, riding, hunting, dancing and shooting with the long bow.'
Huntingdon Grammar School.

'His body was well compact and strong, his stature under six feet, I believe {by} about two inches; his head so shaped as you might see in it both a storehouse and shop of a vast treasury of natural parts. His temper exceedingly fiery, but the flame of it kept down for the most part, or soon allayed ... God made him a heart wherein was left little room for any fear, but what was due to Himself ... yet did he exceed in tenderness towards sufferers. ' John Maidston, Cromwell's steward.

'When he appeared first in Parliament he seemed to have a person in no degree gracious, no ornament of discourse, none of those talents ... As he grew into place and authority his parts seemed to be renewed as if he had concealed faculties till he had occasion to use them.' Clarendon.

'That sloven {Cromwell} whom you see before you hath no ornament in his speech; but that sloven, I say, if we should ever come to a breach with the King, which God forbid, in such a case, I say, that sloven will be the greatest man in England.' 1641. Parliament. John Hampden to Philip Warwick.

'Mr Cromwell, who from a very mean figure of a man in the beginning of this Parliament, rose to that prodigious greatness before the end, said to Sir Thomas Chicheley and myself once in the House in the matters concerning Religion "I can tell you, sirs, what I would not have; tho' I cannot, what I would.' Philip Warwick

'... their troopers {Royalist} are gentlemen's sons, younger sons, and persons of quality. Do you think that the spirit of such base and mean fellows will be ever able to encounter gentlemen who have honour and courage and resolution in them? You must get men of spirit that is likely to go on as far as gentlemen will go ... such men as had the fear of God before them, and made some conscience of what they did.'
1642. After Edgehill, to Hampden.

'I had rather have a plain russet-coated captain that knows what he fights for, and loves what he knows, than that which you call a gentleman and is nothing else. I honour a gentleman, that is so indeed ... no man swears but he pays his twelve pence; if he is in drink he is set in the stocks or worse, if one calls the other 'Roundhead' he is cashiered; in so much that the countries where they come leap for joy at them.' 1643. Cromwell.

'Cromwell's troops {Ironsides} if they prevailed, or though they were beaten and routed, presently rallied again and stood in good order till they received new orders.' Clarendon.

'At this time {1643/44} he had never shown extraordinary parts or do I think he did himself believe that he had them; for although he was blunt he did not bear himself with pride of disdain. As an officer he was obedient, and did never dispute my orders or argue upon them.' Sir William Waller.

'All the counties of England no longer idle spectators, but several stages whereon the tragedy of the civil war was acted; except the Eastern Association, where Mr Oliver Cromwell by his diligence prevented the designs of the royal party.' 1643. Lucy Hutchinson.

'... you know my troubles this way, but the Lord supported me with this, that the Lord took him into the happiness we all pant after and live for.' To Valentine Walton after Marston Moor on the death of his son. Captain Oliver Cromwell, had recently been killed or had died, aged 21.

'He goes farthest who knows not wither he is going.' Cromwell.

'It is an odd thing, Mr Ireton, that every man that wages war believes that God is on his side. I'll warrant God must often wonder who is on his.' To his son-in-law, Henry Ireton.

'Without a more speedy, vigorous and effectual prosecution of the war ... we shall make the kingdom weary of us.' 1644. Speech to Parliament.

'I put a high and true value upon your {Thomas Fairfax} love ... I can say in the simplicity of my heart ... which when I forget, I shall cease to be a grateful and an honest man.' Cromwell.

'Gentlemen, I beseech ye in the bowels of Christ, think it possible ye might be wrong.' Letter to the Elders of the Kirk in Edinburgh.

'One thing I must say to General Cromwell and General Ireton themselves. Your credit and reputation hath been much blasted upon two accounts - your dealings with the King, ... which was to satisfy everybody and has satisfied nobody, and your dealings with Parliament.' 1647. Putney Debates. Edward Sexby.

'O Cromwell, thou art led by the nose by two unworthy covetous earthworms, Vane and St John .' 1647. Lilburne.

'If you prove not an honest man, I will never trust a fellow with a great nose for your sake.' 1648. Arthur Haselrig.

'... imparting to {Cromwell}, to your Fellow-Witches, the bottom of your designs, the Policy of your Actings, the Turns of your Contrivances, all your Falsehoods, Cozenings, Villainies and Cruelties, with full intention to ruin the three kingdoms.' 1648. Denzil Holles.

'A prodigious treason ... they that are implacable and will not leave troubling the land may speedily be destroyed.' 1648. Outbreak of Second Civil War.

'This man {Charles I} against whom the Lord hath witnessed.' 1648.

'We will cut off his head with the crown upon it.' 1648. To Colonel Algernon.

'He {Cromwell} loved a good voice and instrumental music.' Contemp. report.

'At push of pike and butt-end of musket until a troop of horse charged ... the General comes himself in the rear of our regiment ... the Scots all in confusion, and the sun appearing upon the sea, I heard Noll say "Now let God arise, and his enemies shall be scattered", and he following us as we marched I heard him say "I profess they run".' 1650 Dunbar. Rushworth.

'And Dunbar field, resounds thy praises loud,
And Worcester's laureate wreath; yet much remains
To conquer still;
Peace hath her victories, No less renowned than War.' John Milton.

'If we do not make good our interest there {Ireland}, we shall not only have our interests rooted out there, but they will in a very short time be able to land forces in England. I confess I had rather be overrun with a Cavalierish interest that a Scotch interest; with a Scotch interest than an Irish interest;

and of all, this is the most dangerous.' 1649. To the Council of State.

'... pray tell Doll I do not forget her, nor her little Brat. She writes very cunningly and complimentally to me; I wish a blessing upon her and her husband.
'The Lord make them fruitful in all that's good. They are at leisure to write often; but indeed they are both idle, and worthy of blame.'
1650, Scotland. Letter to his daughter-in-law's father, Richard Mayor.

'Eighteen Gloucester bakers had sent to Tewkesbury for the Lord General Cromwell's Army thirteen hundred and odd Dozens of Bread at a shilling the dozen, and that the Mayor and others sent forty barrels of strong beer to the Lord General ... as an argument of the good affection of this Corporation ... and wish prosperous success to you and your Army.
'... appointed the Lord General Oliver Cromwell ... High Steward of the same with an annual rent of 100 shillings.' 1651 Sept. Gloucester City Records.

'At last they call a new House of Commons of Saints ... Old Presbyter Rouse, then Provost of Eaton, being their Speaker ... declared their sitting was no longer necessary and so abruptly left the Chair ... took the Mace with him and marched to Whitehall to Cromwell ...
'Within four days Cromwell is chosen Protector of the Commonwealth of England.' Warwick *Memoirs*

Powick Bridge over the Teme - site of first cavalry skirmish 1642

Warwick Castle - garrisoned for Parliament by Lord Brooke

Charles I at his Trial
print from 1648/49

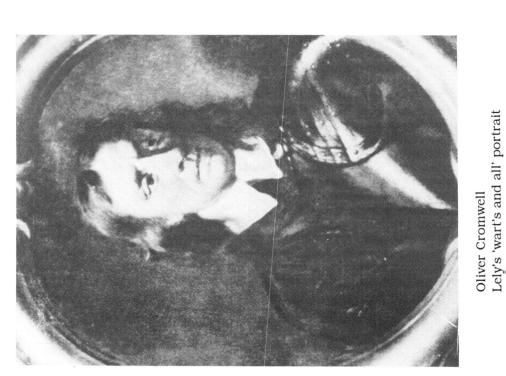

Oliver Cromwell
Lely's 'wart's and all' portrait

Northumberland, Lord High Admiral

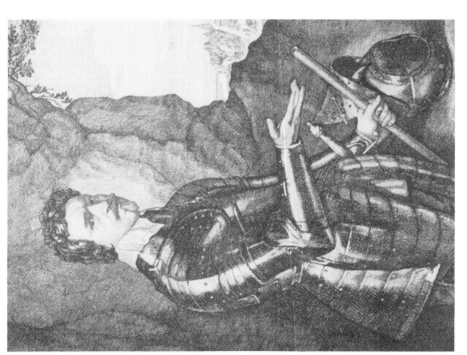

Strafford, Lord Deputy in Ireland

Charles I set out for Hull
from Beverley April 1642

Donnington Castle, guarded the
approaches to Oxford and London

Helmsley Castle. Stormed and
slighted by Fairfax 1644

The Governor, Colonel Hutchinson, held
Nottingham Castle throughout the War

'It's you that have forced me to this for I have sought the Lord night and day that He would rather slay me than put me on the doing of this work.'
1653 April. Dismissal of Parliament.

'By Act of Parliament I was general of all the forces in the three nations of England, Scotland and Ireland; the authority I had in my hand being so boundless as it was.' 1653

'Come again to my house, if thou and I were but an hour of the day together, we should be nearer one to the other.'
1654. Cromwell to George Fox.

'... hoped to make the name of an Englishman as great as ever that of a Roman had been.' Cromwell to the Council of State.

'Truly I will now come and tell you a story of my own weakness and folly. And yet it was done in my simplicity ... It was thought that men of our judgement who had fought in the wars and were all of a piece upon that account {could govern wisely} ... the issue was not answerable to the simplicity and honesty of the design.' The failure of the Barebones Parliament.

'I will not dispute the justice of it {execution of Charles I} when it was done, nor need I now tell you what my opinion is in the case if it were *de novo* to be done.' 1657.

'The Lord cause His face to shine upon you and enable you to do great things for the glory of your Most High God and to be a relief unto His people. My dear son, I leave my heart with thee. A good night.' 1654. Whitehall Palace. Cromwell's mother, aged nearly 90.

'For truly I have, often thought that I could not tell what my business was, nor what I was in the place I stood in, save comparing myself to a good constable set to keep the peace of the parish.' c.1655. Cromwell.

'*Serenissime Potentissimeque Rex, Amice ac Foederate Augustissime ... Majestatis Vestrae Studiosissimus Oliverius Protector Rep. Anglie et.*
Most Serene and Potent King, most close Friend and Ally ... Your Majesty's most friendly Oliver, Protector ... May 26 1658.' To Louis XIV, written by Cromwell's Latin Secretary, Milton.

'The continual troubles and vexations of the poor People of Piedmont professing the Reformed Religion ...'
1658 May. To the ambassador in Paris.

'The cavaliers ... had not patience to stay till things ripened of themselves, but were every day forming designs, and plotting for the murder of Cromwell ... which being contrived in drink and managed by false and cowardly fellows, were still revealed to Cromwell who had the most excellent intelligence of all things that passed, even in the King's closet ...
'To speak truth, Cromwell's personal courage and magnanimity upheld him against all enemies and malcontents.

'... he at last exercised such an arbitrary power that the whole land grew weary of him, which he set up a company of silly, mean fellows, called major-generals as governors in every county.' c.1656. Lucy Hutchinson.

'She lest he grieve, hides what she can her pains,
And he, to lessen hers, his sorrow feigns.'
1658, Summer. Andrew Marvell, on the mortal illness of Elizabeth Claypole.

'At Hampton Court, a few days after the death of the Lady Elizabeth,being then himself under ... that sickness to death, and in his bed-chamber, he called for his Bible ... this scripture did once save my life; when my eldest son died, which went as a dagger to my hear, indeed it did.' 1658 Aug.
Passages concerning his late Highness

'I felt a waft of death come forth... and when I came to him, he looked like a dead man.' 1658 Aug. George Fox.

'I am not able to speak or write, this stroke is so sore ... I can do nothing but put my mouth in the dust and say, It is the Lord.' 1658 Sept. Thurloe.

'His Highness the Lord Protector dyed the 3 day of September. And Lord Richard his sonn was proclaimed in his stead in London on Saturday being the next day, and in Yorke and Hull upon the Tuesday then following.' 1658, Sept. Yorkshire parish register.

'I thought you would hear with joy of the death of that wretch.' 1658, Paris. Henrietta Maria to her sister.

'We shall learn to value him more by missing him than we did when we enjoyed him.' Lady Ranelagh.

'What can be more extra-ordinary than that a person of mean birth, no fortune, no eminent qualities ... should have the courage to attempt, and the happiness to succeed in so improbable a design as the destruction of one of the most ancient and most solid-founded monarchies upon the earth ...
'And ... to bequeath all with one word to his posterity? To die with peace at home and triumph abroad? To be buried among kings, and with more than regal solemnity?' c.1660. Abraham Cowley, Royalist poet.

'A wonderful sudden change in the face of the public; the new Protector Richard {Cromwell} slighted; several pretenders and parties strive for government, all anarchy and confusion. Lord have mercy on us.'
1659, April. Evelyn *Diary*

'Old Mrs Cromwell, Noll's Wife's, petition.' 1661. A document at Whitehall endorsed by Secretary Nicholas.

'He had, I confess served the tyrant Cromwell when a young man, but 'twas without malice, as a souldier of fortune 1672 May. Evelyn, on the death in a naval battle of Edward Montagu, Earl of Sandwich, Admiral of the Blue.

12

SOLDIERS & TROOPERS

'After careless hurrying over their postures with which the companies are nothing bettered, they prepare to give their captain a brave volley of shot at his entrance into his inn; where having solaced themselves for a while after this brave service every man repairs home, and that which is not so well taught them is easily forgotten before the next training.'
1639. Militia officer.

'The trained bands accounted the main support of the realm and its bulwark against unexpected invasion, were effeminate in courage and incapable of discipline, because their whole course of life was alienated from warlike employment, insomuch that young and active spirits were made perfect by the experience of two days ...
  'A small body of desperate cavaliers might overrun and ruin them at pleasure.'   Contemp. report.

'The {trained} bands held it their privilege not to fight outside their own county.' Contemp. report.

'We, the yeomanry, are as free born as any of the gentry of this kingdom, and in this respect we know no privilege they have above us.'
1640. A Hertfordshire protest against compulsory shipment to join the army against the Scots.

'... little men do put on great or tall men's armour and leave little men's armours unfit for great men to put on ... {should} wear their armour just and close to their bodies, soldierlike and neat and fit and not negligently or loosely as though they carried it in a fair or market to sell it.'
Contemp. instructions.

'{The Five Members} retired into the City, and being within a day or two to be brought back to the Houses with the London Trained Bands, which was really treason for them to march thither without the King's Commission'.
1642 Jan. Philip Warwick *Memoirs*

'I found a great concourse of people, yet it was rather like a great fair than a posse and but few were armed. All were so transported by the jollity of the thing that no man was capable of the labour, care and discipline needed.'
Devon. General Sir Ralph Hopton.

'Parliament's soldiers of the Militia not enduring to lie long in the field, it being harvest time, left and went home to their own houses to mind their harvest.' Rushworth *Collections*

'{the train bands} come to their old cry of "home, home"... They are so mutinous and uncommandable that there is no hope of their stay. Yesterday they were like to have killed the Major General and they hurt him in the face. Such men are only fit for a gallows here and hell hereafter.'
1643. Waller after Copredy Bridge.

'... his {chaplain's} duty is to have the care of Souls, and it is well if he meddle with no other business.' Turner *Pallas Armata*

'... clubs, scythes, spits, flails, halberds, sickles and such like rustic weapons.' Contemp. report.

'A soldier died of the raine and snow and extremity of cold.' Hereford.

'We officers wet our halberds with a barrel of strong beer called Old Hum, which we gave our soldiers ... {had a suit} for winter edged with gold and silver lace ... a scarlet coat lined with plush.' 1642. Nehemiah Wharton.

'The Malignants trecherous and Bloody Plot against the Parliment and Citty of London was by God's Providence happily prevented.' 1643 May. Pamphlet with twelve woodcuts.

'... as if they had been thieves not soldiers, ran away with their booty ... pursued after them so fiercely that they redeemed all the prisoners, killed two captains, and took Colonel Stevens {Roundhead} himself with some other men of quality, and so returned again to their own safety, sending their prisoners to Oxford.' *Mercurius Aulicus*

'They {London trained bands] stood like stakes against the shot of cannon ... above half an hour before we could get any of our guns up to us. Colonel Tucker shot in the head with a cannon bullett ... somewhat dreadful when men's bowels and brains flew in our faces ... we kept our ground and after a while feared them not; our ordnance did very good execution upon them for we stood at so near a distance upon a plain field that we could not miss one another.' First Newbury, Sergeant Foster of Essex's Army.

'... to take all from them which are not of their mind (roving soldiers} and to pull down there houses and imprison them, and leave them to the mercy of the unruly multitude. I cannot find that this is the liberty of the subject.' Lady Sydenham to Ralph Verney.

'Our quarter is very poor, our soldiers can get neither beds, bread nor water ... backbiters {bugs} march upon some of them six abreast and eight deep at their open order. I shall be in the same condition 'ere long.' Wharton.

'If you can spare an engineer, to send one hither, having works necessary to be done speedily.' Fairfax to his father.

'An Ordinance for the making of Forts, Trenches and Bull works about the Cittie ... Challen and Tomkins hanged for seeking to betray the Cittie.' 1643.

'A whole file of men six deep with all their heads struck off by one cannon shot.' 1643. First Newbury.

'Be sure you want not any money ... so long as any Roundhead hath either fingers or toes left, within ten miles of the Castle.' 1643. Veteran's advice.

'... at the entering of that church, dreadful to see the enemy, when ready to receive you with their pikes and muskets, the horses slain in the aisles of which the enemy made breastworks, the churchyard as well as the church being covered with dead and wounded.' 1643. Roundhead account of attack on Alton church.

'Oh, dearest Soul, praise God everlastingly. Read the enclosed, ring out your Bells, raise Bonfires, publish these Joyful Tidings, believe these Truths. We march on to meet our Victorious friends and to seize all the Rebells left if we can find such Living.' 1643. Cornish royalist to his wife.

'... my horse was shot in the throat with a musket bullet and his bit broken in his mouth.' A cavalier.

'My son, upon taking Leeds, though he entered it by force, yet he restrained his army from pillaging.
1643. Lord Fairfax to Parliament.

'We stuck together more like a flock of sheep, than a party of horse.'
1643. Captain Atkyns, cavalier.

'As gallant gentlemen as ever drew sword lay upon the ground like rotten sheep.' 1643. Charles I, after Bristol.

'... did so good execution that yester morning 200 Rebels came with Carts to fetch away their wounded and dead men with which they filled their Carts, besides what the Country had buried.'

Of the King's party only three slain, and few wounded.' 1643 Gloucester. *Mercurius Aulicus*

'Pressed all of a heap, like sheep, but not so innocent.' 1644. Defeated Roundhead infantry after Lostwithiel.

'... commander doing his duty like a very worthy person had his leg shot off to the ankle with a great shot, whereof he shortly died.' 1643. Cheriton.

'There began the disorder of the Horse visibly to break in upon all the prosperity of the public proceedings ... {officers} never able to repress the extravagant disorder of the Horse to the ruin and discomposure of all. The best Foot I ever saw for marching and fighting, but so mutinous withal, that nothing but an alarm could keep them from falling upon their officers.' 1643. The Cornish after Grenville's death.

'... soldiers having been promised their pay and a gratuity to spare the plunder of the town, fell into a mutiny upon the failing of the performance ...
'Insomuch that my lord {Essex} was forced to return and quarter his sick and weak army about Kingston and those other towns near London.'
Lucy Hutchinson.

'Pressed men run away as fast as we send them down {to the Navy}... foul weather, naked bodies, and empty bellies make the men voice the King's service worse than galley slavery.'
Contemp. comment.

'Those troops that are to give the first charge are to be at their close order; every left-hand man's right knee must be close locked under his right-hand man's left ham ... swords fastened with a riband unto their wrists, for fear of losing out of their hand if they should miss their blow, placing the pommel on their thigh, keeping still in their close order, close locked as before.' 1644. Cavalry drill *The Young Horseman*

'The souldiers in their passage to York turn into reformers, pull down Popish pictures, break down rails, turn altars into tables.' 1644. Woodcut.

'God so assisting you that you kept in your guts, stopping the hole with your finger.' Contemp. letter.

'The Newark and Belvoir cormorants {garrison soldiers} went into Rutland-shire to plunder and pillage the country, where they took many kine, sheep and horses, from the country people.' 1644. Belvoir Castle.

'In the Castle of Oxford ... {prisoners} detained there for their affection to the Parliament ... I {Ludlow} had a friend in the town who furnished me ... those who had not such means of relief were supplied from London by a collection of three hundred pounds, made for them by some citizens ... neither was Oxford itself destitute of some who contributed ... one Dr Hobbs, an honest man of the episcopal party, usually putting them in mind of it after his sermon.' 1644. Edmund Ludlow.

'... plundering troops killed all the poor countrymen's sheep and swine, and other provisions, whereby many honest families were ruined and beggared.' Lucy Hutchinson.

'I have been plundered of all my horses by special warrant from the chief commanders of the Parliament forces besides other things, and am worse in my estate by £500 with continual payments and billeting of soldiers and such like ... sometimes three or four captains and forty or fifty men, and as many horses four or five days together ... my house hath been in worse care than an inn. This is our condition which I hope God, in his good time, will give us ease of.' 1644, Wiltshire. John Nicholas.

'God hath not for many days past given us a wind serviceable.' 1644. Admiral Warwick to Essex.

'... the soldiers should have a reward {and} the treasurer gave the soldiers a groat {4d} a piece and sixpence a piece to the officers; at which the soldiers, being mad, flung back his money and desired a council of war to do them right.' Lucy Hutchinson.

'We took barns and hedges for our night's repose, after our hard and hot days' marches... grieves me to see men not at all armed, badly horsed, horses spoiled for want of saddles, many men afoot who had their horses killed, and yet all willing and ready to serve you to the uttermost.' 1645. Fairfax to Parl.

'Our pleasure and command to you therefore is, that you immediately provide in that garrison {Belvoir Castle} fit accommodation for General Gerrard's horse, being about 300, besides your own, and that you assist them in levying and bringing in provisions for the supply both of horse and men out of the several townships allotted for their provisions during their stay with you.' 1645, Newark. Charles I to Colonel Gervase Lucas.

'... troopers do commit many outrages in their passage, as firing of towns, ravishing of women stealing or violent taking.' Letter to Henry Oxinden.

'... being well armed within by the satisfaction of their conscience, and without by good iron arms, they would as one man stand firmly and charge desperately.' Whitelocke, on Cromwell's Regiment of Ironsides.

'... he {Colonel Hutchinson} would never condescend to them in anything they mutinously sought, nor suffer them to seek what it was fit for him to provide, but prevented them by his loving care, and while he exercised his authority no way but in keeping them to their just duty, they joyed as much in his commands as he in their obedience ... and {he}would often employ many spare hours with the commonest soldiers.' Lucy Hutchinson.

'... not such as were soldiers or men of estates, but such as were common men, poor and of mean parentage, only

he {Cromwell} would give them the title of 'godly precious men.'
Lord Manchester, commander of the Eastern Association.

'These were of greater understanding than common soldiers {Roundhead Cavalry} ... and making not money, but that which they took for public felicity to be their end, they were the more engaged to be valiant.' Richard Baxter.

'... having been industrious and active in their former callings and professions {Roundhead soldiers} ... afterwards finding the sweet of good pay and opulent plunder and of preferment, suitable activity and merit, the lucrative part made gain seem to them a natural member of godliness.' Philip Warwick.

'... many dangerous hurts, having lost the use of his limbs is not in any way able to work. ' A cavalier sergeant.

'Among Cromwell's soldiers I found a new face of things I never dreamt of ... plotting heads very hot upon that which intimated intention to subvert both Church and State.' Baxter.

'Many of our soldiers are already wasted and do daily moulder away, and that the main of our present strength consists of officers, gentlemen of quality and their attendants.'
1645, Pontefract. Report to Charles I.

'... having ransackt their quarters takes away their best horses & returns back to Cawood with ye prize.' Slingsby.

'Captain Plunket, the vilest villain and ... a notorious Irish rebel, but now, it seemed, come over to fight for the Protestant religion, and who was here made their chief commander in this robbing design, who immediately died of the said wound.' 1644, Lincoln.

'... almost lost the sight of his eyes and almost the use of both arms whereby he is made unable to worke or use any bodily exercise for and towards the gaining of a livelihood and maintenance of himself wife and four children.' Corporal Davyes, a royalist soldier.

'... a necessity, since three armies are to be introduced into one, that some commanders and officers must go out of their employments wherein they now are; and it is not out of any personal disrespect to any of you that shall now go off; therefore, I know you will behave yourselves like men of honour and honest.' 1645. Skippon, on formation of the New Model.

'Two thousand coates and two thousand pairs of breeches at {17s}. Two thousand pairs of stockings at thirteen pence half penny a pair. The coat of a red colour and of Suffolk, Coventry or Gloucestershire cloth ... the breeches of grey or some other good colour and of Reading cloth ... the cloth of both coats and breeches to be first shrunk in cold water. The stockings of good Welsh cotton ... Snapsacks large and of good leather ... bandoliers of wood with whole bottoms, turned within and not bored, the heads to be of wood, and to be laid in oil, three times over, and to be coloured blue with blue and white strings with strong thread twist, and with good belts.' 1645, Feb. New Model Army *Contract Books*

'... a mercenary Army {New Model} ... all of them, from the General except what he may have in expectation after his father's death, to the meanest sentinel not able to make a thousand pounds a year in lands ...
'Most of the colonels and officers mean tradesmen, brewers, taylors, goldsmiths, shoemakers and the like; a notable dunghill, if one would rake into it, to find out their several pedigrees.' Denzil Holles *Memoirs*

'... these new models knead all their dough with ale, never saw so many drunk in my life is so short a time.'

'The best common soldiers he {Fairfax} had came out of our army ... So says he, I found you had made them good soldiers, and I have made them good men.' Warwick *Memoirs*

'7 pieces of ordnance, 17 barrels of gunpowder, 20 cwt musket balls, 8 cwt match{cord}, 70 dozen candles, 30 loads wood, 30 bushels seacoal.' 1643, Oct. Remaining arsenal at surrender of Winchester Castle.

'Few of the common people that cared much for either of the {parties} ... but would have taken any side for pay or plunder.' Thomas Hobbes.

'There is such a universal weariness of the war, despair of the possibility for the King to recover that I protest to God I do not know four persons living, beside myself and you, that have not already given clear demonstrations that they will purchase their own and, as they flatter themselves, the kingdom's quiet at any price to the King, to the Church and to the faithfullest of his party.' 1645, Aug. George Digby.

'We were not merely mercenary soldiers brought together by the hopes of pay and the fortunes of wars, the peace of our country, our freedom from tyranny, the preservation of due liberty, the free course of the laws of the land, the preservation of the King and the privilege of Parliament, and the liberty of the subject, were the main things which brought us together. 1647 *An Apologeticall Declaration concerning the Army*

'They have cast all the mysteries and secrets of government before the vulgar, and taught the soldiers and people to look into and ravel back all governments to the state of nature.' c.1647. Clement Walker.

'Good Service hitherto ill-rewarded, or a Historical Relation of eight Years Service for King and Parliament in and about Manchester and those parts.' 1649. Pamphlet title, by an engineer with pay long in arrears.

'He spake Welch, English, French, High Dutch and Low Dutch, but never a one well... a little man not many degrees above a dwarfe... smoaking a Pipe, and did cry out to the Soldiers, when angry with them 'Sirrah, I'll cleave your skull.' John Aubrey, of Sir Thomas Morgan, Governor of Gloucester.

' Sir, said he, I care not for your Cause, I come to fight for your halfe-crownes and your handsome women ... I have fought for the Christians against the Turkes, and for the Turkes against the Christians ... he was an admirable Horse officer, and taught the Cavalry of the army the way of fighting with Horse... {Essex} saved him from hanging twice for Ravishing, and he was not content to ravish himself, but would make is soldiers doe it too, and he would stand by and look on.' Croatian mercenary. After changing sides twice, he was finally hanged at Oxford.

'You must be careful before you march with your Army into the Field to see your Soldiers well Cloathed, well Armed and well disciplined; and that you be stored with Shoes and Stockings for the March.' George Monk.

'The daubing of a coat with lace of sundry colours, I do neither take to be soldierlike nor profitable for the coat.'

'Stripp'd and carried in scorn to Worcester, but escaped, took to the trees in the day-time ... was retaken and sentenced to be shot ... escaped, lived three weeks in an enemy's haymow, went on crutches to Bristol ...' 1660. Cavalier's petition to Charles II.

Provisions

'... daily two pound of Bread, one pound of Flesh or in lieu of it, one pound of Cheese, one pottle of Wine, or in lieu of it, two pottles of Beer. It is enough, crys the Soldiers, we desire no more.' Turner *Pallas Armata*

'The ministers, moved by a motion from the honoured, pious and prudent Lord Mayor {Pennington} ... encourage the people to spare some part of their diet, ready dressed to bestow it upon the soldiers {at Turnham Green}... whereupon after the sermon was done ... an hundred loads of all manner of good provision of victuals, bottles of wine and barrels of beer instantly carried to them accompanied by honest and religious gentlemen to see it faithfully distributed to them.'
1642 Nov. *Parliamentary Chronicle*

'150lbs cheese, 800 lbs butter, 140 quarters meal, 10 quarters salt, 20 bushels oatmeal, 70 cwt biscuit, 14 sheep, 38 hogsheads salt meat, 4 quarters fresh beef, 3 hogshead wine, 112 hogsheads beer.' 1643 provisions of the garrison of Winchester Castle.

'1000 sheep and 60 head of cattell, taken from malignants and papists. 87 sheep was allotted for our red regiment {trained band}, but we lost them all when we came to fight.'
1643. Londoner's report.

'We think it best to stay here and not draw down into Yorkshire, to eat up that small remainder of provisions that is left, and by that means do your lordship more prejudice than the enemy can do.' 1643. Colonels Gell, Cromwell and Hotham to Lord Fairfax.

'Victuals of one pound bread and half a pound in cheese to each man ... to deliver Biscuit, to be put into sacks and laden in carts to be carried away towards His Majesty's Army.' 1644. Order for a royalist garrison.

'... at old Radnor, when the King was at eating a pullet and a piece of cheese, the room without was full, but the men's stomach's empty for want of meat; the goodwife troubl'd with continual calling upon her for victuals and having but the one cheese, comes into the room where the King was, and very soberly asks if the King has done with the cheese for the Gentlemen without desired it.' 1645. Slingsby.

'... the Scottish policy to defeat their enemies sooner by famine than by the sword ... to make the country a verier wilderness so that the soldier hath little to subsist upon besides his own provender which he carries in his knapsack; and therefor about 7 dayes hence we expect their return back here.' 1650 Sept. *Mercurius Politicus*

'Furnish the Horse with 14 days provisions, the soldiers snapsacks with 7 days bread and cheese to be carried on horseback, and as much bisquett besides the cheese as the horse can well carry.' 1654. Order from Monk.

13

BATTLES

'The King went to Beverley, in order to besiege Hull. When he was within two hour's march of the place Sir John Hotham floated {flooded} the country about it, and Sir John Meldrum sallying out of the town with five hundred townsmen made the King's party retreat to Beverley.'
1642 April. Contemp. report.

'... the King's Council of war broke up the siege {Hull} from whence the King went back to York, and about the middle of August came to Nottingham where he set up his standard royal {22 August 1642 } ... hither his two nephews, Prince Rupert and Prince Maurice, came to him and were put into commands.' Lucy Hutchinson.

'Get somebody to buy six carbines for me and some twenty pounds of powder I hope that will be enough to defend us here, if it be not powder enough, as much as you think fit ...
'There came in few or none at all after the standard was set up {at Nottingham}, it seems the King sent and gave much of his monies to the trained bands of Yorkshire and other places, thinking to make them sure to him, and when he would have had them they all fell off and said they would not fight against their brethren, and every day his army lessens.'
1642. Lady Sussex to Ralph Verney.

Edgehill - 23 October 1642

'The King marching through Nottingham, Derby and Leicestershire called together the trained bands, disarmed those counties and marched to Shrewsbury and there set up a mint and coined the plate that had been brought in to him ... marching into Warwickshire he there fought his first battle at a village called Keynton {Kineton}; it not being yet agreed who gained the victory that day.' Contemp. report.

'My Lords and Gentlemen here present, if this day shine prosperously for us we shall be happy in a glorious victory. Your King is both you cause, your quarrel and your captain. Now show yourselves no malignant parties, but with your swords declare what courage and fidelity is within you. Come life, come death, your King will bear you company, and ever keep this field, this place, and this day's service in his grateful remembrance.' Charles I.

'They shall have me with it if they carry it away. Traitor, deliver the standard.' Captain John Smith retrieved the King's captured standard, and was knighted by the King on the field. He was killed in 1643 at Cheriton.

'I fear them not.' Charles, Prince of Wales. With his brother James, Duke of York, he sheltered under a hedge in the care of Dr William Harvey, who is said to have read a book throughout the battle and ignored his charges.

'... The battle was bloody on your side {Parliament} for your horse ran away at the first charge and our men had the execution of them for three miles; it began at 3 o'clock and ended at six. The King is a man of the least fear and the greatest mercy and resolution that I ever saw, and had he not been in the field we might have suffered. My Lord of Essex is retired in great disorder ... it is said there was killed and run away since, eight thousand of his army.' Edward Sydenham to Ralph Verney.

'... of all nations the English stick the closest to their officers and it's hardly seen that our common soldiers will turn their backs, if they who commanded them do not first show them the bad example, or leave them un-officered by being killed themselves.' Later comment of James II, of Edgehill.

'... the Earl of Lindsey, general for his Majesty, who was killed in the field; and his Majesty, notwithstanding the treachery of his chief gunner, the loss and retaking his standard, the over-eager pursuit of the Parliament's wings of horse by Prince Rupert, whose soldiers too soon fell to plunder, remained sole master of the field, and the next day had advantage of the rout.' Contemp. Royalist pamphlet.

'On Sunday last I saw the Battle which was the bloodiest I believe the oldest soldiers in the field ever saw. We have routed utterly their horse and slain & chased away so considerable a party of their foot that the enemy is very weak ... the Earl of Lindsey, Willoughby and Colonel Lunston, the Lord St John with the Lord Feilding are slain, with many others. My Lord Essex escaped us by being in an alehouse. We have his coach and much money in it ... At the beginning of the fight two double troops came over to the King's party commanded by Sir Faithfull Fortescue & fought on our side ... Marquis Hertford is now on the march with ten thousand men armed out of Wales and intends to meet the King at Oxford. Sir R Hopton and Mr Rogers bring as many from the West Country.' Letter to William Sancroft at Cambridge, later Archbishop of Canterbury.

'As cold {a night} as a very great frost and sharp northerly wind could make it ... congealed the blood of the wounded and many a life was saved.'

'Strange and portentuous Apparitions of two jarring and contrary Armies ... with Ensignes display'd, Drummes beating, Musquets going off, Cannons discharged, Horses neyghing ... on Christmas night appeared the same tumultuous adverse Armies fighting with as much spite and spleen as formerly ...

'His Majesty at Oxford despatched Colonel Kirke and three other Gentlemen ... they heard and saw, distinctly knowing the apparitions or incorporeal substances by their faces, as that of Sir Edmund Verney and others that were slaine.' 1643 Jan. *Apparitions and Prodigious Noyses of War and Battels seen on Edge-Hill*

'Monday morning we marched into Warwickshire ... being ready all night, early in the morning we went to meet them with a few troops of horse and six field pieces, and being on fire to be at them we marched through the corn and got the hill of them, whereupon they played upon us with their ordnances, but them came short. Our gunners took their own bullet, sent it to them again and killed a man and a horse. After we gave them 8 shott more, whereupon all their foot companies fled and offered their armes in the towns adjacent for twelve pence apiece.' Account of a skirmish by a soldier in Essex's army.

*

'Then the enemy {Roundhead} gave ground apace ... the four parties ascended the hill between three and four of the clock, they all met together upon ground near the top of the hill, where they embraced with unspeakable joy ... being possessed of some of the enemy's cannon they turned them upon the camp and advanced together to perfect their Victory.' General Hopton's report of Stratton.

'... the fertility whereof is ascribed to the virtue the land received from the blood of the slain men and horses and the trampling of their feet in this battle.' Stratton. Contemp. report.

'We were then seated like a very heavy stone upon the very brow of the hill {Lansdown}, which with one lusty charge might well have been rolled to the bottom.' Slingsby.

'When I came to the top of the hill, I saw Sir Bevil Grenvile's stand of {Cornish} pikes, which certainly preserved our army from total rout, with the loss of his most precious life; they stood as upon the eaves of an house for the steepness, but as unmovable as a rock on which side of their stand of pikes our horse were I could not discover, for the air so darkened by the smoke of the powder that ...

'There was not light seen, but what the fire of the volleys of shot gave ...

'I found {Hopton} miserably burnt {by an explosion} and his horse like parched leather ... the fire had got within {Sheldon's} breeches, which I tore off as soon as I could ... from as long a flaxen head of hair as ever I saw, in the twinkling of an eye his head was like a blackamoor.' Captain Atkyns.

'... wanted Chirugeons much ... seven cartloads of dead men were carried from the place.'

First Newbury - Sept 1643

'My Lord of Falkland did me the honour to ride in my troop this day ... more gallantly than advisedly {he} spurred his horse through the gap, where both he and his horse were immediately killed.' Nicholas Byron.

'... they could not find his body (Falkland); it was stript and trod-upon and mangled ... there was one that wayted on him to know it, by a Mole his Lordship had in his neck, and by that marke did finde it.' Aubrey *Lives*

'The enemy is mighty and master of the field, plentifully supplied from His Majesty and the Papists and malignant parties, with money and all necessities.' 1643. Lord Fairfax to Parliament.

'To My Lord {Leven} ... I cannot but admire that your Lordship hath so near beleaguered the City on all sides ... without signifying what your {Scots army} intentions are, and what you desire or expect, which is contrary to the rules of all military discipline and customs, therefore I have thought fit to remonstrate ... , your Lordship's humble servant, William Newcastle.' 1644 June, York.

'Manchester works his mines under St Mary's Tower without Bootham Bar {York} and raised a battery against the manor wall ... begins to play his cannon and throws down piece of the wall. We fall to work and make it up with earth & sods ... at noon they spring the mine under St Mary's Tower & blows up one part of it, which falling outwards made the access more easy. Then some at the breach, some with ladders, getts up & enters, near 500.
'Sir Philip Biron was killed as he opened the doors into the bowling green whither the enemy was gotten ... we soon beat them out again, having taken 200 prisoners and killed many of them as might be seen in the bowling green and garden. The Scots the while busy about the mine & we busy in countermining.' Slingsby.

'... the {Royalist} soldiers in York, being in a raging mutiny in the town for their pay ... {marched} but with much unwillingness.' Arthur Trevor.

'My lord, I wish you had come sooner with your forces, but I hope we shall yet have a glorious day.' Rupert to Newcastle on his troops late arrival.

'God and the King' - 'God with Us'
Field words

'Be them two fall'n out then?' alleged remark of a yokel before Marston Moor

'By God, Sir, it is very fine on paper, but there is no such thing in the field.' Lord Eythin, on Rupert's battle plan.

'Our soldiers did drink the wells dry, and then were necessitated to make use of puddle water.'

'The noble commander {Leven} exercised his martial abilities with unwearied activity and industry. He hasted from place to place to put all his forces in battle array, which he did to the satisfaction and admiration of all that beheld it.' Manchester's chaplain.

'... seeing the ditch must disturb their order, and the other be ready in good ground to charge ... had two such armies drawn up so close departed without fighting ... it would have been as a great a wonder as hath been seen in England.' Scout-Master Watson.

'The enemy ... in Marston corn fields falls to singing psalms. The Prince's Horse had the right wing, my Lord Goring the left, the Foot disposed of with most advantage to fight, some of them drawn off to line the hedges of the field ... The enemy's forces consisting of 3 parts, the Scots, Manchester and Fairfax ... Cromwell having the left wing drawn into 5 bodies of Horse, came off to charge our Horse & upon their first charge routed them; they fly along by Wilstrop woodside as fast & as thick could be, yet our left wing presses as hard upon their right wing & pursued them over the Hill ... here I lost my nephew, Colonel John Fenwick & a kinsman, Sir Charles Slingsby, both slain in the field ...

'The former could not be found to have his body brought off, the latter was found & buried in York Minster ... They {the enemy} pursued not, but kept the field as many as were left, for they were fled as fast as we, & their 3 Generalls gone, thinking all had been lost.' Slingsby *Diary*

'... soe taking the signall {white cloth} out of my Hatt, I {Fairfax} passed through for one of their owne Commanders, and soe gott to my Lord Manchester's Horse, in the other Winge; only with a cut in my cheek and a shot my horse received.' Fairfax, *Memorials*

'... colonel Cromwell, with the brave regiment of his countrymen and sir Thomas Fairfax, having rallied some of his horse.' Whitelocke *Memorials*

'Swounds, do you run, follow me.' Rupert to the broken right wing.

'We {Ironsides} came down in the bravest order and with the greatest resolution that ever was seen. In a moment we were past the ditch into the Moor, upon equal grounds with the enemy, our men into a running march ... The Enemy seeing us come in such a gallant posture to charge them, left all thought of pursuit and began to think that they must fight again for that victory which they had already got ... Here the business of the day, nay of the kingdom, came to be determined ...

'They stood at the sword's point a pretty while, hacking one another, but at last he {Cromwell} broke through them {Rupert's cavalry}, scattering them like a little dust.' Scout-Master Watson.

'Seeing us thus pluck a victory out of the enemy's hands, could not too much commend us, and professed Europe had no better soldiers.' General David Leslie, Scots cavalry commander.

'... our {Roundhead} broken forces were rallyed againe .. in which service the Earle of Manchester and Lieutenant Generall Cromwell have merited most, and Sir Thomas Fairfax very much.' Captain Thomas Stockdale.

'... Sir Thomas Fairfax commandit in cheiff, ane brave commander, but his Horse ansered not our expectation, nor his worth.' Sir James Lumsden, a Scots officer.

'Spare the poor deluded countrymen, oh spare them, I pray, who are misled and know not what they do.' Fairfax.

'If Goring's men had been kept close together as did Cromwell's and not dispersed themselves in pursuit, in all probability it had come a drawn battle at worst.' Sir Hugh Cholmley.

'This victory was one of the greatest and most bloody since the war began, and I hope hath let out much of that ill blood that hath so long distempered the state.' Thomas Stockdale.

'An honest man that overlooked the dead thought that there were two gentlemen slain to one ordinary soldier that was slain.' *Weekly Account*

'Therefore thinking it not fit to hazard the town {York}, having no hopes to be relieved we capitulate on article ... & upon very good conditions if they had been kept, for we were to march out with our armys & with flying colours, to have convoy until we came within 12 miles of the prince {Rupert} ...

'Upon these article we march out, but find a failing in the performance at the very first, for the soldier was pillaged, our Waggons plundered, mine the first day & others the next. Thus disconsolate we march, forced to leave our country {county} unless we would apostate, not daring to see mine own house, nor take a farewell of my Children, although we lay the first night at Hesset within 2 miles of my house.' 1644, 16 July. Slingsby.

'A Dogs Elegy or Ruperts Tears.' For the late defeat given him at Marston-Moore near York by the Three Renowned Generalls. Alexander, Earl of Leven, Generall of the Scottish Forces, Ferdinando Lord Fairfax and the Earle of Manchester, Generalls of the English Forces in the North. Where his beloved Dog named BOYE was killed by a Valliant Souldier who had skill in necromancy {witchcraft}.' July, London. Roundhead pamphlet.

'My Lord of Newcastle and Lieutenant General King {Eythin} going to Scarborough, where they took shipping to go beyond sea. Thus we were left at York, out of all hope of relief ... fain to give out false reports, that the Prince had fallen upon the enemy and routed them and was coming back to the Town.' 1644 July. Slingsby.

'This people, yesterday and today were much discouraged and fainting; but this night are triumphing. We dare not be too much exalted, only we bless God from our heart.' Baillie.

'... the like was never done, or heard, or read of before, that two great Generals, whereof one {Rupert} had still a good Army left ... and the other, {Newcastle} having the absolute Commission over the Northern Counties, should both agree in nothing else but in leaving that good City {York} and the whole country as a prey to the Enemy, who had not yet the Courage to believe that they had the Victory.' Clarendon *History*.

'Truly England and the church of God hath had a great favour from the Lord in this great victory given unto us, such as the like never was since the war began ... The Left Wing, which I commanded, being our own horse, save a few Scots in our rear, bet all the Prince's horse. God made them as stubble to our swords ...' Cromwell to Colonel Valentine Walton.

'The loss of York, (succeeding the bloody battle fought by his Highness Prince Rupert and the English and Scottish rebels}, your excellency {Ormond} may well imagine what prejudice we suffer in the North, and how insolent those rebels are become upon it. But as his Highness hath now no less than 10,000 together in Lancashire, so as his Highness hopes to give a very good account of the rebels that pursue him.' July, Oxford. Secretary Nicholas.

Second Newbury - Oct 1644

'The King's regiment drove at them, which made them wheel off, all their bodies of horse in confusion, killed many, besides musketeers that had lined the hedges and played us up in the chase till we cut their throats.' Captain Symonds, cavalier.

'This accident trouble me exceedingly, he {Gabriel} being one who had expressed great affection to me, and of whom I had great hopes that he would be useful to the public.' Death of Ludlow's young cousin by cannon shot.

'Their cannon made the ground very hot {from Donnington}, there was no way left but to fall on with Horse and Foot, and that without delay.' Waller.

'Carry away the Castle walls themselves if you can but, with God's help, I am resolved to keep the ground they stand on.' Sir John Boys, Royalist Governor of Donnington.

*

'To consider of a frame or model of the whole militia.' 1644 Nov. House of The Commons to C'tee of Both Kingdoms.

'The New Noddle Army.' Royalist jibe.

'Their new-modelled army consists for the most of raw, unexperienced, pressed soldiers. Few of their officers are thought capable of their places ... if they do great things, many will be deceived.' 1645, Spring. Baillie.

'Ten regiments of horse of 600 men, twelve regiments of foot of 1,200 men, 1,000 dragoons ... assessment of £56,000 a month for its maintenance ... Sir Thomas Fairfax appointed general by 101 votes to 69.' Cromwell and Vane, tellers for the 'yeas'.

'There are very few of us, but have most of this world's interest in the Citie of London, being chiefly and principally raised thence, and verie many, especially of our officers, being citizens themselves having their wives and children therein.' 1647. *Vindication of the Army ... intending sack of London*

'... two Summers past over, and we were not saved: our Victories so gallantly gotten were put into a bag with holes; what we wonne one time, we lost another ... the Game however set up at Winter, was to be new played again the next spring.' 1645, Spring. Sprigge.

'{Leicester's governor refused Rupert's summons to surrender} ... and the same night a general assault with the whole army, in several places, but principally at the breach, which was defended with great courage and resolution insomuch that the King's forces were twice repulsed ... another party on the other side of the town entered the town and made way for their fellows to follow them so that by break of day the King's army entered the line ... and miserably sacked the whole town, without any distinction of persons or places.'
1645, 30 May, Clarendon.

Naseby - 14 June 1645

'Queen Mary' - God our Strength'
Field words.

'{Cromwell} with the greatest joy received by the General and the whole army. Instantly orders were given for drums to beat, trumpets to sound to horse, and all our army to draw to rendezvous.' 1644, 13 June.
Kislingbury, Northampton. Sprigge.

'{New Model} were better Christians than soldiers, and wiser in faith than fighting.' Sprigge.

Let us, I beseech you {Fairfax}, draw back to yonder hill which will encourage the enemy to charge us.' Cromwell.

'Upon a Saturday ... the enemy's horse upon another Hill, which was the same on which Naseby stood ... {Rupert} perceived General Fairfax intend'd not to quitt the advantage of the Hill ... that they could easily observe in what body we drew up our men ... they lay without our sight having ye Hill to cover them ...' Slingsby 'Diary'

'The Foot on either side scarcely saw each other until they were within carbine-shot, so only gave one volley.'

'... the wind blowing somewhat Westwardly ... it was evident {the Cavaliers} designed to get the winde of us: which occasioned the General {Fairfax} to draw down into a large fallow field on the Northwest side of Naseby flanked on the left hand with a hedge, which was a convenient place for us to fight the Enemy ... {Cavaliers fought on} with incredible courage and resolution.' Sprigge.

'It fell upon Prince Rupert to charge at the disadvantage, and many of the Regiment were wound'd by shot from {Sulby} hedges {by Okey's dragoons}... but our Northern horse who stood upon the wing and the Newark horse being out fronted & overpour'd by their assailants after they were close joined ... and presently made our whole horse run ... our foot left nak'd were forced to lay down their arms.' Slingsby.

'... would not stir so long as a man should stand.' The injured Skippon rejecting Fairfax's advice to retire.

'... standing with incomparable courage and resolution ... until such time as the General {Fairfax} called up his own regiment of foot which immediately fell in with them with butt end of muskets, the General charging them at the same time with horse, and so broke them.' Contemp. report.

'Sir, had you seen him {Fairfax} and how his spirit was raised it would have made an impression on you never to be obliterated; God knows I speak truth and do not hyperbolise.' A Roundhead officer after Naseby. (The same was said of Wellington at Waterloo)

'The enemy did not pursue, and the Prince on the one hand and Sir Marmaduke Langdale on the other, the King yet being upon the place, got together as many as they could, made an offer of a charge ... they being horse and foot in good order, and we but a few horse only, and those mightily discourag'd.' Slingsby.

'This success was astonishing, being obtained by men of little experience in affairs of this nature, and upon that account despised by their enemies {Cavaliers}.' Ludlow.

'I saw the field {Naseby} so bestrewed with the carcasses of men and horses as was most sad to behold ... but most of them professed enemies of God and his Son ... The bodies lay slain about four miles in length, the most thick on the hill where the King stood. I cannot think there were less than four hundred men slain there, and truly I think not many more, and three hundred horses.' Contemp. account.

'Sir, this is none other but the hand of God, and to him alone belongs the glory... The General {Fairfax} served you with faithfulness and honour ... honest men served you faithfully in this action ... they are trusty, I beseech you in the name of God, not to discourage them ... he that ventures his life for the liberty of his country, I wish he trust God for the liberty of his conscience, and you for the liberty he fights for.' Cromwell to Speaker of the Commons.

'... saw now that Fairfax's Army would master both King and Parliament too; and rule as the Roman Emperors ... in despite of the Senate.'
Mr Hales, a Fellow of Eton.

'... the King pitched upon that fatal resolution {after Naseby}, recommended to him by Lord Culpeper, of besieging Gloucester, thinking it a good policy not to leave a strong town behind him ... had the King struck at London, he had raised such confusion among the two Houses ... if they had fought him most probably be had been victorious.' Warwick.

'I have thought of one means more to furnish thee {Henrietta} with for my assistance ... It is that I give thee power to promise in my name to whom thou thinkest most fit that I will take away all the penal laws against the Roman Catholics in England as soon as God shall enable me to do it, so as by their means, or in their favours, I may have so powerful assistance as may deserve so great a favour and enable me to do it.' 1645. *The King's Cabinet Opened*.

War in the West

'The dragoons on both sides seeing us so mixed with their men that they could not fire at us, but they might kill their own men as well as ours, took horse and away they run also ...

'We charged them {Roundheads} and they made as it were a lane for us, being as willing to be gone as we ourselves. In this charge there was but one of my troop killed, and eight hurt. For the wounded men of my troop, and also of my division I received 20s a man of Sir Robert Long, then Treasurer of the Army, which was all the money I ever received for myself, or troops, during the war.' 1643. Capt. Richard Atkyns.

'To ye inhabitants of ye county of Cornwall ... to be printed and published and one of them read in every church and chapel therein and to be kept for ever as a record ... {of} ye extraordinary merits of our county of Cornwall, of their zeal for our Crown, and for ye defence of our person ... {and} great and eminent courage.' 1643, Sudeley Castle. Charles I to his Cornish subjects.

'If you offer to plunder our Cattell, be assured we'll give you Battell.' 1645. West Country Clubmen

'Clubmen who would not suffer either contributions or victuals to be carried to the Parliament's garrisons ... Fairfax treated them civilly for they were strong at that time.' 1645. Rushworth

'This is the most mutinous army that ever I saw, not only horse but foot.' 1644 Aug, Exeter. George Digby.

'The enemy upon them {Cavaliers} before the men could get upon their horses, they being then feeding in a meadow, so that this body was entirely routed and very many taken.' 1645 July. Ilminster. Clarendon.

'The cannon played their part as gallantly as ever I saw gunners in my life.' Langport. Col. Robert Lilburne.

'The greatest gallantry imaginable ... the bravest that ever their eyes beheld.' 1645 July. Fairfax & Cromwell of Major Bethell's charge at Langport.

'I wish that he may not go unlamented to his grave who was so full of God ... he lived without pride and died full of faith.' 1645 Sept. Bristol. *The Army's Tears over Major Bethell*.

*

Second Civil War

'That the King may be restored to his due Honour and Just Rights ... that he may be forthwith established on the

Throne, according to the Splendour of his Ancestors ...

'That he may for the present come to Westminster with Honour and Safety to treat personally for composing of Differences. That the freeborn subjects of England may be governed by the known Laws and Statutes ... that the War beginning may be prevented ... that the Ordinance for preventing Free quarter may be duly executed and speed made in disbanding all Armies having their Arrears due paid them.' 1648 May. Petition to Westminster from Surrey.

'Very numerous, but likewise very disorderly.' George Goring's garrison at Maidstone garrison. Clarendon.

'Friends, I have been nearer to you when you have missed me.' Lisle.

'Under this marble lie the bodies of the two most valiant Captains Sr. Charles Lucas and Sr. George Lisle, knights, who for their eminent loyalty to their Soverain were on the 28th day of August 1648, by the command of Sr. Thomas Fairfax, then General of the Parliament Army, in cold blood barbarously murdered.' Colchester. Fairfax had the two officers shot under the Articles of War, but his later request to Charles II to have the memorial's wording altered was rejected.

'This summer the revolt was not greater at land than at sea ... many of the great ships set the vice-admiral on shore, and sailed towards Holland to Prince Charles ... to reduce these revolted ships, and preserve the rest of the navy from the like, the Earl of Warwick was made lord high admiral of England.

'But at the same time his brother, the Earl of Holland, who had floated up and down with the tide of the times, rose also against he Parliament and appeared in arms, with the young Duke of Buckingham, Lord Francis Villiers, his brother, ... making about five hundred horse at Kingston upon Thames. Here some of the Parliamentary troops, assailing them before they had time to grow, totally routed and dispersed them ... Lord Francis Villiers was slain, the Earl of Holland flying with those he could rally was fought with at St Neots; Dalbier and other of his associates were slain, and himself taken prisoner and carried to Warwick Castle.' 1648 Lucy Hutchinson.

Preston 17-19 August 1648

'Lancashire was a close country, full of ditches and hedges, which was a great advantage the English would have over our raw and undisciplined musketeers ... while on the other hand Yorkshire was a more open country and full of heaths, where he might both make better use of our horse, and come sooner to push of pike ... {Hamilton} was for the Lancashire way.'

'Want of intelligence helped ruin us, Sir Marmaduke was well near totally routed before we knew that it was Cromwell attacked us.' 1648 Aug. Sir James Turner.

'... surrender himself {Lt-Gen Baillie} and all his officers and soldiers prisoners of war, with all his arms and ammunition and horses ... giving quarter for life, and promising civil usage.' Cromwell's demand to the only Scot's commander left in the field after the flight of the generals.

'Ten men will keep a thousand from running away.' Cromwell.

'But now, my pikemen being demented, as I think we were all, would not hear me; and two of them ran full tilt at me. One of their pikes, which was intended for my belly, I gripped with my left hand, the other ran me nearly two inches in the inner side of my right thigh, all of them crying of me and the Horse 'They are Cromwell's men.'
'I desired {the Horse} to charge through their Foot ... the pikemen threw down their pikes, and ran into the houses. All the Horse galloped away, and as I was afterwards told, rode not through, but over, our whole Foot, treading them down.' Turner.

'The faint and weary soldiers who lagged behind we never saw again.' Scots officer in retreat.

'There {at Warrington} we conceived we might face about having command of a town, and a bridge. Yet I conceive there was but few of us thought we might be beaten before we were masters of any of them ...
They {a last stand} were commanded by a little spark in a blue bonnet, who performed the part of an excellent commander, and was killed on the spot.' Turner.

'If I had a thousand horse that could but trot thirty miles I should not doubt but to give a very good account of them, but truly we are so harassed and haggled out in this business that we are not able to do more than walk at an easy pace after them.'
Cromwell to the Commons.

'The weakness, rawness and undisciplinedness of our soldiers, our want of artillery and horse to carry the little ammunition we had, the constant rainy, stormy and tempestuous weather which made all highways impassable for man and beast, our leaving our Irish auxiliaries so far behind us, and our unfortunate resolution to waive Yorkshire and march by Lancashire all ... made us a prey to Cromwell's veteran army.' Turner.

'You have left God, so He hath now left you {Army} ... poor wretches, though angry at you, my soul pities you, never were men caught in such a snare of the devil as you are.' 1648 Dec. *Justice upon the Army's Remonstrance*

'To Whitehall at last; where he {the King} end'd his good life ... Thus I ended these commentaries or book of remembrance, beginning in the year 1638 and ending in the year 1648 ...
A year fatal and very remarkable in which the Scots lost their army and the English their King.' Slingsby *Diary*

Dunbar 3 September 1650

'The great misery and calamity of having an army of Scots without our country, that there will be war between us I fear is unavoidable. Your Excellency will soon determine whether it is better to have this war in the bowels of another country or of our own, and that it will be one of them, I think it without scruple.' 1650 June. Cromwell to Fairfax, who refused to invade Scotland and resigned his commission. Cromwell became commander in chief.

'... an engagement very difficult. The enemy has blocked up our way at the Pass at Copperspath through which we cannot get without almost a miracle ... our lying here daily consumeth our men, who fall sick beyond imagination.' 1 Sept. Cromwell to Haselrig.

'How will you fight when you have shipped off half your men, and all your great guns?' Leslie to a prisoner.

'... often coming to push of pike and close firing, and always making the enemy to recoil .. the enemy making, though he was worsted, very stiff and sturdy resistance.' 1650. Cromwell's report to Parliament

'The regiments ... scarce exceeded half their number, and not the fifth man could handle pike or musket. The horse were the best mounted that ever Scotland sent out, yet most of the troopers were raw and undisciplined.' Scots report.

Worcester

'For me it is a crown or a coffin.' Charles II.

'Sultan Oliver appeared with a great body of horse and foot on Red Hill within a mile of Worcester. And as they had few persons of condition among them to lose, so no rebels but Quartermaster General Morley and one captain Jones were worth taking notice of to be slain in that battle.'
1651 Sept. Thomas Blount *Boscobel*

'We had such a number of beaten men with us, of the horse, that I strove ... to get from them; and though I could not get them to stand by me against the enemy, I could not get rid of them now I had a mind to it.' Charles II to Pepys.

'22 Sept. Arrived the news of the fatal battle at Worcester, which exceedingly mortified our expectation.
'29 Oct. Came news and letters to the Queen of his Majesty's miraculous escape after the fight at Worcester.
'21 Dec. Came to visit my wife, Mrs Lane, the lady who conveyed the King to the seaside at his escape from Worcester.' Evelyn in Paris.

'It is, for aught I know, a crowning mercy.' Cromwell's Worcester despatch to Parliament

'Say you have been at Worcester, where England's sorrows began, and where they are happily ended.'
1651. Hugh Peter. Powick Bridge, near Worcester.

14

CASTLES, GARRISONS & SIEGES

'The Manner of Framing a Sconce ... with a strong situation, as great Rivers or upon a Rock, or flankered from the Bulwarks of a Fort ... the Bulwarks and Curtains are to be made very high, thick and strong, that it may endure the battering of the Enemy's Ordnance.' 1639. Manual on defensive works.

'We shall do little good on this town {Gloucester} for they begin to contain us, which will make it a work of time; wherefore we shall endeavour to fight with Essex as soon as may be ... the greatest care will be to meet him before he reaches the hedges.'
1643 Sept. Charles I to Rupert.

'The King reduced that most important trading town, Bristol, commanded by a Gentleman, Mr Nathaniel Fiennes.' 1643. Warwick.

'The countrymen came so slowly with their assessments that the Horse belonging to the garrison was employ'd wholly in fetching it and such persons as refus'd ... sometimes would injure those that were well affected & had duly paid ... I eased the tax the former governour had imposed, 3d upon every horse load of Corn duly paid.' Slingsby

'Prince Rupert with 4,000 horse and foot marched by Sudeley Castle to Cirencester where the magazine of the county lay; this he took putting the Earl of Stamford's regiment and many others to the sword, took 1,000 prisoners and 3,000 arms. Then the prisoners were led in triumph to Oxford, where the King and Lords looked on them, and too many smiled at their misery, being tied with cords, almost naked, beaten and driven along like dogs.' Whitelocke *Memorials*

'I have a command from my lord to keep it, and I will obey that command.' 1643 May. The Royalist Lady Arundel refusing to surrender Wardour Castle to Sir Edward Hungerford.

'... dangerous and unprofitable to this state to keep up forts and garrisons which may foment rather than finish a war ... the Low Countries found by experience during these three hundred years that losses are entailed by places being fortified ... If there be a garrison kept at Liverpool there must be at least three hundred men, which will make the jealousies and emulation amongst these {local} gentlemen endless and chargeable.' 1644. Sir John Meldrum, a veteran's advice to Parliament.

'... the late dishonour in suffering the relief of Donnington; also to desire them {Manchester, Waller etc.} not to go to their winter quarters as long as the enemy is in the field, and to have a care to prevent the relief of Basing.' 1644. Committee of Both Kingdoms.

'{Evesham} stormed and taken for want of men to defend the works.'

Broughton Castle - Parliamentary stronghold of Lord Saye & Sele

Rockingham Castle - Royalist fortress close to Naseby

For King ....

Sir Edward Hyde
Sir Edmund Verney

Sir Jacob Astley
Sir Philip Warwick

Or Parliament ...

Colonel John Hutchinson
Speaker William Lenthall

General Sir William Waller
The Lord General Essex

Scarborough changed hands by treachery 1643, & assault 1645 and 1648

Newark on Trent, key Royalist fortress in the Midlands, surrendered 1646

'If any inconvenience should come to the State by not keeping such castle and houses from relief, we conceive the error lies in the first undertaking such sieges, and the loose prosecuting of them.' 1644 Nov. Basing House. Response by Manchester etc.

'... spend time unprofitably before a town, whilst the King hath time to strengthen himself and by terror to enforce obedience where he comes.' 1645 May. Fairfax besieging Oxford.

'... the high sheriff of the county of Lincoln had taken Belvoir Castle for his Majesty, an house belonging now and long since to the earls of Rutland, and which by reason of the situation on an hill of difficult access ... is thought to be of special consequence and importance.' 1643 Jan. Oxford.

'I was not placed here by the king to surrender to rebells, and for the effusion of blood you mention, the crime will be your own, not mine; therefore I will not give one inch of ground I am able to maintain with my sword, against all your attempts made against the place, and your servant {Colonel} Gervase Lucas.' 1645 Nov. Belvoir. To Maj-General Poyntz.

'... not the part of a souldier ... to endeavour the holding of a place not tenable; when not the least hopes of being relieved. Which act in you will by all men be interpreted, rather an obstinacy than a souldierly resolution.' 1646 Jan. Second summons to Belvoir.

'The strong and almost impregnable garrison, called Belvoir Castle, being one of the strongest and fairest building in the kingdom ... which had 66 steps or ascents unto it, and therefore might well overlook the country ... is now reduced to the obedience of the Parliament, for Gervase Lucas, the governor thereof, with all the commanders, officers, and souldiers therein, having permission to march away to Lichfield, upon more honourable terms indeed that they deserved.' Contemp. report. The Castle was demolished, allegedly with the Earl of Rutland's agreement, but his compensation was 'not exceeding £1000.'

'... of great strength {Devizes}, having been an old fortification, raised on a huge mount of earth ... {the Royalists} added to the strength of its natural situation ... having cut out of the main earth several works commanding one another, and so strong that no cannon could pierce them; besides that being pallizadoed, and stockaded in most places it was a matter of extreme difficulty to storm it ... some of the granadoes breaking in the midst of the castle killed several of their men, and much endangered the blowing up of the magazine, which so startled the enemy that they sounded a parley.' 1645. Sprigge.

'The only considerable port the King had in the whole kingdom, for shipping and trade, and which being withall his magazine for all sorts of ammunition.' 1645 Sept. Siege of Bristol. Sprigge.

'During the whole of the siege he never received any intelligence.'
Prince Rupert after Bristol.

'... two were condemned and most perfidiously executed ... Captain Leicester, an officer from Ireland, told me that I only conditioned {accepted quarter} for my soldiers, and that these who ran from them were not mine, but theirs.' 1643. Ludlow, after the surrender of Wardour Castle the Royalists hanged two men they claimed were deserters.

'I have received this night the hamper with the powder and match, but I have not yet the muskets ... my Cousin Davis tells me that none can make shot but those whose trade it is, so I have made the plumber write to Worcester for fifty weight of shot ... I thank God, I am not afraid, it is the Lord's cause ...

'Their aim {Cavaliers} is to seize upon my house and cut our throats by a few rogues, and then say they knew not who did it ... tell me that then I shall be safe, but I have no cause to trust them ... if I put away the men I shall be plundered, and if I have no rents I know not what course to take. If I leave Brampton all will be ruined ...

'If I had money to buy corn and meal and malt, I should hope to hold out, but then I have three shires against me ... pray for me that the Lord in mercy may preserve me from my cruel and blood-thirsty enemies.'
1642/43, Brampton Castle. Lady Brilliana Harley to her husband in Parliament at Westminster.

'... their wives came to the castle, there they weep and wring their hands and with clamorous oratory persuade their husbands to come home and not, by saving others, to expose their own houses to spoil and ruin.' 1644.
Corfe Castle. Contemp. report.

'Lady Bankes, wisely and like herself, despatched messengers to Dorchester and Poole to entreat the small pieces {cannon} might remain ... there were but five men in the Castle ... yet assisted by the maid servants at their Ladies' command ... and loading one of them they gave fire ... which small thunder so affrighted the seamen that they all quitted the place and ran away.' 1643. Corfe Castle.

'Where the Queen had putt in 3 ships load'd with armes & ammunition ... had cast up 2 works either side of the Harbour & raised 2 Batteries, & Drakes to discharge upon the ships.' 1646. Bridlington. Slingsby.

'Nature and Religion forbid and our soul abhors ... let no Woman presume to counterfeit her Sex by wearing man's apparel under pain of the severest punishment which Law and our displeasure shall inflict.'
1643 July. Proclamation.

'He {Charles I} caused 14 boats to be made for transporting his artillery ... makes trial upon the river at Oxford how these boats would carry these guns, causing two of the biggest to be drawn over by them'. Oxford. Slingsby.

'Take care, these thieving rats are friends of those outside. Our supplies must last until relief arrives now that York has fallen and Black Tom {Fairfax} with his Godless force is camped outside, our plight is grim.' 1644 Oct. Letter smuggled out from besieged Helmsley Castle.

50 officers and gentlemen, 80 horses and supplies of meat and salt were captured after breakout of Royalist troops on 12 November 1644. Ten days later Sir Jordan Crosland surrendered to Fairfax on honourable terms - '200 men, 9 pieces of ordnance, 300 muskets, 6 barrels of powder, money and silver plate' fell into Parliament's hands. The East tower, curtain wall and main gates were 'slighted' to render Helmsley untenable.

'The Surrender and Delivery of the said Castle {Skipton} with the Cannon, Ammunition, Goods ... for the use of King and Parliament ....
Article 4. That the {garrison} march out according to the Honour of a Soldier, with Colours flying, Trumpets sounding, Drums beating, Matches lighted on both ends, and Bullets in their mouths. Every Trooper and every Foot Soldier three charges of powder, and the Officers to march with their wearing apparel that is properly their own in their Portmantles, and not have anything taken from them, and that the Common soldiers shall not march away with any Bag or Baggage.' 1645 Dec. Skipton Castle. Colonel Thornton's terms to the Royalist commander, Sir John Mallory.

'2 demi-cannon and 3 whole culverins ready at Windsor and Northampton ... 1200 spades and shovels, 300 steel spades, 500 pickaxes, 200 scaling ladders, 500 barrels of gunpowder, 40 tuns of match, 30 tuns of bullet, 300 granadoe shells, 1000 hand grenades, 50 tuns of round shot. 20 carriages for provisions,, 200 horse harness. Grand total £6,172.10s.' Fairfax's prepares to besiege Oxford in 1645.

'Fling me up half a mutton, and I will fling you down a lord.' 1645 Oxford. Royalist sentry to Roundhead besieger.

'... when Oxford surrendered the first thing General Fairfax did was to set a good guard of soldiers to preserve the Bodleian Library. 'Tis said there was more hurt done by the cavaliers, during their garrison, by way of embezzling and cutting off chains of books than there was since. He was a lover of learning, and that noble library had been utterly destroyed, had he not taken this special care, for there were ignorant senators enough who would have been contented to have had it so.' Aubrey *Lives*

'Nothing but salt beef tainted, a little quantity of bread and wine almost spent ... We urge nothing for ourselves, not the rest of your loyal servants here who are now poorly clothed and sickly fed upon bread and water {and horseflesh}.' 1645. Pendennis Castle.

'If the King had no more ground in England than Basing, I would venture as I did ... Basing is called 'loyalty' ... I hope that the King may have a day again.' 1646, Oct. Marquis of Winchester after the destruction of his house that had withstood years of intermittent sieges. Inigo Jones was among the captured.

'You are not now at Bletchingdon.' 1645 Faringdon. Col. Burges to Cromwell. Francis Windebanke had surrendered Bletchingdon House after a very brief siege fearing for the safety of his young wife and her friends. He was court-martialled on his return to Oxford, and shot on the King's orders.

'Cavaliers, citizens, seamen and water-men ... very numerous but likewise very disorderly.' 1648 Maidstone.

Siege of Colchester

'... the season which was wonderful wet, and that for the greatest part of the summer.' 1648. An Essex parson.

'... their bodies in the streets and hedges as infallible witnesses of what had been done; yawning out their souls to receive their arrears in another world, for their religious rebellion in this.' 1648 June. Matthew Carter, a Royalist officer. Many popular officers were killed in the first Roundhead assault, and revenged in the second.

'They {Barkstead's regiment} fell on like madmen, killing and slaying them {Royalists} in a terrible manner, even in the cannon mouths.'

'For some satisfaction to military justice and with the advice of the chief officers ... caused two, who were rendered at Mercy, to be shot to death.

'Sir Charles Lucas had forfeited his parole, his honour and faith, being his prisoner upon parole, and therefore not capable of ... trust in martial affairs ... the satisfaction of military justice ... avenge for the innocent blood they have caused to be spilt, and the trouble, damage and mischief they have brought upon {Colchester} this county and the kingdom.' 1648 Aug. Fairfax on the verdicts on Lucas and Lisle.

'Duke Hamilton, the Earl of Holland and that excellent person, Lord Capel, {surrendered at Colchester} suffered {execution}.' 1649. Warwick.
*

'Victualled with two hundred and twenty or forty fat cattle ... {Royalists in Pontefract} are resolved to endure to the utmost extremity, expecting no mercy, as indeed they deserve none ... one of the strongest inland garrisons in the kingdom; well watered, situated upon a rock in every part of it, and therefore difficult to mine. The wall very thick and high, with strong towers, and if battered very difficult of access.' 1648 Nov. Cromwell.
*

'The Scotch take all movables, cows, sheep and all household stuff to the very pothooks; they take children and make their parents pay ransom for them, and force women before their friends' faces.'
1650 Newcastle. Haselrig.

15

LILBURNE & THE LEVELLERS

'I am the son of a gentleman, and my friends are of rank and quality in the country {Northumberland} where they live.' 1638. John Lilburne.

'Captain John Lilburne {of the trained bands} both faithful, able and fit to be a captain of a troop of horse, having shewed his valour at the battle of Kineton {Edgehill}.' Earl of Warwick.

'I am as free from covetousness or cowardliness as your self, I will take my horse and post away to Brentford to your regiment and fight as resolutely tomorrow as your Lordship shall.' 1642 Oct. Lilburne to Lord Brooke.

'A mad fellow ... a base fellow.' 1644 July. Manchester of Lt-Colonel John Lilburne, officer in the Eastern Assoc.

'... to show the maladies and remedies of this sick, swooning, bleeding and dying Nation.' 1645. John Lilburne *Englands Birth-right Justified*

'I build upon the Grand Charter {*Magna Carta*} of England. I have as true a right to all the privileges that do belong to a freeman, as the greatest man in England ... I speak that which I will stand to, and live and die by, humbly submitting my body to your pleasure.' 1645 July. Lilburne on accusations of slandering the Speaker.

'As if they intended to level men of all qualities and estates.' Richard Baxter.

'... we never had it in our thoughts to level men's estates, it being the utmost of our aim that the Commonwealth be reduced to such a pass as that every man may with as much security as may be enjoy his propriety.' John Lilburne.

'Public-spirited men stood up in parliament and the army declaring against these factions and the ambition of the grandees of both ... they were nicknamed levellers ... there rose up afterwards with that name a people who endeavoured the levelling of all estates and qualities, which these sober levellers were never guilty of desiring.' Lucy Hutchinson.

'... I was robbed of my trade, and in greater bondage by my fighting for justice, liberty and freedom than I was before. I was at a mighty stand with myself what to do to provide for myself and family ... what have we fought for all this time?' 1645. Lilburne.

'All the war I have made, hath been to get victory on the understandings of men.' William Walwyn, Merchant Adventurer, and Leveller.

'{Walwyn with} a great white and brown basket-hilted beard, and with a set of teeth in his head all staring and standing some distance one from another, as if they had not been good friends; it may be conjectured, he picks

them twice a day with a bed-staff, they look so white and clean.'
1645. Dr John Bastwick.

'It is was observed by some that a Victorious Army, out of imployment is very inclinable to assume power over their Principals.' 1647. Whitelocke.

'Let two horsemen go presently to Colonel Rainsborough to Oxford, and be very careful you be not overwitted.' 1647 May. Instructions from Sexby.

'A Remonstrance of many thousand Citizens of England to their owne House of Commons, occasioned through the illegall Imprisonment of John Lilburne.' 1647 June.

'... men instrumental in bringing this War to a conclusion ... the Army's honour and reputation turned into reproach and scandal. Here the power of the Army, which I once had, was usurped by the forerunners of confusion and anarchy, viz. the Agitators...
'At Nottingham ... I took notice of it, by the soldiers' meetings to frame a Petition to Parliament about their arrears. The thing seemed just, but ...
'... created the thoughts of a New Government, which in time attained the name of a Common Wealth ... being sometimes democratical, sometimes oligarchical, lastly anarchical ...'
{1647} Fairfax Memorials

'The Army now did all, the Parliament was but a cipher and only cried amen.' 1647. London. Denzil Holles

'The old, beaten, subtle foxes of Westminster.' 1647 July. Richard Overton.

An Humble Representation of the Dissatisfaction of the Army.
1647 June. Newmarket.

The Solemn Engagement of the Armie. 1647 June. The Council of the Army, consisted of two officers, and two common soldiers from each regiment, the elected agitators {agents}.

'An Agitator is a late spurious monster ... begotten of Lilburne with Overton's help.' The Character of an Agitator

'Trust your great officers no farther than you can throw an ox.' Lilburne.

'... though you have given me little encouragement {of keeping quiet} ... such is the affection I bear you, as you shall see, I will not be wanting in my best endeavours to procure your liberty of the Parliament.' 1647 Aug. Cromwell to Lilburne in the Tower.

The Heads of Proposals offered by the Army. 1647, 1 Aug. The Case of the Army Truly Stated. 1647 Oct.

The Agreement of the People as presented to the Army. 164, 28 October.

England's Freedom - Soldiers' Rights. 1647 15 Nov. Corkbush Fields, Ware. The mutineers were overawed by Cromwell, but only one, Richard Arnold, shot as an example.

'I do hear nothing at all that can convince me why any man that is born in England ought not to have his voice in elections {to Parliament} ... why Almighty God gave men reason, it was that they should make use of that reason.' 1647 Nov. Colonel Thomas Rainsborough. Putney Debates.

'It is by right of Nature? If you will have forth that as your ground, then I think you must deny all property too, and this is my reason ...{if} one man hath an equal right with another to the choosing of him that shall govern him, by the same right of nature he hath the same equal right in any goods he sees, meat, drink, clothes, to take and use them for his sustenance. He hath a freedom to take to the land, to exercise it ....' Henry Ireton. Putney Debates.

'I wish you {Ireton} would not make the world believe we are for anarchy.' Rainsborough.

'There are many thousands of us soldiers that have ventured our estates, yet we have had a birthright. But it seems now, except a man hath a fixed estate in this Kingdom, he hath no right in this Kingdom. I wonder we were so much deceived.' Agitator Edward Sexby.

'{Parliament} could take no cognizance of their petition, they being women, and many of them wives, so that the Law took no notice of them.' An MP to Mrs Chidley, leader of a crowd of Leveller women at Westminster.

'The Whalebone Inn, behind the Exchange ... the Mouth in Aldersgate ... two new Houses of Parliament of the London Levellers.' 1647.
Mercurius Pragmaticus

'Dost thou not think this fear of the Levellers (of whom there is no fear},'that they would destroy Nobility' has caused some to take up corruption and find it lawful to make this ruining hypocritical Agreement ...' 1648 Nov. Cromwell to Colonel Robin Hammond.

'The true Levellers ... the Diggers ... work together, eat bread together.' 1649. Inspired by Gerrard Winstanley and William Everard the Diggers started cultivating St George's Hill, Surrey as communal land.

'I did not think that you had such heathenish and barbarous principles in you as to obey your officers in murdering me.' 1649 April, London. Richard Lockier, Leveller mutineer.

'It is our day today, it may be yours tomorrow.' 1649 May, Leveller mutin-eers at Burford. 400 were arrested and three shot.

'And what, shall then honest John Lilburne die!
Three-score thousand will know the reason why!'
1653. Lilburne was imprisoned, yet again, 'for the peace of this Nation'. He died, a Quaker and at liberty, 1657. Similar defiant verses, 'And shall Trelawney die', attacked James II.

16

MIGHTIER THAN THE SWORD

'Witches Apprehended, examined and Executed for notable villainies by them committed both by Land and Water. With a strange and most true triall how to know whether a woman be a Witch or not. Printed at London for Edward Marchant, and sold over against the Cross in Pauls Churchyard. 1613.'

'The Old, Old, Very Old Man or the Age and long Life of Thomas Parr ... borne in the raigne of King Edward the Fourth in the yeare 1483. Hee lived 152 yeares nine moneths and odd dayes and departed this Life at Westminster the 15 of November 1635 and is now buried in the abby at Westminster. Imprinted for Henry Gosson at his Shop on London Bridge neere to the Gate.' 1635.

'Tho.Parr of ye County of Sallop. Borne in Ad 1483, he lived in the reignes of Ten Princes, viz: Kg. Edw IV, K. Ed V, K. Rich 3, K. Hen VII, K. Hen VIII, K. Edw 6, Q. Ma, Q. Eliz, K.Ja. & K.Charles, aged 152 yeares & was buried here {Westminster Abbey} Novemb. 15 1635.'

'The Principles of the Art Militarie, Practised in the Warres of the United Netherlands, represented by Figure, the Word of Command and Demonstration. Composed by Henry Hexham, Quarter-Master to the Regiment of the Honourable Colonell Goring, Governor of Portsmouth. London. Printed by Robert Young at the signe of the Starre upon Bread street hill. 1639.'

'With taxes and monopolies oppressed,
Ship-money, soldiers, knighthood and the rest,
The Coat and Conduct money was no jest,
Then think, good neighbours, how much we are blest,
In the Great Counsel of the King.

Who did regard our poverty, our tears?
Our wants, our miseries, our many fears?
Whipt, stript and banished as appears,
You that are masters now of your own ears,
Bless the Great Counsel of the King.'
Satirical ballad.

'Master PYM in Parliament on Wednesday the fifth of January 1641 concerning the Vote of the House of Commons for his discharge upon the Accusation of High Treason, exhibited against himselfe, and the Lord Kimbolton {Manchester}, Mr John Hampden, Sir Arthur Haselrig, Mr Strowd, Mr Hollis, by His Majesty. The true effigy {woodcut} of Mr John Pym, Esquire. London. Printed for I.W. 1641.' By the New Style calendar, Jan 1642.

'The Citie Trained Bands and the brave Seamen with Barges and Long-Boates adorn'd with streamers, drums and trumpets and furnished with ship guns & other warlike instruments, guard the Lord & Commons safely to Parliament by Land & Water.

'The Countie of Buckinghamshire cometh to London the very same day of the Lords & Commons so guarded with their Petition to the Parl.

'Carrying the Protestation on their staves on horseback, and the Counties of Essex, Hertford, Barkshire, Surrey & others followed them in like manner shortly after.' 1642. Pamphlet with two woodcuts.

'A True and exact Relation of the manner of his Majesty's setting up of His Standard at Nottingham, on Monday the 22 of August 1642. 'First, the forme of the Standard as it is here figured, and who were present at the advancing of it. 'Second, the danger of setting up of former Standards, and the damage which ensued thereon ... 'Sixtly, the Cavaliers resolution and dangerous threats which they have uttered, if the King concludes a peace without them, or hearkens unto his great Council the Parliament; moreover how they have shared and divided London amongst themselves already.' 1642. Pamphlet with woodcuts.

'A Collection of Records of the great Misfortunes that hath happened unto Kings that hath joined themselves in a near alliance with foreign Princes with the happy success of those that have only held Correspondency at home.' 1642. Pamphlet title.

'Grand PLUTOES Remonstrance or The Devil Horn-mad at Roundheads and Brownists, wherein his Hellish Majesty (by advice of his great council ... pleaded to declare how he differs from Round-head, Tattle-head or Prick-care. His Copulation with a holy sister. His dear affection for Romish Catholiks and hate to Protestants. His oration to the Rebells. 1642. An obscene tract.

'... Fire and Blood, {and} the rattling of the Drum, the shrill sounding of the Trumpet, the confused neighing of the Horse ... cries of the pursuing and groans of the dying, are heard into every corner of the Kingdom.' 1644. *Perfect Weekly Account*

'Sir Jacob {Astley}, lately slain at Gloucester, desires to know was he slain with a musket or a cannon bullet?' Royalist satire.

'Do you not know a fortnight ago, They bragged of a Western Wonder? When a hundred and ten slew five thousand men, with the Help of lightning and thunder. There Hopton was slain, again and again, Or else my author did lie. 1643 April. Denham on Waller's defeat at Roundway Down.

'A Declaration and Vindication of Isaak Pennington, now Lord Mayor of the Cittie, Colonell Venn, Captain Manwaring and Mr Fowke.'
1643. *A Humble Remonstrance to the King's Most Excellent Majesty*

'A Dialogue between the DEVIL and Prince RUPERT ... before Chester upon Rupert's coming to relieve the said City ... Written by E.B. London, printed for T.B. 1644.'

'Sad, Cavaliers, Rupert invites you all that do survive, to his Dog's {Boye's} funeral. Close mourners are the Witch, Pope and devill, That much lament your late befallen evill.' 1644, July. Roundhead pamphlet after Marston Moor.

'The Scout' is clapt here up for some unadvised expressions, he is not this week to be heard of.' 1645 Feb. Sir Roger Burgoyne.

'England's Miraculous Preservation Emblematically Described, erected for a perpetuall Monument to Posterity.
'Though England ARK has furious storms indur'd
By Plotts of foes and power of the Sword.
Yet to this day by Gods almighty hand
The Ark's preserv'd and almost safe to land.' 1646. The Commons floats on a sea of drowning Cavaliers, surrounded Essex, Warwick, Manchester, Leslie, Fairfax and Cromwell.

'The Rebels' Almanack ... for the use of all loyal subjects ... wherein is discovered a new nest of old monsters.' Royalist pamphlet.

'To Newmarket now I am by my Army led,
They'll sell me better than your brethren did.
Else seek to make me shorter by the head,
Never was grief like mine.'
1647 July. Parody on Charles I's removal from Holdenby House.

'Send me the 'Moderate Intelligencer' weekly ... for we have no news at all here {in France} ... a printed book or two concerning my Lord of Essex and the chronicle of these times ...'
1647. Ralph Verney to Dr Denton.

'The World turn'd upside down, or a brief description of the ridiculous Fashions of these distracted Times. By T.J. a well-wisher to King, Parliament and Kingdom.' 1647

'I believe in no God save Oliver ... Cromwell, the Father of all Schisms, Heresy and Rebellion, and in his only son Ireton.' 1647. *The Parliament's Ten Commandments*

'Prince Rupert, not ashamed to profess that, provided he may ruin and destroy the English interest ... he cares not whether he get a farthing more than what will maintain himself, his confederates and his fleet.' 1649. Report.

'The Declaration and Standard of the Levellers of England. Delivered in a speech to the Lord General Fairfax ... at White-Hall by Mr Everard, a late Member of the Army ... before his Excellency, the manner of his deportment with his Hat on, and his severall speeches the manner of his deportment with his Hat on, and his severall speeches when commanded to put it off ... Together with a List of the severall Regiments of Horse and Foot that have cast Lots to go for Ireland. London, April 13 1649.'

'O Cromwell. O Ireton. How hath a little time and success changed the honest shapes of so many Officers.' 1649. Leveller pamphlet. *Hunting of the Foxes from Newmarket ... to Whitehall, by five small beagles*

'Hosanna, or a Song of Thanksgiving, sung by the Children of Zion set forth in three notable speeches at Grocer's Hall.
'The First, Alderman Atkins, the Second, Alderman Isaac Pennington, the Third, Hugh Peters.' 1649 June. Royalist satire on the City.

'The confession of Richard Brandon, the Hangman, (upon his Death Bed), concerning his beheading his late Majesty CHARLES the first of Great Britain ... and his Protestations and Vow touching the same; the manner how he was terrified in conscience; the Apparitions and Visions ... the great judgment that befell him three days before he dy'd; and the manner he was carryed to White-Chappell Churchyard on Thursday night last; the Strange actions that happened thereupon.' 1649 June. Pamphlet

'... John Rooten did acquaint me with this; that he was in Rosemary Lane a little after the execution of the King, drinking with the hangman ...,
"God forgive me," said the hangman, "I did it, and I had forty half-crowns for my pains".' 1660 Oct. Account of the trial of William Hulet.

'A new and more exact Mappe or Description of New Jerusalem. Unto the Court of Parliament, who are Supreme in England, Ireland and elsewhere. Unto the Armies faithfull leaders and unto the faithfull under their command.' 1652. Pamphlet.

'To His Highnesse Oliver Lord Protector of The Commonwealth ... and Dominions thereof. This Humble Petition of the Hebrews at Present reziding in this citty of London whose names are underwritten humbly sheweth:
'That acknowledging the manifold favours and protection your Highness hath been pleased to grant us ... desirous of being favoured more ... to meet at our own private devotions in our particular Houses without fear of molestation to our persons, family or estates ...' 1655 March. Expelled in 1290, the Jews, after negotiations between Cromwell and Rabbi Manasseh ben Israel of Amsterdam, had returned to England.

News-sheet & pamphlet titles

In 1640 a London bookseller saved 24 different publications, in 1641 some 720 and in 1642 over 2100. The British Museum now houses this huge archive of *Thomason Tracts*

*

Mercurius Aulicus - Mercurius Rusticus - Mercurius Pragmaticus Mercurius Politicus - Mercurius Elencticus - Parliamentary Scout Perfect Diurnall - The Kingdom's Weekly Intelligencer - True Informer

*

The Beginning and Proceedings of the English Plantation at Plimoth in New England   1622

The Discovery of a Swarm of Separatists 1641

A New Discovery of the Prelates Tyranny   1641

England's Weeping Spectacle 1641

God's Providence in Ireland   1642

New Lambeth Fayre   1642

The Midwives Just Petition   1643

True Relation of the State of the Business of Soap 1643

Rupert's Burning love to England in Birmingham's Flames 1643

Mad Verse, Sad Verse, Glad Verse, Bad Verse 1644 John Taylor.

Relation of Massacre at Bolton 1644

The King's Cabinet Opened   1645

More exact Relation of the great Victory in Naisby Field 1645

The Happy Success of the Marquis of Montrose 1645

Resolutions of the Club-men   1645

Free-man's Freedom Vindicated 1646

The Humble Remonstrance of the Company of Stationers   1646

London's Liberty in Chains 1646

An Unhappy Game of Scots and English 1646

The Devil in his Dumps   1647

Gold Tried in the Fire 1647

Killing No Murder   1647

Mournfull Cries of many Thousand Poore Tradesmen 1647

The Fountain of Slaunder   1649

Baiting of the Bull of Bashan 1649

Light Vanquishing Darkness, some truths formerly Declared   1650

Cromwell's Bloody Slaughter-House 1660

17

LAW and ORDER

'Who rules the kingdom? - the King. Who rules the King? - the Duke of Buckingham. Who rules the Duke? - the Devil. Let the Duke look to it, or he will be served as his doctor was served.' c.1626. Dr Lambe, suspected of sorcery, was lynched by the mob.

'... the Duke of Buckingham then coming out of a parlour ... having about him diverse Lords, Colonels and Captains ... was by one Felton, once a lieutenant in our army, slain at one blow, with a dagger-knife. In his staggering he turned about, uttering only this word 'villain', and never spoke a word more ... the blood came gushing from his mouth and the wound so fast that life and breath at once left his begored body.' 1628 Aug. Portsmouth. Contemp. letter.

'I am forced to make bold with the gallows, for nothing else will put life into an Irishman.' 1630s. Strafford's answer to piracy in the Irish Sea.

'Unless you hang up some of them you will do no good with them {City aldermen}.' 1641. Strafford to the King.

'{Sir Allen Apsley}... was a father to all his prisoners, sweetening with such compassionate kindness their restraint that the affliction of the prison was not felt in his day.' Lucy Hutchinson's father, when Lieutenant of the Tower.

'Severely whipped before he was put in the Pillory. Being set in the Pillory he had one of his Ears cut off. One side of his nose slit. Branded on one cheek with a red-hot iron 'S.S.' signifying 'Stirrer up of Sedition'. Carried back again prisoner to the Fleet to be kept in close custody.

'On that day seven nights, with Sores upon his back, ear, nose and face, not being cured he was whipped again at the Pillory in Cheapside ... cutting off the other Ear, slitting the other side of his Nose, and branding the other Cheek.' 1630s. Sentence of Court of Star Chamber on a libellous preacher and doctor, Alexander Leighton. Punishment sanctioned by William Laud, then Bishop of London.

'Anne Diplock was whipped for a rogue. John Palmer and Alice his wife were whipped for rogues. Thomasina Hemming, John Ballard, Margery Oiler, Robert Spray whipped.' 1633. Wadhurst, Sussex.

'Thomas Tomlinson and Dorothy his wife of Wakefield or thereabout, were taken begging at Bakewell, and whipped according to the law, and he sent home.' 1636. Derbyshire.

'... persons of honour and great quality were prosecuted to their shame and punishment (which they called an insolent triumph upon their degree and quality and levelling them with the common people).' Clarendon *History*.

'{Katharine Hadley} churlishly used by the matron {of Bridewell} and put among the common sluts ... a hell upon earth to one that fears the Lord.'

'Mr Prynne hath printed a book against the whole Kingdom ... he would have a new Government, a new Church, a new King, new laws and all the people discontented.' 1637. Verdict of thew Court of Star Chamber.

'From the plague, pestilence and famine, from bishops, priests and deacons, good Lord deliver us.' 1637. Dr John Bastwicke. Along with Prynne and Henry Burton he was fined, pilloried, had his ears cropped by the common hangman and imprisoned for life. Such punishments were unheard of for gentlemen, and all three became heroes to the Londoners.

'The intention of these men, was and is to raise sedition, being as great incendiaries in the State as they have ever been in the Church.' Archbishop Laud

'A sharp sentence against Prynne in the Star Chamber, by which that unhappy bigot was to be imprisoned for life, fined five thousand pounds, expelled from Lincoln's Inn and disbarred, deprived of his University degree, set in the pillory and have his ears cut off while his book was burnt by the common hangman.' Bulstrode Whitelock *Memorials*

'... there are thousands that their place of birth is utterly unknown, they had never any abiding place in their lives, but were and are vagrants by descent ... a sturdy beggar, lawfully whipped ... some are very desperate and envious; if a farmer give them not alms they care no more to set his Barn and Ricks of corn on fire than to light a Pipe of Tobacco.' Contemp report.

'There's a waterish Tree at Wapping, Where sea-thieves or pirates are catch'd napping {hanged}.' John Taylor, the 'Water Poet'.

'Beware of beastly drunkenness, drinking begets challenges and quarrels and occasioneth the death of many ... hence are Newgate and the Compters filled with our young heirs and swaggering gallants; to the sorrow of their friends and the joy of their jailors ...
'Drunken men are apt to lose their hats, cloaks or rapiers, not to know what they have spent and full oft have their pockets picked by whores and knaves. There is less danger in recreations as shooting, bowls, riding and tennis.' 1642 *Harleian Miscellany*

'... in a sad condition having little or nothing whereby to maintain himself, his wife and six little children but is in much debt and like to be cast into prison.' Contemp. report.

'All men that can work, want work, and are without work, shall be given work according to their abilities.' Ralph Verney.

'Many do blow and puff up sundry kinds of flesh as beef, mutton, veal, lamb and pork which flesh so blowed and puffed up is very deceivable and being but winde and oftentimes unwholesome to be eaten, being blowed and puffed up with foul and stinking breathes, {penalty} twelve pence of lawful money to the Master of the Butchers' Company.'

Hannibal Baskervyle, near Oxford 'so great a cherisher of wandering beggars that he built a large barn to receive them, and hung up a little bell at his back door for them to ring when they wanted anything.' Anthony a Wood.

'The necessitous people of the whole kingdom will presently rise in mighty numbers and set up for themselves, to the utter ruin of all the nobility and gentry.' 1642, Hull. Sir John Hotham.

'The gentry, they say, have been our masters a long time, and now we chance to master them ... now they know their strength it shall go hard but they will use it.' 1643. Royalist letter

'Military punishments which reach not to Death, are the Strappado, hanging up by the thumbs that only the Delinquents' Toes can touch the ground; the laying Muskets on their Shoulders; riding the Wooden Horse, hands tyed, Muskets or other weights tyed to his feet; ... to be turned out of the Army by the Hang-man, to have their ears cut off {and} their swords broke by the Hang-man.' Turner *Pallas Armata*

'Richard Chamberlen made an assault on Robt. Becket, and with a Sword. in English called a Fauchyn, of the value of 12d, had drawn blood upon the body of the said Robert, and forthwith rescued from the same Robert one horse of the value 50s.' 1648. Manorial Court, East Dereham. Norfolk.

'He made a speech at the gallows, which I send you with these, according to a copy I had from one of the same profession a priest, who stood under the gallows ...
'There were four coiners hanged, drawn and quartered with Mr Southworth. He was clothed in a priest gown, and had a four-cornered cap ... The quarters {dismembered} the Spanish ambassador bought of the hangman for forty shillings.'
1654. French ambassador's despatch, after the execution of the Catholic Father John Southworth at Tyburn.

Lawyers

'The wisest, brightest, meanest of mankind.' c.1620. Said of Francis Bacon, the Lord Chancellor.

'Mr Selden got more by his Prick then he had done by his practise. He was no eminent practiser at the Bar.' Aubrey.

'... of later times the judges of the land are so awed with the power and greatness of the prelates {bishops}... that neither *Habeas Corpus* nor any other lawful remedy can be had.' London petition.

'Nothing could lessen Sir Edward Coke's character more than his conduct at this Trial ... the Insolence and Violence and Scurrilous language he used to run down a man of Quality and Honour ... To see him Wrestling and perverting the Law ... to come at the Blood of an Innocent Man; and this either to make his Court to the new King, or out of Malice to the Prisoner, must give every Man a poor Opinion of this Lawyer.' 1603. Winchester. Trial of Sir Walter Raleigh. Attorney General Coke was crown prosecutor.

'That if a Man took a maid by Force and ravished her, and she afterwards gave her Consent, and married him, this would not purge the Offence, but it was still a Rape.'
1631. Lent Assizes Wiltshire.

'Friend John, I desire thee to be so kind as to go to one of those sinful men in the flesh, called an attorney, and let him take out an instrument with a seal fixed thereunto, by means whereof we may seize the outward tabernacle of George G. and bring him before the lambskin men {judges} at Westminster and teach him to do, as he would be done by. I rest thy friend in the light, R.G.' To a London Quaker

'If it be not Reason, the pronunciation of 10,000 judges cannot make it law.' 1647. John Cook.

'In the great herd of common lawyers many pragmatical spirits, whose thoughts and observations had been contracted to the narrow limits of the few books of that profession, or within the narrower circle of the bar oratory.' Clarendon.

'... although Judge Rolle was of the Parliament party he never would obey Committee Law, and when Counsel would allege the plaintiff or defendant was a Cavalier he would be peevish ... "What is this to the cause before us?" All who knew him in that station will say that he never warped his administration of justice.' Aubrey Lives.

'A London scrivener is a creature begot by a pen and hatched up in an inkpot ... the Attorney may have the honour to go to Hell on horseback, while the base Knave fairly foots it after him. Where they once get they spread like the itch and become as universal the Sickness.
'Had a Scrivener been among the Israelites, there needed no other punishment to have forced them out of Egypt; Pharaoh himself would have fled, not pursued them.'
Contemp. Oxford pamphlet.

'... being moved and seduced by the instigation of the devil, then and there, to wit on the 4th day of June 1655, took into his hand a certain piece of bedcord, value one penny, and did then and there fasten one end of the said bedcord to a pillar of the window and the other end around the neck of him, William Toomes ... {and} feloniously, wilfully, and as a felon himself did hang, choke and strangle himself.'
1655, London. Coroner's inquest.

Witchcraft

'This treatise of mine ... against the damnable opinions of one man called {Reginald} Scot, and Englishman, not ashamed in public print to deny such a thing as witchcraft.' 1597. James I *Demonologie*

'If all the old women in the world were witches we should not have a drop of rain nor blast of wind the less for them.

'... some say they fly in the air, dance with devils and take the form of asses, wolves, apes ... lycanthropia is a disease, not a transformation.'
Reginald Scot *Discoverie of Witchcraft*

'The land is full of witches, their malice is great, if we do not convict them they will in a short time over-run the land.' 1602. Mr Justice Anderson.

'The witch ... hath bound herself by other laws to the service of the emmies of God and his church ... death is his portion justly assigned him by God.' 1608. William Perkins *Discourse on Witchcraft*

'Where is it written in the Old or the New Testament that a witch hath power to kill by witchcraft or to inflict infirmity?' 1656. Thomas Ady, *A Candle in the Dark*

'I have been plants among, hemlock, henbane, adders tongue, nightshade, moonwort, leopardsbane.' Ben Jonson.

'Witches themselves are imaginative and believe oft times they do that which they do not; and people are credulous and ready to impute accidents and natural operations to witchcraft. The great wonders they tell of, carrying in the air, transporting themselves into other bodies are still reported to be wrought, not by incantations and ceremonies, but by ointments and anointing themselves all over.' Francis Bacon.

'A withered, spent, decrepit creature ... the rankest hag that ever troubled daylight ... accused of working woe.' Mother Demdike and Old Chattox, two of the accused Witches of Pendle.

'A young woman two years after her death returned again in human shape, and went up and down in the house, sat at table, but ate little. A certain Magician came who said to the beholders "this woman is but a dead carcase carried about by the Devil", and took from under her right arm hole the charme, which he had no sooner done, but she fell down a filthy carcase.

'Two witches were taken which went about by tempest, hail and frost to destroy all the corn in the country. These women stole away a little infant of one of their neighbours, and cutting it in pieces, put it in a cauldron.' c. 1610. Dr Thomas Beard, *The Theatre of God's Judgement*. Cromwell was a pupil when Beard was headmaster of Huntingdon Grammar School.

127

'... particulars of the afflictions of my poor children given in evidence at two sundry assizes and two several juries ... the Judge at last told the jury that the evidence reached not to the point of the statute, and withdrew the offenders {accused witches} from their trial by the jury of life and death, and dismissed them at liberty, at which manner of proceedings many wiser men than I am, greatly wondered.' 1621. Edward Fairfax, *A Discourse of Witchcraft*

'Buried, Katharine Roose, apprehended for a witch.' 1630, Reading.

'I have ever believed in, and do now know, that there are Witches; they that doubt of these, do not only deny them, but spirits; and are obliquely and upon consequence, a sort not of Infidels, but of Atheists.' Sir Thomas Browne, *Religio Medici*

Witches' familiars: 'Holt, a white kitten ... Jamara, like a fat spaniel without any legs ... Vinegar Tom, a long-legged greyhound with a head like and ox, a long tail and bored eyes ... Sack and Sugar, like a black rabbit ... News, like a polecat. All these vanished away in a little time.' 1647. Matthew Hopkins, self-styled Witch-Finder General *Discovery of Witches*

'The magistrates sent their bell-man through the town, crying all people that would bring any complaint against any woman for a witch ... thirty women were brought into the town hall and stripped, and then openly had pins thrust into their bodies, and most of them were found guilty, near twenty-seven of them by him, and set aside.' 1649, Newcastle.

'These parties hereunder named were executed in the Town Moor for witches. Matthew Bonner, Isabel Brown, Katharine Welsh ... The same day were hanged nine thieves, and Jane Marten for a witch, the millers wife. Mari Dunn, was kounted {named} for a witch.' 1650/51, Northumberland.

'A Scotchman, who pretended knowledge to find witches, by pricking them with pins, where he should try such who should be brought to him and to have 20s.a piece for all he could condemn as witches ... upon the gallows he confessed that he had been the death of above two hundred and twenty women in England and Scotland, for gain of twenty shillings a piece, and beseeched forgiveness, and was executed.' 1655. *England's Grievance Discovered*

'Unheard of stories of the universal increase of Witches in New England, men, women and children devoting themselves to the devil.' 1693. Evelyn.

' ... not far from Cyrencester was an Apparition. Being demanded whether a good Spirit or bad, returned no answere, but disappeared with a curious Perfume and most melodious Twang. Mr W Lilly believes it was a Fairy.' John Aubrey *Lives*

18

TRIAL OF CHARLES I

'What court shall their King be tried in - who shall be his peers - who shall give sentence - what eyes be so impious to behold the execution - what arm be stretched out to give the stroke against the Lord's Anointed and shall not wither.' 1648. Royalist pamphlet.

'That the said Charles Stuart, being admitted King of England ... out of a wicked design to uphold in himself an unlimited and tyrannical power to rule according to his will and to overthrow the rights and liberties of the people ... hath traitorously and maliciously levied war against the present Parliament and the people therein represented ...

'Upon or about 30th June 1642 at Beverley in the county of York; 24th August at the county of the town of Nottingham where and when he set up his standard of war; also on 23rd October at Edgehill or Keynton-field in the county of Warwick; 30th November at Brentford ... 30th August 1643 at Caversham Bridge near Reading; 30th October upon the city of Gloucester; 30th November at Newbury; 31st July 1644 at Copredy Bridge, Oxon; 30th September at Bodmin and other places adjacent in the county of Cornwall; 30th September at Newbury; 8th June 1645 at Leicester; also on 14th of the same month at Naseby-field

'... hath also renewed the said war against the Parliament and good people of this nation in 1648 in the counties of Kent, Essex, Surrey, Sussex, Middlesex and many other counties ...

'... the said Charles Stuart hath been the occasioner, author, and continuer of the said unnatural, cruel and bloody wars and therein guilty of all the treasons, murders, rapines, burnings, spoils, desolations, damages and mischiefs to this nation, acted and committed in the said wars.'
Indictment of Charles I.

'Having already made my protestations, not only against the illegality of this pretended Court, but also, that no earthly power can justly call me, who am your King, in question as a delinquent...
'... But how the House of Commons can erect a Court of Judicature, which was never one itself, I leave to God and the world to judge. And it were full as strange, that they should pretend to make laws without King or Lords' House, to any that have heard speak of the laws of England.'
Charles I's refusal to acknowledge the Court in Westminster Hall.

'Sir, you are not to dispute our authority ... it will be taken notice of that you stand in contempt of the Court, and your contempt will be recorded accordingly ... Sir, you ought not to interrupt while the Court is speaking to you.' John Bradshaw.

'I do know law and reason, though I am no lawyer professed ... Sir, I am, not an ordinary prisoner.' Charles I.

'Here a Malignant Lady interrupted the Court .. it is affirmed that Lady Fairfax said with a loud Voice " 'tis a lye, not the tenth part of the People are concerned in it, all's done by the Machinations of that Traitor Cromwell."

'The Lord Fairfax was not there in person, that he never would sit among them and they did him wrong to name him.' Contemp. reports.

At the High Court of Justice for the Trying of Charles Stuart, King of England. Anno Dm. 1648{49}

'Whereas Charles Stuart, King of England, is and standeth convicted, attainted and condemned of high treason and other high crimes; and sentence upon Saturday last was pronounced against him by this Court, to be put to death by the severing of his head from his body ...

'These are therefore to will and require you to see the said sentence executed in the open street before Whitehall upon the morrow, being the thirtieth day of this instant month of January between the hours of ten in the morning and five in the afternoon ... and these are to require all officers, soldiers, and others, the good people of this nation of England, to be assisting unto you in this service.

'To Colonel Francis Hacker, Colonel Huncks and Lieutenant Colonel Phayre. Given under our hands and seals
  Jo.BRADSHAW, Tho.GREY,
  O.CROMWELL, Edw.WHALLEY,
  John OKEY, Jo.BOURCHIER,
  H.IRETON, Har.WALLER,
  J. HUTCHINSON, Wm.GOFFE,
T.HARRISON, J.HEWSON, R.I.DEANE, Ad.SCROPE, Edm.LUDLOW, Henry MARTEN, Rich.INGOLDSBY, J.BARKSTEAD, Valentine WALTON, Symon MAYNE, J.JONES, C.FLEETWOOD, Rob.LILBURNE,Tho.CHALLONER, Tho.SCOT, Jo.CAREW, Gregory CLEMENS, Miles CORBET {etc.}.'
59 men signed the Death Warrant;41 were still alive at the Restoration.

'Black Fairfax can climb no further,
Than Heaven will give him leave.
Red Cromwell no more can murder
Nor the Saints more deceive.'
  Royalist pamphlet.

'Never was such a damnable doctrine vented before in the world for the persons of sovereign princes have ever been held sacred, even among the most barbarous nations ...

  'In many kingdoms Kings have been regulated by force of arms and sometimes deposed and afterwards privately murdered, but in no history can we find a parallel for this, that ever the rage of rebels extended so far to bring their sovereign lord to public trial and execution, it being contrary to the law of nature, the custom of nations and the sacred scriptures.'
Contemp. report.

'The King and his party being conquered by the Sword, I believe the Sword may justly remove the power from him, and settle it in its original fountain, next under God, the people ... {but} I know not how it may justly be done.' Major Francis White.

Marston Moor, Yorkshire
Obelisk - Parliamentarian position & Cromwell's Plump

Naseby, Northamptonshire
Obelisk near the battlefield - inscription

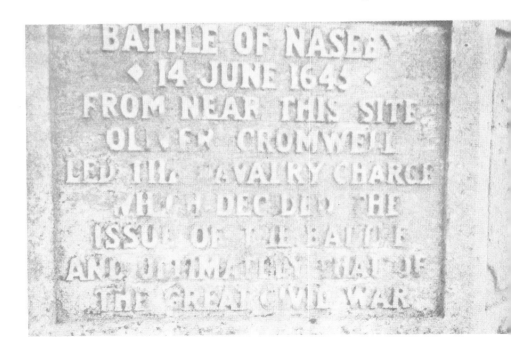

BATTLE OF NASEBY
◆ 14 JUNE 1645 ◆
FROM NEAR THIS SITE
OLIVER CROMWELL
LED THE CAVALRY CHARGE
WHICH DECIDED THE
ISSUE OF THE BATTLE
AND ULTIMATELY THAT OF
THE GREAT CIVIL WAR

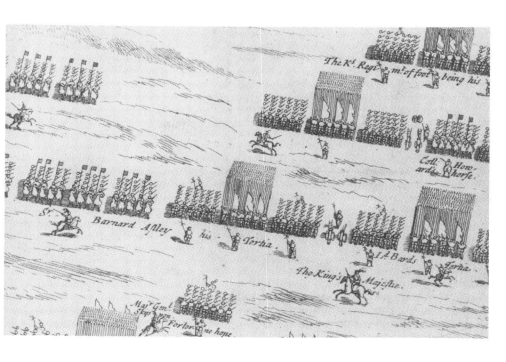

Details from *The Battail of Nasble 1645*

Edgehill memorial pillar
on Radway - Kineton road

The Commandery, Worcester
Charles II's HQ in 1651

'Let me have a shirt on more than ordinary by reason the season is so sharp as probably may make me shake, which some observers will imagine proceeds from fear. I would have no such imputation. I fear not death. Death is not terrible to me.' 1649 30 Jan. Whitehall.

'If I would have given way to an arbitrary way, for to have all the laws changed according to the power of the sword, I need not have come here; and therefore I tell you, and pray to God, it be not laid to your charge, that I am a martyr of the people ...

'I have delivered my conscience, I pray God you do take those courses that are best for the good of the kingdom, and your own salvation ...I go from a corruptible to an incorruptible Crown, where no disturbance can be, no disturbance in the world.' Charles I on the scaffold.

'Fetched out of bed by a troop of horse ... paid thirty pounds, in silver half-crown pieces.' Richard Brandon of Whitechapel, the masked executioner?

'{The Earl of Pembroke} told me himself that out of his chamber window he looked upon the King as he went up the stairs from the park to the gallery in the way to his place of death ...

'That he should not have done, but have retired himself to pray for him and to lament his misfortune, to whom he has so great obligations.

'As I remember, the Earl of Salisbury, hath told me that he was with Pembroke at the same time. It would have become him also to have been away, whose father and himself were as much bound as any man to the said late King, and his father King James.' 1649 Jan. Earl of Leicester *Diary*

'Charles the first, King of Great Britain, France and Ireland, Defender of the Faith, suffered Martyrdom upon a Scaffold before the Gate of the Royall Palace of Whitehall in Westminster. The memory of the just is blessed.' 1649. A Shropshire parish register.

'The villainy of the rebels ... struck me with such horror, that I kept the day of his martyrdom as a fast.' Evelyn.

'We are not traitors, nor murderers, nor fanatics, but true Christians and good Commonwealth men fixed and constant to the principles of sanctity, truth, justice and mercy, which Parliament and the Army declared and engaged for.' 1660. John Cook, regicide, before his execution.

'The deed should live and remain upon the record to the perpetual honour of the English state, who took no dark or doubtful way, no indirect course, but went in the open and plain path of justice, reason, law and religion.' Another regicide.

'I do not come to be denying anything but rather to be bringing it forth to light ... It was not a thing done in a corner.' 1660. Major-General Thomas Harrison, at his own trial as a regicide.

19

LONDON

'The want and misery is the greatest here {London} that ever any man living knew, no trading at all, the rich all gone, housekeepers and apprentices of manual trades begging in the streets.' 1625. Plague epidemic.

'... the City of London was in great splendour and full of wealth, and it was a glorious sight to behold the goldsmiths shops all of one row in Cheapside from the end of the street called Old Change near Paternoster Row, unto the open place over against Mercers Chapel at the lower end of Cheap.' 1629. John Rushworth.

'... for that he {Thomas Palmer} hath broke Henry Bourefelde, his apprentice, head without any just cause.' City merchant's complaint in court.

'To the right honourable Lord Mayor of City of London ... We have considered the Wheelwrights and Coachmakers inhabiting the City of London & suburbs ... do find that many frauds and deceits are daily used ... much young & unseasoned timber {used} which when it is fitted for wheels or frames for coaches are shrunk and thereby being disjointed both coach and wheels quickly decay whereby ... journeys are disappointed and lives many times endangered.' 1631. Wheelwrights' Petition seeking incorporation.

'The King, and his dearest consort the Queen, the nobility, and other of place and degree were disturbed in their passage, that the pavement was destroyed and the streets pestered by the number of coaches for hire. The King began by limiting the power of hiring hackney coaches to persons who wanted to go three miles out of town ... allowed licences to fifty persons, each holding twelve horses ... the Master of the Horse, Lord Hamilton being at the head.' 1638. *Patent for London Coaches*. Since 1625 a hackney stand stood at the 'Maypole in the Strand'

'An infernal swarm of trade-spoilers who like grasshoppers or caterpillars of Egypt, have so overrun the land that we can get no living on the water; for ... every day, if the court be a Whitehall, they rob us and carry five hundred and sixty fares daily from us.

'Note the streets and the chambers of lodgings in Fleet Street or the Strand, how they are pestered with coaches, especially after a masque or play at the court, where even the very earth shakes and trembles and the casements shatter, tatter and clatter.' John Taylor, Thames waterman and poet. *The World Runs upon Wheels*

'Carroches, coaches, jades and Flanders mares,
Do rob us of our shares, our wares, our fares;
Against the ground, we stand and knock our heels,
Whilst all our profit runs away on wheels.' John Taylor

'These frogs of Egypt ... they sup in our cup, they dip in our dish, they sit by our fire, we find them in the dyevat the wash bowl and the powdering tub.' 1641. Complaint against monopolists.

'God save the King, confound the Queen and her children, and send the Palsgrave to reign over us.' 1640. London mob. The protestant Elector Palatine, was Charles I's nephew.

'The oyster women locked their fish up, and trudg'd away to cry No Bishop.' 'There stand redcoats, a knot of papists.' 1641. London mob.

'Were not your Parliamentary officers so busy in stopping and opening Letters, I would presume to write oftener to you. But I hate to have my secrets laid open to everybody's view ... for a private conference betwixt one friend and another should be read openly in Westminster Hall ... or proclaimed at {Paul's} Cross.' 1642 Sept. Captain Thomas Gardiner.

'If a man at Constantinople or some other remote part shall send a letter to his parents, master or friends that dwell at Nottingham, Derby, Shrewsbury or Exeter or any other town in England, then this book will give instructions where the carriers do lodge that may convey the same letter,
'The carriers that go to Exeter may send daily to Plymouth or to the Mount in Cornwall ... places are served betwixt London and Lincoln, Boston, Yarmouth Oxford, Cambridge,

Walsingham, Dover, Rye and many other place of the King's dominions with safe and true carriage of goods and letters.'
The Carriers' Cosmography

'... the Accused {the Five Members}... sequestered from the House. The next day being Tuesday, many of the Citizens of London, hearing the news did shut up their shops, fearing some Insurrections would ensue upon this occasion of disaster in the Parliament House.' 1642 Jan. Pamphlet.

'What hope his Majesty can have of safety there while Alderman {Isaac} Pennington, their pretended Lord Mayor, the principal author of these calamities which so nearly threaten the ruin of that famous City, Venn, Foule and Mainwaring commit such outrages in oppressing, robbing and imprisoning all such His Majesty's loving subjects.' 1642. Charles I to the City.

'Farewell little Isaac, with hey,
Farewell little Isaac, with ho.
Thou hast made us all like asses,
Part with plate and drink in glasses
Whilst thou growest rich, with two
Shilling passes. With hey, trolly lolly lo.'
Ballad against the Lord Mayor.

'The riches of the City of London, and the trading Ports, the armes, and magazines of powder, ammunition ... the great zeale of the Presbyterian, Phanatick and Parliamentarian party, supported with the wealth of the King ... the revenue of the Church ... and of the confiscated estates of the Nobility and Gentry gone over to the King, and the heavy taxes laid upon the subjects in divers shapes and distinct titles, (as if three groats {4d} were less than a shilling {12d}).' Warwick *Memoirs*

'Going to taverns, seeing plays, and now and then to worse places, let a monied man or gentleman especially beware those over-hot and crafty daughters of the sun, your silken and gold-laced harlots everywhere, have been and are daily the ruin of thousands ... allure and entice him only to cheat him and pick his pocket to boot

'In the meantime his creditors, if they be of the inferior sort, nay their scolding and clamorous wives and every saucy apprentice, will be ready to disgrace him ... what you call for, pay for, without going upon the score {credit}, especially in city ale-houses, where you shall be torn out of your skin, if it were possible, even for a debt of two-pence, though you have spent twenty or forty pounds in their houses.' 1642. *The Art of Living in London*

'But I have writ too much, I am afraid, especially if my letter be intercepted, which is not ashamed, however of any light.' 1642. Letter from London to Henry Oxinden.

'... thought fit and ordained by the Lords and Commons in this Parliament assembled that while these sad causes and set times of humiliation continue, public stage-plays shall cease and be forborne.' 1642.

'Oppressed with many calamities and languishing to death under the burden of a long and an everlasting restraint, we the comedians, tragedians and actors belonging to the famous private and public houses within the city of London and the suburbs thereof ... do we in all humility present this our humble and lamentable complaint ... to be restored to our pristine honour and employment.' 1643. *The Actors Remonstrance*. Theatres were closed for security as much as moral reasons.

'... this day an act of Common Council passed that the Cross in Cheapside should be pulled down; if that takes now, then Paul's is soon after to follow, and so other churches by degrees; windows in St Margaret's Westminster were battered to pieces on Tuesday last.' 1643. Letter to Henry Oxinden.

'The 2 May 1643 the Crosse in Cheapeside was pulled downe, a Troope of Horse and 2 Companies foote wayted to garde it and at the fall of the top Crosse drums beat, trumpets blew and multitudes of capes were throwne in the ayre and a great Shout of People with joy;

'The 2 May, the Almanack sayeth was the invention of the Crosse and ... at night was the Leaden Popes burnt in the place where it stood with ringing of Bells, a great acclamation and no hurt done in all these actions.' Pamphlet with etching of the scene by Hollar.

'... where wild-fire is, milk, urine, sand, earth or dirt will quench it ... if many houses are endangered by a mighty fire, before it can be quenched or choked with earth, then you may pull down the next house, opposite to the wind, and then earth and rubbish being cast upon the fire will choke the violence of the fire, besides the water you may get to do the like ...

'Every parish should have hooks, ladders, squirts, buckets and scoops in readiness, upon any occasion ...

'Let the very sight of fire and candle put us in mind to prevent the like miseries that have come by fire, both in London and the parts of England.' 1643. *Seasonable Advice for preventing the Mischief of Fire*, ordered to be printed by the Lord Mayor, invented by William Gosling, Engineer.'

'The City hath many courts of guard with new barricadoed posts and they strongly girded with great chains of iron ... daily musters {trained bands} shows of all sorts of Londoners here were wondrous commendable.' 1643 *The Present Survey of London*.

'The assembly of the members of the two Houses sit here {Oxford} daily very diligently ... they are now raising of a hundred thousand pounds for the King, and taking order for recruiting and arming his Majesty's forces in all places.

'They have sent several messages to London for a Treaty for accommodation but have been still refused, whereupon the Londoners say that at Oxford sit the Parliament for Peace, and at Westminster the Parliament for War.

If the Scots shall once retire out of the Kingdom, it is said that London will suddenly declare for the King, which God grant.' 1644. Secretary Nicholas

'Behold now ... the shop of war hath not there more anvils and hammers working to fashion out the plates and instruments of armed justice in defence of beleaguered truth than there be pens and heads there, sitting by their studious lamps, musing, searching, revolving new notions and ideas.' 1644 London. Milton *Areopagitica*

'... men and women to travel from London to the principal towns of the country, that the like hath not been known in the world, that is by stagecoaches, wherein anyone may be transported sheltered from foul weather and foul ways, and this at the low price of about a shilling for every five miles.' Carrier's advertisement.

'The Assize of Bread set forth by Order of the Lord Mayor ... A penny Wheaten Loaf to contain Nine Ounces and a half, and three halfpenny White Loaves the like weight.'

'Order that the garden be made into grass, the Clerk to allow clothes drying at certain times without molestation of users.' 1644. The Drapers Company.

'That the Committee of Weavers' Hall may be called to account how they have issued out £200,000, not above £40,000 of it having come to this Army.' 1647 July. Rushworth.

'... after so many warnings for non-payment of arrears {to the army} ... ordered Colonel Hewson that so soon as he hath the list of persons in arrear, he shall quarter the soldiers only upon such.' 1647. Fairfax to Lord Mayor.

'The Orphans Cry, we perish we die.
For the Lord's sake, some pity take.
Lay not this sin to their charge.
  I am sick, I die.
As we you see, so may yours be.
  Dead in the street.'
1649. *London's Charity Enlarged*

'News from Powles {St Paul's} ... a colt was foaled in the cathedral in London, and how it was publicly baptized by Paul Hobson's soldiers, one of them pissing in his helmet and sprinkling it, in the name of the father, son and holy ghost ... because it was a bald colt, was called Baal-Rex. With a catalogue of the blasphemies, murders, cheats, lies and jugglings of the independent party.' 1649. Royalist pamphlet.

'Ordered by the Parliament ... that the Markets be kept {open} tomorrow, being the five and twentieth day of December. And that the Lord Mayor and Sheriffs of London and Middlesex, and the Justices of the Peace for the City of Westminster and the Liberties thereof do take care that all such persons as shall open their shops on that day be protected from Wrong or Violence and the Offenders punished.
'Resolved ... that no Observation be had of the day commonly called Christmas-Day, nor any Solemnity used or exercised in Churches upon that day.' 1652. Printed by John Field, Printer to the Parliament of England.

'Carriers, waggons, foot-posts and higglers do usually come from any parts, towns, shires and countries of the kingdoms of England, as also from the kingdom of Scotland and Ireland. With nomination of what days of the week they do come to London and what days of the weeks they return; whereby all sorts of people may find direction how to receive or send goods or letters into such place as their occasions may require.
'As also where the ships, barks, tilt-boats, barges and wherries do usually attend to carry passengers and goods to the coast towns of England, Scotland and Ireland or the Netherlands; and where barges and boats are ordinarily to be had that go up the river of Thames westward from London.'
The Carriers' Cosmography

'Twelve years Observations upon the Times ... concerning the lamentable Game called Sweepstake, acted by General Plunder and Major General Taxes. With his exhortation to the people, a description of that oppressing Ringworm called Excise, and the manner how our high and mighty Christmas-ale that would formerly knock down Hercules ... 'Keep out you, come not here' {puritan}; 'O, sir, I bring good cheer'{Christmas}; 'Old Christmas, welcome, do not fear'{citizen}.' 1653. Imprinted at London.
The Vindication of Christmas

'All Gentlemen, Merchants and other Persons may please to take notice that upon Tuesday night, the eighteenth day of January 1652 the Letters were sent from the old Post-House, at the lower end of Threadneedle-street by the Stocks in London at the Rates of twopence the single Letter within eighty miles of London, and three-pence the single Letter above eighty miles within Commonwealth and so proportionably for double Letters and Packets and Packets of printed Books, or two shillings the pound, and the State Packets and Letter carried free;

'... and so continue going forth Tuesdays and Saturday nights, and Answers expected Mundays and Fryday mornings, as formerly accustomed.

'Letters may be received in for conveyance by the old Post at those rates at the several places accustomed. VIZ.

... the *Sarizans Head* in Westminster
... the *White Hart* at Charing Cross
... Porter of the Gate at the Savoy
... the *Gun* in the Strand
... the *Crown* at Temple Bar, Stationer
... the *Marygold* against Fetter lane
... the *White Horse* in Fleet street
... the Stationer at Staple Inn
... *White Lyon* by stairs at Wapping
... Tower Hill next the Navy Office
... the *Cock* in Ratlef {Ratcliffe}
... over against the Gun in Woodstreet

'The Persons that leave Letters at any of these places are desired to bring them in thither before ten of the clock, Tuesdays and Saturday nights;

'and at the Post-house by the Stocks by twelve a clock.' 1652.

'An Ordinance Touching the Office of Postage of Letters, Inland and Foreign. Saturday September 2. 1654.

'Ordered by his Highness the Lord Protector, and His Council, That this Ordinance be forthwith Printed and Published.

'Henry Scobell, Clerk of the Council. London. Printed by William du-Gard and Henry Hills, Printers to His Highness the Lord Protector, 1654.'

'... I rode negligently till, within three miles of Bromley two cut-throats started out, and striking with long staves at the horse threw me down,, took my sword and hauled me into a deep thicket where they might securely rob me, as they soon did ...

'... they took two rings, one an emerald with diamonds, the other an onyx, a pair of buckles set with rubies and diamonds .. and after all bound my hands behind me, and my feet, having pulled off my boots ... I rode to Colonel Bount's ... who sent out hue and cry immediately.

'Next morning, I went to London and got 500 tickets printed and dispersed by an officer of Goldsmith's hall, and within two days had tidings of all I had lost, except my sword, which had a silver hilt, and some trifles ...

'The rogues had pawned one of my rings for a trifle to a goldsmith's servant ... the other was bought by a victualler, who brought it to a goldsmith, but he having seen the ticket seized the man ... Thus did God deliver me from these villains, not only so, but restored what they took.' 1652. Evelyn.

'This day was more observed by people going a-maying than for divers years past; and indeed much sin committed by wicked meetings with fiddlers, drunkenness, ribaldry, and the like; great resort to Hyde Park, many hundreds of coaches and gallants in attire, but most shameful powdered-hair men and painted and spotted women ...

'But his highness, the Lord-Protector went not thither, not any of the lords of the commonwealth, but were busy about the great affairs of the Commonwealth.' 1654 May.
The Moderate Intelligencer

'Sir A Haslerig came out very angry ...{to} the City to Guildhall where the Hall was full of people expecting Monk and the Lord Mayor to come thither, and all very joyful. Met Monk, coming out of the chamber where he had been with the Mayor and Aldermen, such a shout I never heard in all my life 'God bless your Excellence!' Here I met Mr Locke and took him to an alehouse.' 1659 Feb. Pepys.

'...That this glorious and ancient City should wrap her stately head in clouds of smoke and sulphur, so full of stink and darkness, I deplore with just indignation; ... buildings composed of such a congestion of misshapen and extravagant houses ... streets so narrow and incommodious in the very centre ... so ill and uneasy a form of paving under foot, so troublesome and malicious a disposure of the spouts and gutters overhead, are ... worthy of reproof and reformation.' Evelyn.

'Pardon me, therefore, if I do not judge the City by Furs, and gold Chains, Births and Bruit, Port and Portalls, Means and Merchandise, no, not by Wit and Worship, Sermons and Services, but by soft Brests, sound Vitales, pure and operative Spirits ...

'Oh, what great affection, what great Care, great Zeal ought we to use for this great City. we had need to bring forth our strongest Shore to underset this Building, and lay down our whole Estate to redeem this Jewell. Citizens! Then where are your City Bosoms, City Bowells, City Grones and your City Cries?' 1657. Thomas Reeve of Chancery Lane. *God's Plea for Nineveh*

'A large whale was taken betwixt my land {Deptford} butting on the Thames and Greenwich which drew an infinite concourse, by water, horse coach and foot from London and all parts ...

'... after a long conflict it was kill'd with a harping iron, struck in the head, out of which spouted blood and water by two tunnels, and after an horrid grone it ran quite on shore and died .. no teeth, but suck'd slime only as thro' a grate of that bone which we call whalebone ... a mouth so wide diverse men might have stood upright in it ... all of it prodigious, but nothing more wonderful than that an animal of so great a bulk should be nourished only by slime.' 1658 June. Evelyn.

'... that they {the bears} be shott to death by a company of soldiers.'
Commonwealth Order for the closing of the Bear Garden in Southwark.

20

STUART WOMEN

'I married three times, never with entire satisfaction.' Contemp. widow.

Lady Suffolk 'had the smallpox which spoiled that good face of hers, which has brought to others much misery, and to herself greatness, which ended in much unhappiness.'
1619. Lady Anne Clifford *Diary*

'If my daughter shall approve thereof she is provided of a gentlewoman reported to be extraordinarily qualified towards performance of more than is required, be it in the kitchen, larder, buttery ... her ambition is to sit at table the first course, and then to rise and attend my daughter's commands.'
1641. Christopher Browne.

'... such as are of the poorest condition come to the city, compelled by necessity to try their fortunes ... young maids, who never knew ill in their lives, enticed by bawds to turn common whores, poverty itself is no vice, but by accident.' 1642. Henry Peacham,

'When I was a child (and so before the Civill Warres) the fashion was for old women and mayds to tell fabulous stories nighttimes, of sprights and wailing of ghosts.' John Aubrey.

'Whether my Lady Vere disliked me, the conditions or us both I cannot tell, but she put me off with an unwillingness to marry her daughter {Anne} ... whether I should proceed further in this business or no, I leave to you.'
1637. Thomas Fairfax to his father.

'I am so acquainted with delays as I am very impatient of them, we are free in our offers, and I hope my lady will consider it; if not, she hath her moneys, and we our wares ...
'Your son hath forgotten to write to me, but be remembereth his old wont, not to write.' 1637. Lord Mulgrave, Thomas' maternal grandfather, to Ferdinando Fairfax.

'The marriage intended private was made too public; a very great feast and many at it. I hope she {Anne} will prove a good wife; her affection to her husband, and her demeanour in these few hours promiseth well.' 1637. Ferdinando to Lord Fairfax, his father.

' ... his second lady {Lady Denham} had no child: was poysoned by the hands of the Countess of Rochester, with Chocolate.' Contemp. account.

'When the first child was born, the father, mother and child could not make one and thirty years old ... she had some after that child-birth which distempered her.' Lucy Hutchinson.

'... holding up my petticoats to the calves of my legs, to show my fine coloured stockings and how trimly I could foot it in a new pair of corked shoes.' *Willy Beguiled*

'... strive by straight-lacing to attain into a wandlike smallness, never thinking themselves fine enough until they can span their waist ... they by strong compulsion shut up their waists in a whalebone prison or little-ease, they open a door to consumptions and a withering rottenness.'
The Artificial Changeling

'... if she will have cloth, she begins at the seed, she carrieth the seed into the ground, she gathereth flax, of her flax she spinneth a thread, of her thread she weaveth cloth, and so she comes by her coat.' Marriage sermon.

'Anne Wilding to be flogged. Before she is released she must find surety for a moiety of the expense of keeping her bastard.' Parish report.

'Women are cruel this year; Saturn reigns with strong influence. Another wife has given her husband a poison of melted lead but{only} because he came home drunk.' Letter from Germany.

'His father found a rich Wife for him whom he {Henry Marten} married something unwillingly. He was a great lover of pretty girls, to whom he was so liberall that he spent the greatest part of his estate ... he lived from his Wife a long time, she was sometime distempered by his unkindnesse to her ... He was as far from Puritan as light from darknesse.' Lucy Hutchinson.

'A beautiful desirable Creature {Venetia Stanley}... a celebrated Beauty and Courtezane kept as a Concubine ... a most lovely and sweet turn'd face ... cheeks just that of the Damask rose.' Aubrey *Lives*.

'... Elizabeth Hampden ... tender Mother of a happy Offspring in 9 hopeful Children ... the stay and comfort of her neighbours, the love and glory of a well-ordered family, the delight and happiness of tender parents, but a crown of Blessing to a husband ... a loss invaluable ... John Hampden, in perpetuall testimony of his conjugal love hath dedicated this Monument.' 1634. Great Hampden.

'Most in this depraved later Age think a woman Learned and Wise enough if she can distinguish her Husband's bed from another's.' Hannah Woolley.
The Gentlewoman's Companion

'It was wondered by some that knew him {Van Dyck}, that having been in Italy he would keep a mistress of his in his house, Mistress Lemon, and suffer {Endymion} Porter to keep her company.' c.1638. Richard Symonds.

'... Sir Vandyke will do my picture, I am loth to deny him but truly it is money ill bestowed ... I have some sables with the clasp of them set with diamonds, I think would look very well ... but tis no great matter for another age to think me richer than I was ... let me know whether Vandyke was content with the fifty pounds ... the face is so big and fat that it pleaseth me not at all.' Lady Sussex .

144

'{Mary} has been extremely froward since I have been ill; I did not think that she would have been so choleric. I pray God, if ever you {Ned} have a wife, she may be of a meek and quiet spirit.' 1639. Lady Brilliana Harley.

'We never had but one mind throughout our lives ... our souls were wrapped up in each other, our loves one and our resentments one.'
Anne Fanshawe, a Royalist wife.

'... the short portrait is for my Lady of Carlisle set to the frame which I appointed for it, and so let it stand with Sir Anthony {Van Dyck} till you have waited upon her Ladyship and known her pleasure.' 1636. Strafford.

'... that busy Stateswoman the Countess of Carlisle, who had now changed her gallant from Strafford to Mr Pym, and was become such a She-Saint that she frequented sermons and took notes.' 1642. Philip Warwick.

'Active and tempestuous {Carlisle}, a very pernicious instrument.'

'... inclined to be choleric {Carlisle} yet doth so kindle and fire her wit that it has a sharpness and strength and taste to disrelish, if not to kill, the proudest hopes you have of her value of you. She more willingly allows the conversation of men than women, yet when she is amongst those of her own sex her discourse is of fashion and dress, which she always had so perfect on herself.' Sir Toby Mathew.

'The She-Wedding or marriage between Mary, a seaman's mistress and Margaret, a carpenter's wife. A cunning intrigue carried on to hide the discovery of a great belly and make the parents of her sweetheart provide for the same; for which the said parties were both committed; one remains in the Round House at Greenwich, the other being bailed out.' Pamphlet.

'I rejoice that your father is well, and that is my comfort in his absence. I could wish I could undergo some of the pains for him ... which lie upon him.' 1641. Lady Brilliana Harley.

A husband questioning the loss of her purse at the playhouse. "Wife, did I not give you warning of it, how much money was there in it?"
Quoth she, "truly, six shillings and silver tooth-picket."
Quoth her husband, "where did you put it." "Under my petticoat, between that and my smock."
"What, did you feel no body's hand there?"
"Yes, I felt one's hand there, but I did not think he had come for that."
1642. Henry Peacham, pamphlet.

'She hath ever drawn so evenly in her yoke with me as she hath never prest before or hung back and behind me, nor ever opposed to or resisted my will, and yet truly I have not in this or anything else endeavoured to walk in the way of power with her, but of reason ... though her love will submit to either, yet truly my respect will not suffer me to urge her with power unless I can {not} convince her by reason.' Sir Bevil Grenvile of his wife.

'Lord Grandison ... married to a lady so jealous of him and so ill-natured in her jealous fits, to anything that was related to him, that her cruelties to my mother exceeded the stories of step-mothers.' Lucy Hutchinson.

'On Friday last I received your welcome present of four Guinea birds for my wife, whereby you have made her a proud woman. She desired me to present to you her affectionate thanks for that great rarity.'
1641 July. Edward Nicholas.

'My cousin, much weakened at present by a hard bargain, though, thanks be to God, well delivered of a pretty, lively boy, last Friday morning.'
1642. Christopher Browne.

'It is hard to get children with good courage when one is melancholy ... be in good health and then you may till your ground, otherwise it will be time lost if you enter the race frowningly.'
Sir Theodore Mayerne.

'A woman hazards her life {bearing children} and hath the greatest share of trouble in bringing them up.' Margaret, Duchess of Newcastle.

'Sir Charles Lucas could find none that would undertake to carry it {a letter} to the castle {Nottingham}, whereupon they took the mayor's wife and with threats compelled her to undertake it.' Lucy Hutchinson.

'The women of Wem and a few musketeers,
Beat the Lord Capel and all his Cavaliers.' 1643. Cheshire.

'Tell that insolent rebel he shall have neither persons nor house; when our provision is spent we shall find a fire more merciful than {Colonel} Rigby; and then if the providence of God prevent it not, my goods and my house shall burn in his sight. My self, children and soldiers, rather than fall in his hands will seal our religion and loyalty in the same flame.' 1644. The Countess of Derby at Lathom House.

'... remembered both her lord's honour and her own birth, conceiving it more knightly that {Fairfax} should wait upon her than she upon him ... though a woman and a stranger, divorced from her friends and robbed of her estate, she was ready to receive their utmost violence.' Countess of Derby.

'... some reflection on the Parliament itself as much as the miscarriage of a Member cast on it, when Millington, a man of sixty and professing religion and having but lately buried a religious matronly gentlewoman, should go to an alehouse to take a flirtish girl of sixteen.' Lucy Hutchinson.

'I was dumb and held my peace, because God did it.' Mary Boyle on the death of her son from smallpox.

'She being an ingeniose woman and loving men, would let him (Selden) lye with her, and her husband knew it. After the Earle's death he married her.

'He did lye with Mrs Williamson, one of my Lady's women, a lusty bouncing women who robbed him on his death-bed ... they did talk also of my Lady's Shee Blackamore.' Aubrey *Lives*

'That noble lady and phoenix of women died in peace. Though surrounded with drums and noise of war, yet she took her leave in peace. The sword had no force against her as long as God preserved her, he preserved the place where she was.' 1643 Oct. Death of Lady Brilliana Harley at besieged Brampton Castle.

'Did you ever heare the like, Or ever heard the same,
Of five Women-Barbers, that lived in Drury Lane?' Ballad of the whores who shaved off a rival's pubic hair for poxing one of their husbands.

'... of the lowest extraction, without either wit or beauty ... not at all hand-some, nor cleanly ... ever a plain, homely dowdy ... had been kind to him, in a double capacity.' Nan Clarges, a laundress, married Monk on his release from the Tower. She was said to have been one of the above whores.

'... those wretched men, not only conniving at and permitting the wicked-ness of others but themselves {two MPs} conversing in taverns and brothels till ... ensnared that married a couple of alehouse wenches to their open shame.' Lucy Hutchinson.

'The most accomplished Cavalier, a goodly handsome person {Sir Kenelm Digby}, gigantique and great voice ... had he drop't out of the Clowdes he would have made himself respected... married, much against his Mother's consent, that celebrated Beautie and Courtezane, Mrs Venetia Stanley, whom the Earle of Dorset kept as his Concubine and had children by her ...
'Sir Kenelm would say that a hand-some lusty man that was discreet might make a vertuose wife out of a Brothell-house. This Ladye carried herself blamelessly, yet, he was jealous of her.' Aubrey *Lives*

' ...the day of his birth {Thomas Hob-bes} was April 5th 1588, which that yeare was Good Fryday ... his mother fell into labour upon the fright of the Invasion of the Spaniards.' Aubrey.

'Sweet madam, if you make any stay in Paris and see any pretty things that is not too chargeable, fitt for my wearing being a widow, send me word.' 1645. Lady Sussex to Lady {Ralph} Verney.

'My solitary condition and want of help in managing household affairs made me think of a gentlewoman for assist-ance and comfort. Her virtue ... was the much commended by the parents and friends of her former husband ... she was {a widow} whose father was a citizen ... she has five children, but provided for in such manner as I hope

147

will not be burdensome.

'I heartily wish I could have had the advice of children, brothers and near friends, but I hope {this} ... will not be cause of offence.' 1646 Oct. Yorks. Ferdinando Fairfax to his brother.

'A pamphlet called *The Parliament of Ladies*' spread abroad that abominable and dangerous Doctrine that it was far cheaper and safer to lye with common Wenches than with Ladies of Quality.'

'{Bess} lost her Mayden-head to a poor young fellow, then I beleeve handsome. Her father locked her up in the Turret, but she getts down by a rope and away to London and did sett up for her selfe. A most exquisite beautie ... and her price was very deare. At last she grew common and infamous and gott the Pox, of which she died.' Aubrey.

'... {had I died} then my Wife and children might have enjoyed my fortune Freely, for Widdowes and Orphans are rarely made Delinquents.' 1647 Dec. Ralph Verney in exile to Dr Denton.

'I am soe full of griefe for the Death of my poore children ... 'tis true they are taken from us, but wee shall goe to them, that shall bee our comfort.'1647 Dec. Mary Verney from England.

'For Serjeant {Judge} Rolle was just, but by nature penurious; and his wife made him worse.'

'... in St James's park, the Lady Lambert, as proud as her husband, came by, and as the present princess always hath presidency of the relict of the dead prince, so she put my Lady Ireton below; who notwithstanding her piety and humility, was a little grieved at the affront.' 1653. Lucy Hutchinson. Lambert had been voted Deputy in Ireland on the death of Henry Ireton.

'He {Suckling} made a magnificent entertainment for a great number of Ladies of Quality, all beauties and young, which cost him many hundreds of poundes ... Silk Stockings and Garters, and I thinke also Gloves.

'The greatest Gamester, Bowling and Cards, no shopkeeper would trust him with 6d ... His Sisters, come to the bowling green crying he should loose all their Portions.' Aubrey.

'First, that she hath taught her sexe that there are more ways than one to avoid idleness, the devil's cushion on which so many sit and sleep their last. They that will not use the Distaff, may improve a Pen.

'A holy, modest and painful spirit runs through her endeavours ... in this dress you shall see neither naked Brests, black Patches, nor long Trains; but an heart breathing after the coming of Christ and the comfort of Saints.' 1657. Hugh Peter's preface to Mary Cary's *The Little Horne's Doom*.
The Fifth Monarchists sect believed the Second Coming was imminent, and Charles I's kingdom, the fifth monarchy, would crumble like Babylon, Persia, Greece and the Roman Papacy. Thomas Harrison was a convert.

21

HOME & FAMILY

Children

'I sent from London, against Easter, a suit of clothes for my son Thomas, being the first breeches and doublet that he ever had & made by my tailor, Mr Miller.. It was too soon for him to wear them being but 5 years old, but yet his mother had a desire to see him in them, how proper a man he would be.' 1641. Slingsby *Diary*

'By the time I {Lucy Apsley} was four years old I read English perfectly, and having a great memory I was carried to sermons ... when I was about seven years of age I remember I had at one time eight tutors in several qualities, languages, music, dancing, writing and needlework, but my genius was quite averse from all but my book ... my father would have me learn Latin, and I was so apt that I outstripped my brothers who were at school, although my father's chaplain that was my tutor, was a pitiful dull fellow.

'As for music and dancing, I profited very little in them,, and would never practise my lute or harpsichords but when my masters were with me, and for my needle I absolutely hated it. Play among the other children I despised, and when I was forced to entertain such as come to visit me, I tired them with more grave instructions that their mothers.' Lucy Hutchinson.

'... {Thomas Hobbes} at fower yeer old went to Schoole in Westport church ... at 8 he could read well and number ... after he went to Parson Evans. After him he had for a Schoolemaster, Mr Robert Latimer, a young man of about nineteen or twenty newly come from the University who then kept a private schoole ... used to instruct him and two or three youths more in the evening till nine a clock.

'When he was a Boy he was playsome enough. His haire was black, and his schoolfellows were wont to call him Crowe.' Aubrey *Lives*

'Mr Cheney, his schoolmaster, doth begin to teach him {Thomas} his primer; I intend he shall begin to spell, and Read Latin together with his English ...

'He could last year, before he was 4 years old tell the Latin words for the parts of his body & of his clothes, and I find him duller to learn this year ... the cause be too much minding Play, which takes off his mind from his books ...

'They do ill that do foment & cherish that humour in a child & by inventing new sports increase his desire to play which causeth a great aversion to their books ...

'I will make trial of this way Teaching my Son Latin, that is without Rule or grammer, & herein I do follow the Pattern of Michel de Montaigne, a frenchman ... but I want the means he had, having those about him that could speak nothing but Latin.' 1640. Slingsby

'... your sweet child {Anna Maria, aged four} is going apace to a better world, she has but a short time to stay with us ... make all haste to your good wife who wants your comfort.'
Sir Edmund Verney to Ralph.

'I am glad little Dick is become so stout a horseman. Upon notice that he dares shoot off a gun, I will send him a brass cannon ... I long to know how he hath borne himself in this time of your carnivals and with what countenance he hath entertained those strange disguises. I doubt not but Moll hath adventured to dance with the ugliest vizards {masks} in the troop. I pray God bless them.' 1641, Feb. Christopher Browne.

'Mrs Hutchinson {herself} was brought to bed of her eldest daughter; which by reason of the mother's and the nurse's griefs and frights, in those troublesome times, was so weak a child that it lived not four years, dying afterwards at Nottingham Castle ... about this time the battle was fought at Edge Hill.' 1642. Lucy Hutchinson.

Education

'... swearing and drinking, rioting and hatred of all piety and virtue.'
1620. Cambridge

'... my precious Library, in which I have stored up with great care, cost and industry, divers originals and autographs ancient coins of gold, silver and brass, manuscripts or written books.

... keep it entire and not sell it nor divide or dissipate it, neither would I have it locked up from furthering the public good, but all lovers of learning might have access to it at seasonable times.' 1639. Will of a gentleman.

'In the village where I was born there was four readers successively in six years, ignorant men and two of them immoral in their lives ... another, an attorney's clerk, and a common drunkard and tippled himself into so great poverty that he had nothing to live ... these were the schoolmasters of my youth ... taught school and tippled on the week days and whipped the boys when they were drunk, so that we changed them very oft.' Richard Baxter.

'Oxford and my Tutor I {'Mun Verney} like very well. The Vice-Chancellor spoke to me very courteously when I came to be matriculated, as he could not find fault with my Hair, because I had cut it before I went to him.

'There is a Proctor for every house during the King's continuance in Oxford, the chiefest thing they will amend is the wearing of long hair. The Principal protested that after this day he would turn out of his house whomsoever he found with hair longer than the tips of his ears. I believe this severity will last but a week.' 1636. Letter to his father at Claydon.

'{New College} much given to drinking and gaming and vaine, brutish pleasures, so that they degenerate in learning.' Student of Merton.

'There is over Balliol College a dingy, horrid, scandalous alehouse. Here the Balliol men continually and by perpetual bubbing add art to their natural stupidity to make themselves perfect sots.' Student at Christ Church.

'Dr Busby was a great man. He whipped my grandfather. I should have gone to him myself if I had not been a blockhead. A very great man.' Richard Busby was headmaster of Westminster School for fifty years.

'My dear Ned ... If your tutor doth not intend to buy you silk stockings to wear with your silk shirt, send me word and I will bestow a pair on you ... I send expressly to your Tutor... your father by no means would have you go any where without him ... be diligent in the way in which you are to store yourself with knowledge, for this is your harvest in which you must gather the fruits which bear; It is a sorrowful repentance to repent for the loss of that which we cannot recall, which many men do in sorrowing over their lost time.' 1638. Lady Brilliana Harley. to her son at Magdalene Hall, Oxford

'I am now by your fatherly goodness brought to Oxford, for the bettering myself in learning, which, God willing, shall be my endeavour as far as he shall enable me. And next to the service of Him, I shall not be wanting in my humble duty to you, and my dear mother, for whose health shall ever be the hearty prayers of, Your most obedient Son, John Nicholas.'

'Upon the first news at Oxford that the armies were going to fight, {a student} left his gowne at the town's end and ran to Edgehill, did his Majesty good service, and returned on horse well accoutered and afterwards was made an officer in the King's army.' Contemp. account.

'Masters of Arts, yea Divines also, were served out with a pike .' 1642 Oxford.

'Students were ... much debauched and became idle by their bearing arms, and keeping company with rude soldiers.' 1643. Letter from Oxford University.

'The core of the rebellion ... are the universities, which nevertheless are not to be cast away, but to be better disciplined. That is to say that politics there taught be made to be such as are fit to make men know that it is their duty to obey all laws whatsoever that shall by the authority of the king be enacted.' Thomas Hobbes *Behemoth*

'The apprentices are harlotry-minded, high-stomached and wanton-conditioned, not knowing their duty to their superiors.' Contemp. Newcastle

'Every man strains his fortunes to keep his children at school. The cobbler will clout it till midnight, the porter will carry burdens till his bones crack again, the ploughman will pinch both back and belly to give his son learning, and I find that this ambition reigns nowhere so much as is this island.' 1640s. James Howell.

A Farmer's Estate

'Weak in body, but whole in mind and memory.' 1639. Will of Agnes Hayne.

Funeral expenses of Agnes Hayne:
'2 oxen seized for the lord for herryotts {heriot = landlord's claim to best beasts}, 2 funeral sermons and mortuaryes, 12 dozen of bread, to clerk for grave and ringing knells, coffins, wyne and sugar for met at prising {pricing?} of goods, for ten payre of {mourning} gloves, servants wages due, to vicar for ground in churchyard'... approx. £18.

Inventory of Gregory Hayne:
'Kitchen: 5 brass pots, 4 brass kettles, 2 furnaces, 2 skillets, 1 brewing tub, 1 kneading trough.
Hall: 1 table, 1 form, 2 fowling pieces, 1 musket, 5 spits, 2 dripping pans.
Parlour: 1 table, 1 form, 4 joined stools, 1 joined chair.
Milk House: 1 dozen truggs, 2 churns.
Loft over kitchen: 1 flock bed, 4 plain chests, 2 feather beds, 2 joined chests, 4 bolsters, 4 blankets, 2 coverlets, 2 pillows, 1 set curtains, 1 warming pan.
Loft over parlour: 1 feather beds, 1 flock bed and joined bedstead, 2 bolsters, 2 pillows, 10 pair sheets, 1 holland sheet, 20 pair flaxen sheets, 2 dozen of diaper{diamond pattern} linen napkins, 2 diaper towels, 3 diaper table clothes, 1 flaxen table cloth, 2 dozen flaxen napkins.
Parlour: 3 dozen pewter dishes, 3 brass candlesticks, 1 pewter candlestick, 1 flagon, 2 dozen of spoons, 1 silver bowl.

Farm: 4 oxen, 3 steers, 7 cows and calves, 5 younger beasts, 2 horses, 2 colts, 15 couples of sheep and lambs, 1 barren sheep, 2 hogs, 5 pigs ... wheels, ploughs, harrows, chains, implements. One parcel of hay, wheat upon the ground, tares sown upon the ground.' 1646 March. *Memoir of Richard Hayne, by his seventh male descendant 1899*

'Sick of body, but of good and perfect remembrance.' 1656 March. Will of Elisabeth Pollard.

Gardens

'Men can more easily build stately than garden finely.' Francis Bacon.

'To licence those in the use or exercise of the Art or Mystery of Gardening ... to seize plants, herbs and roots {on sale} unwholesome, dry, rotten, deceitful or unprofitable ... engage in planting, grafting, fencing and the removing of plants, herbs, seeds, fruits, stocks, sets and contriving the conveyances of the same {wheelbarrows?}.' James I, Charters of the Gardeners Company.

'{Have} a gathering apron like a poke made of purpose, or a wallet hung on a bough, or a basket with a sieve bottom or skin bottom, with lathes of splinters under, hung in a rope to pull up and down; bruise none, every bruise is to fruit death; if you do, use them presently. An hook to pull boughs to you is necessary, break no boughs.' *Country Housewife's Garden*

'A fountain in the midst to convey water to every part of the Garden, either in pipes under the ground, or brought by hand and emptied into large cisterns or great Turkey jars place in convenient places, to serve as an ease to water the nearest parts thereunto.' John Parkinson.

Place on the garden 'all manner of soap suds, or other suds, and washings, which shall proceed from the laundry.' Contemp. advice.

'... he {Edward Broughton} considering the grounds improved by Compost, he made an experiment of improving by soape-ashes, having land neer the City, and mightily emproved it.'

'I wish also in the very middle a fair Mount, with three ascents, and alleys enough for four to walk abreast; and the whole Mount to be thirty feet high, and some fine Banqueting House with some chimneys neatly cast, and without too much glass ...

'At the end of both the side grounds I would have a Mount of some pretty height, leaving the Walk of the enclosure breast high, to look abroad in the Fields.

'Closely mown Lawns, because nothing is more pleasant to the eye than green grass kept finely shorn.

'Pools mar all, make the garden unwholesome and full of flies and frogs.

'For aviaries, I like them not, except they be of that largeness as they may be turfed and have living plants and bushes set in them, that the birds may have more scope and natural nestling and that no foulness appear on the floor of the aviary.' 1625.
Francis Bacon *Of Gardens*

'... she {the Queen Mother} had some fruit which came from my brother's presented unto her; I saw her take a pear, and her two dogs drink some water, but was somewhat disdainful in regard the glass was not brought upon a silver plate, which was much inquired for.' Henry Oxinden.

'It is usual ... after they get all the pease pulled or the last grain down, to invite all the workfolks and their wives that helped them that harvest to supper, and then they have puddings, bacon, or boiled beef, flesh or apple pies, and then cream brought in a platters, and every one a spoon, then after all they have hot cakes and ale.' Contemp. account.

'Hoppes dried without touch of smoake ... Moulte {malt}, Wheate, Beanes, Peases, Oates, Flaxe, Hempe or whatsoever may be dryed with Fyre.'
17th century oast house.

'Touching the digging of the old orchard ...
'John and Lewes have already digged the mount, and planted it with beans and pease and are to be sharers in the benefit ...If you desire any Canary wine I have now a quarter cask of that which is good, and at a reasonable rate.' Christopher Browne, letter.

'... being almost melted with the double heat of the weather and her {Lady Gardiner} hotter employment, because the fruit is suddenly ripe and she is so busy preserving.

'I pray tell your mother I will do up her sugar if she hath currants enough, for this last week the winds have been so high that most of them were blown off the trees.' 1639. Verney letters.

'... embroidered also the borders with varieties of herbs and flowers. Only the two mulberry trees and great walnuts languish, I fear, past hope of recovery. Our damask roses also have been much blasted with easterly winds, the red have escaped better ... have tasted our strawberries, as for raspberries we are like to have a great store; and sugar being so abundantly cheap at this time our chief want will be a skilful preserver.' Christopher Browne.

'... thank her for her oranges, lemons potatoes and other things.' 1637.

'Pawsley, sorrill, spinnidge, sputs, leeks, sallat, horse rydish and Jerusalem hawty chorks.' Vegetable garden at Knole, Sevenoaks.

'Every housekeeper, that should be last up, see to the fire and candle, and shut the cellar-windows, doors, casements, garret-windows and stop holes and sinks that fire may not come in ... If you will use candle all night, let your candlestick be a pot of water brim-full. Then light a candle, and stick a great pin in the bottom and let it slowly into the water and it will burn all night without danger.' 1643. Pamphlet, *Seasonable Advice*

'Several ways Houses, Towns and Cities have been set on Fire ... bad hearths, chimneys, ovens, by shooting off pieces, by tinder or matches, by setting candles under shelves, by leaving candles near beds, by tobacco-snuffs & burnt papers, by drunkards, by warming beds, by looking under beds with candles, sparks fallen upon gunpowder, by warm sea-coal, by cinders put in baskets ...

'Some have been burnt without either fire or candle, as by wet hay, corn, straw or by mills, wheels or such like; by carelessness ... some have been fired of purpose, by villainy and treason.' 1640s. *Harleian Miscellany*

'Spaw water and change of ayre aideth a swift conceptyon.' Medical advice.

'Take red herrings and, cutting them to pieces burn the pieces on the molehills, or you may put garlick or leeks in the mouths of their hill.' Contemp. advice.

'Put butter in your dish, lay on herring and on them dates, gooseberries, currants and butter. Close it up and being baked, liquor it with butter, verjuice and sugar.' Family recipe.

' ... the Earl of Pembroke has 52 Mastives and 30 greyhounds, some Beares and a Lyon, and a matter of 60 fellowes more bestiall then they.' The menagerie at Wilton, near Salisbury.

154

Ferdinando, Lord Fairfax
when Governor of York 1644-48

Bulstrode Whitelocke
MP, author of *Memorials*

Elizabeth of Bohemia

Lady Sussex

Elizabeth Cromwell

Bridget Ireton

Oliver Cromwell's wife and daughter

Two poets, an 'arrant mountebank' and a gardener

Andrew Marvell

Sir Kenelm Digby

Sir John Suckling

John Tradescant

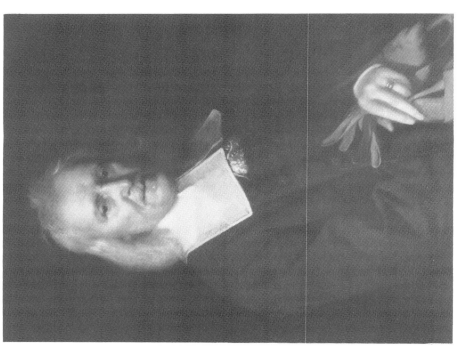

Izaak Walton, a 'contemplative man' author of *The Compleat Angler*

Thomas Hobbes, philosopher author of *Leviathan*

22

MEDICINE & SURGERY

'The wife of Maurice Clun, she prac-
tiseth surgery, but lycensed or noe,
they knowe not.' c.1600. Norfolk.

As paedants out of the schoole-boyes
breeches, doe clawe and curry their
owne itches.' c.1610.

'Sciatica he cured by boyling his
Buttock.' Sir Jonas Moore, tutor to the
Duke of York.

'Much troubled with Flegme, sitting by
the fire spitting and spawling, he tooke
a fine tender sprig and tied a ragge at
the end and putt it downe his throat
and fetch-up the Flegme ... he made
this instrument in Whale-bone ... if
troubled with the wind it cures you
immediately, with a blast as when a
Bottle is un-stopp't.' Walter Rumsey,
lawyer and judge. Contemp. report.

'The Fearfull Summer or London's
Calamitie, the Countries Discourtesie
and both their Miserie. Printed by
Authoritie in Oxford, in the last great
Infection of the Plague 1625 ... reprinted 1636 ... grievous and afflicted
famous Towne of New-Castle upon
Tine, with some other visited Townes
of this Kingdome.' 1636. Tract.

'Dose of purging pills 3/6; a purge for
your worship 3/6; chalybeate wine 4/.'
1634. Apothecary Thomas Hicks.

'The smallpox appeared upon his
Majesty, but God be thanked, he had
a very gentle disease of it ... {Queen}
kept him merry in a warm room with
a furred gown on his back.' 1632.

'Dried flesh of vipers seemed one of the
usefullest cordials I took ... a {plague}
preventive be the kernel of a walnut,
five leaves of rue, a grain of salt beaten
together and roasted in a fig ... take the
lungs of a fox, dry it to a powder and
put a spoonfull into a little almond
milk or broth, and it is good to preserve the lungs ... from a Pigeon pluck
the tail feathers very bare and set the
tail to the sore to draw out the venom
till it die.

'Also a chicken or hen is good ... take
a handful of rue, mandrake, feaverfew,
sorrell and burnet, wash them clean,
and seeth by a soft fire with running
water. Strain and if it be bitter put to
it sugar candy, and take this cordial
before the Purples do arise.'
17th century remedies.

'The Cobler may cure your sciatica ...
your new name for an owld ache.'
Sir John Leeke to Sir Edmund Verney.

'Juniper berries he extols in the wind,
cholic and many other distempers, a
commendation of berries in dropsies,
gravel, coughs, consumptions, gout,
stoppages of the monthly courses ...
rising of the lights, stopping of the
stomach ... epilepsies, palsies and
lethargies in which there are often an
ill appetite, bad digestions and obstruc-
tions.' Contemp. medical tract.

'Tobacco is found to cure mangy and ulcerous diseases ... highly commend tobacco clysters {enemas} in the most violent colic pains, water of tobacco against agues; the curious Dr Grew found the success of the oil in the toothache, a lint being dipped in it and put into the tooth, and daily smoking of it, if subject to catarrhs, rheums, and pains then there may be a temptation to venture upon it ... a French author commends it in convulsions, in pains and for bringing on sleep; he extols {the oil} in curing deafness, being injected into the ear, also against gouty and scorbutical pains of the joints being applied in a liniment.

'A lixivium prevents the falling off of the hair, and is famous for curing the farcy or leprosy of cattle.'
The Natural History of Tobacco

'Take a great Onion, hollow it and put in a fig, rue, and a dram of Venice Treacle. Put it close stopped in wet paper and roast it in the embers, apply hot unto the tumour, let three or four one after another, and let lie three hours.' Plague remedy from the Royal College of Physicians.

'Whether doctored by degree or courtesy because of his {Dr Napier's} profession I know not ... He conversed with the Angel Raphael {who} told him if the patient were curable or incurable. At some times he had conversation with {the Angel} Michael, but very rarely ... cured the falling sickness perfectly by constellated rings, some diseases by amulets etc. ... lent whole cloakbags of books ... no justice of the peace being permitted to vex him.

'Tis certain he told his own death to a day and an hour, and died praying upon his knees being of a very great age, on April 1st 1634 ... His knees were horny with frequent praying.'
Aubrey *Lives*

'God in one moment alienated her most excellent understanding in a difficult child-birth; all the art of the best physicians in England could never restore her understanding, yet she was not frantic ... her ravings were more delightful than other women's most rational conversations.'
Lucy Hutchinson *Memoirs*

'It will become a gentleman to have some knowledge in medicine, especially the diagnostic part, whereby he may take more timely notice of a disease, and by that means timely prevent it.'
Lord Herbert of Cherbury.
Having taken a course of physic {laxatives}', he later regretted being unable to leave home to join the King's army.

'Soft surgery makes foul sores.'
17th centiury medical opinion.

'... often troubled with the Gowte ... {William Harvey's} Cure was thus; he would then sitt with his Legges as if it were a Frost on the leads (roof) of the house, putt them into a payle of water till he was almost dead withe cold, and betake himselfe to his Stove, and so 'twas gone.' Aubrey.

'After a fit of the stone, fell into an ague, which hath held him (Thomas Fairfax) ever since with somewhat long fits each other day ...

'My daughter, (Anne) with watching and cold she got, is fallen into a fever, which is more to her, because she hath never had any sickness ... I cannot much blame my daughter in case of so much fear and danger of a husband so dear to her.' 1637 London.
Lady Vere to Lord Fairfax.

'After his {Harvey's} book on the Circulation of the Blood came out, he fell mightily in his practice and that 'twas believed by the vulgar that he was crack-brained and all the physicians were against his opinion and envied him ...

'In about 20 or 30 years it was received in all the universities in the world, and as Mr Hobbes says in his book *De Corpore* he {Harvey} is the only man, perhaps, that ever lived to see his own doctrine established in his life-time'. Aubrey.

'A most splenetic man {Cromwell}, and had fancies about the cross in the town {Huntingdon}, and that he had been called up to him at midnight, and such unseasonable hours, very many times, upon a strong fancy that made him believe he was then dying {c.1630s}.' Dr Symcott, Cromwell's physician.

'Excessively melancholic.' Dr Theodore Mayerne of Cromwell.

'Arrived in the first ship that ever cast anchor in this place ... my thankfulness for your helpfulness to my little one in carrying him in your coach to Sir Theodore Mayerne for advice about his neck.' 1639. Rev. Davenport to Lady Vere from Quinnipiack, New England.

Elizabeth Bedell 'was very famous and expert in chirurgery, which she continually practised upon multitudes that flocked to her without respect of poor or rich.' Contemp. report.

'My Lady Howland had a cancer in her Breast, which he (Harvey) cutt-off and seared, but at last she dyed of it.'

'I am glad you prosper so happily in Issue Male, God send the good Woman well again, which my wife prays for as an encouragement for her journey which she shall shortly be ready for.' 1637. Clarendon to Whitelocke.

'A massive fellow trod on his toe {John Hoskyns} which caused a Gangrene which was the cause of his death ...

'An experienced Chirurgeon who had formerly been in the Warres was sent for to cure him, but his skill and care could not save him, his Toes were first cutt-off.' Aubrey.

'Afflicted with an angina and sore throat that it had almost cost me my life ...

'Old Salvatico, the famous physician, made me be cupped and scarified in the back in four places, which began to give me breath and consequently life.' 1645. Venice. Evelyn.

'There was besides a young physician {Dr Plumtre} who was a good scholar and had a great deal of wit but withal a professed atheist, and so proud, insolent and scurrilous a fellow ... that he was thrown out of familiarity with the great people of the country {county}, though his excellency in his profession made him to be taken in again.' Lucy Hutchinson.

1639 The long illness of Lady Slingsby:
'It did at first puzell the Physitians to understand what she ailed; they thought it had been the cholick, then the Cardiaca Passio, then the Jaundize, then the Spleen; and every one gave her according as they judged the disease. Dr Parker gave her a vomit, but she had fainting fits in her stomack and after that her pain increasing.

'A succession of doctors advised 'take thin broth with Cream of Tartar in it ... rhubarb powder ... heat wine and after it drink some beer ... Pills of Castor to take bedward against fumes ... an ounce of Holland powder to take the weight of a groat or sixpence in a posset ale some Morning instead of the Rhubarb powder.

'Also to drink her beer hot at Meales, first boiled, then scummed putting to it a sprig or 2 of Seawormwood, to strengthen the Stomach ...'
Sir Henry took her to London where 'after she had given over Dr Fryer she was told of a skilfull woman for the Spleen, who they call Mistress Kelway ... she practised Chimistry and out of that art had extracted certain oyles and salts which she applied to all diseases

... sewing up a certain quantity thereof in a Taffity bagg, so applying it upon the spleen ... after a month's Tryall my wife finding no good at all gave her over, bestowing on her for her pains a Diamont ring.

'My dear wife departed this life after she had endured a world of misery, her many infirmities at last turning to a consumption ... the loss is beyond expression, both to her children & all that knew her, but chiefly to myself, who hath enjoyed happy days in her company & society which now I find a want of;

'She was a woman of a very sweet disposition, pleasant & affable. When anything moved her to anger or yet she conceived any injury done to her, she would easily forgive & be the first that would offer terms of reconsilement.'
1641 Dec. Slingsby *Diary*

'A true note of all those wounded souldiers cured by George Blagrave and his sonne, for which he demandeth pay as follows:
Hugh Bande, a thrust in the arme with a tuck and shott in the back - 13s 4d
John Bullock, a very sore cut in the forepart of his head which caused a peece of his scull to be taken forth, also a very sore cut hand - £1.10s.
Richard Becke, a scalded foot - 5s.
For cureing 10 Cavaliers taken at the fight at Ashe whereof one was shot in the elbow joint and the bullet taken forth in the wrist near the hand. The rest sore cut in their heads & thrust in the back - £5. {total} £12.5s.'
1645. Military surgeon's account.

'... God hath taken away your eldest son by a cannon shot. It brake his leg. We were necessitated to have it cut off, whereof he died ... He was a gallant young man, exceedingly gracious. God give you his comfort ... he was exceedingly beloved in the army of all that knew him, but few knew him, for he was a precious young men, for God.' 1644. Cromwell to Colonel Valentine Walton, after Marston Moor.

'What is the physician or surgeon but dame Nature's handmaid to be aiding and assisting to her, but the great God has ordained and appointed several diseases which are incident to men ... I have done what I can for the sick and wounded according to my best judgement.' c.1645. Military surgeon.

'A seizure of paralysis in the legs and all over the body, it seems as though my bowels and stomach weighed more than a hundred pounds, and as though I was so tightly squeezed in the region of the heart that I was suffocating... at I can scarcely stir, and am doubled up. This same weight is also upon my back, one of my arms has no feeling, and my legs and knees are colder than ice. This disease has risen to my head, I cannot see with one eye.' July 1644, Exeter. Henrietta Maria to Charles I.

'Went to Padua to be present at the famous Anatomy Lecture, which is here celebrated with extraordinary apparatus, lasting almost a whole month. During this time I saw a woman, a child and a man dissected with all the manual operations of the chirurgeon on the human body.

'I purchased those rare tables of Veins and Nerves and caused him to prepare a third of the Lungs, Liver and Nervi with the Gastric Veins, which I sent into England, and afterwards presented to the Royall Society, the first of that kind that had been seen there, and for aught I know in the world.

'When the Anatomy Lectures, were ended, I went to see cures done in the Hospitals, and certainly as there are the greatest helps and the most skilfull physicians, so there are the most miserable and deplorable objects to exercise upon.' 1646. Italy. Evelyn.

'They that play much at tennis impair their health and strength and wasting their vital spirits through much sweating.' Duchess of Newcastle.

'Dr Farrar, a Physician, a man of a pious heart but fanciful brain, would have had King and Parliament decide their business by lot.' 1649 Warwick.

'At the first fight at Newbury was shot in one of his legs by means whereof he lay in the Hospital of Bartholomew near Smithfield by the space of half a year, lame and sore diseased ... in a chirurgeon's hand having had above three score splinters of the bone of his leg at several times taken out, to his great pains ... continually in intolerable pain thereof, of which he cannot hope of remedy during his life.' 1650s. Old soldier's petition to the Justices.

23

WORDS & MUSIC

'The Bodleian Library, a work rather for a king than a private man ... As long as I remained at Oxford I passed whole days at the library; for books cannot be taken out, but the library is open to all scholars for seven or eight hours every day. You might always see, therefore, many of these greedily enjoying the banquet prepared for them, which gave me no small pleasure.' 1606. Isaac Casubon, a contemporary of Thomas Bodley.

'This island {England} seems to me to be a spectacle worthy of the interest of every gentleman, not only for the beauty of the countryside and the charm of the nation; not only for the splendour of the outward culture, which seems to be extreme, as of a people rich and happy in the lap of peace, but also for the incredible quantity of excellent pictures , statues and ancient inscriptions which are to be found in this Court.'
1629, London. Peter Paul Rubens.

'The Benchers agreed to have their Solemnity performed in the noblest and most stately manner ... Forty lutes at one time, besides other instruments and voices of the most excellent musicians in consort ... flambeaux in their hands, which with the torches gave such a lustre to the paintings, spangles and habits that hardly anything could be invented to appear more glorious' 1633. Candlemas Masque of the Inns of Court presented to Their Majesties at the Banqueting House, Whitehall.

'Stage plays, the very pomps of the Devil, are sinful, heathenish lewd, ungodly spectacles.' 1633. Prynne.

'A Maske presented at Ludlow Castle 1634 on Michaelmasse Night, before the Right Honourable, John Earle of Bridgewater, Viscount Brackly, Lord President of Wales, and one of His Majesties most honourable Privie Counsell. Printed for Humphry Robinson, at the signe of the Three Pigeons in Pauls Churchyard.'

'I have one {Wenceslaus} Hollar with me, who draws and etches prints in strong water quickly, and with a pretty spirit.' 1636. Earl of Arundel on the Bohemian engraver.

'For music you must pay besides ... teachers for viol, singing, lute and virginals.' School prospectus.

'A follower of a great lord was wont to say that he had in effect as much as his lord, though he were owner of little or nothing, considering how he had the use of his lord's garden and galleries to walk in, heard his musick with as many ears as he did ...' 1625, John Robinson *Observations*

'We had our grave Musick, fancies of 3, 4, 5 and 6 parts to the Organ with some pavanes, allamegnes, solemn and sweet delightful airs ... as divine raptures powerfully captivating all our unruly faculties and affections, and disposing us to solidity, gravity and a good temper; making us capable of heavenly and divine influences ...

'And these things performed upon so many equal and truly-sized viols, and so exactly strung, tuned and played upon, as no one part was any impediment to the other.' Thomas Mace . *Musik's Monument*

'The fantazia manner held thro' his reign {Charles I's} and during ye troubles and when most other good arts languished, Musick held up her head, not at Court nor, in ye cant of those times, profane theatres, but in private society, for many chose rather to fiddle at home, than to go out and be knocked on the head ...

'Not only in country but city families, in which many Ladies were good consortiers and in this state was musick daily improving more or less till the time, in all other respects but Musick, the happy restoration.' Roger North.

'The Sheriffs of the City of London with their officers went thither {Salisbury Court Theatre} and found a great number of people, some young lords and other eminent persons; and the men and women with the boxes {box office} fled. The Sheriffs brought away Tim Read, the Fool, and the people cried out for the monies, but slunk away like drowned Mice without it.' 1642. *Perfect Occurrences*

'O England, full of sin, but most of sloth;
Spit out thy phlegm, and fill thy breast with glory.George Herbert 1593-1633

What though the German drum
Bellow for freedom and revenge,
The noise, concerns us not,
Nor should divert our joys;
Nor ought the thunder of their carabins
Drown the sweet airs of our tun'd violins.' Thomas Carew 1595-1639

'Give me a kiss, and to that kiss
a score;
Then to that twenty add a
hundred more:
A thousand to that hundred;
so kiss on,
To make that thousand up a million.
Treble that million, and when that
is done,
Let's kiss afresh, as when we
first begun.'
Robert Herrick 1591-1674

'Gather ye rosebuds while ye may,
Old Time is still a-flying:
And this same flower that smiles today
Tomorrow will be dying ...
'Then be not coy, but use your time
And while ye may, go marry.
For having lost but once your prime,
You may for ever tarry.' Herrick.

'Why so pale and wan, fond lover
Prithee, why so pale
Will, when looking well can't move her
Looking ill prevail.
Prithee, why so pale.
John Suckling 1609-1642

'I could not love thee, Dear, so much,
Lov'd I loved not honour more.'
Richard Lovelace 1618-1658

'Stone walls do not a prison make,
Nor iron bars a cage.'
Minds innocent and quiet take
That for an hermitage.
If I have freedom in my love,
And in my soul am free,
Angels alone, that soar above,
Enjoy such liberty.'   Lovelace.

'The most amiable and beautiful
person that eye ever beheld {Lovelace}.
Having consumed all his estate he grew
very melancholy, which at length
brought him into a consumption,
became very poor in body and purse,
was the object of charity, went in
ragged clothes, whereas when he was
in his glory he wore cloth of gold and
silver, and mostly lodged in obscure
and dirty places, more befitting the
worst of beggars than poorest of
servants.' Anthony a Wood.

'Captain, or Colonel or Knight in arms.'
*When the Assault was intended on the
City*   John Milton 1608-1674

'Peace hath her victories,
No less renowned than war.'
'To the Lord General Cromwell.'

'Methinks I see in my mind a noble and
puissant nation rousing herself like a
strong man after sleep, and shaking
her invincible locks ... an eagle mewing
her mighty youth and kindling her
undazzled eyes ...'   Milton.

'But at my back I always hear
Times winged chariot hurrying near.
And yonder all before us lie
Deserts of vast eternity.'
Andrew Marvell 1620-1678

'{Sir John Denham begged the King
not to hang Captain George Withers}
for that whilst he lived, he {Denham}
should not be the worst Poet in
England ...
'After Edgehill fight his Poeme was
printed at Oxford, in a sort of browne
paper, for then they could gett no
better.' Aubrey.

'When civil fury first grew high,
And men fell out they knew not why.
...
The trenchant blade, Toledo trusty,
For want of fighting was grown rusty,
And eat into it self, for lack
Of some body to hew and hack.'
...
Has not this present Parliament
A Legar to the Devil sent,
Fully empower'd to treat about
Finding revolted witches out:
And has not he, within a year
Hang'd threescore of them in one Shire
Samuel Butler *Hudibras*

'Who would true valour see
  Let him come hither.
One here will constant be
  Come wind come weather.
There's no discouragement
Shall make him once relent
His first avow'd intent
To be a Pilgrim.'
John Bunyan 1628-1688

166

'Words are wise men's counters; they do but reckon by them: but they are the money of fools.

'Geometry, which is the only science that it hath pleased God hitherto to bestow on mankind.

'The Papacy is not other than the Ghost of the deceased Roman Empire, sitting crowned upon the grave thereof.

'No arts; no letters; no society; and which is worst of all, continual fear and danger of violent death; and the life of man, solitary, poor, nasty, brutish and short. *Leviathan* or the Matter, Forme and Power of a Commonwealth Ecclesiastical and Civil. Thomas Hobbes of Malmesbury. London printed for Andrew Crooke. 1651.'

'Doubt not, therefore, sir, but that angling is an art, and an art worth learning; the question is rather whether you be capable of learning it? For angling is somewhat like poetry, men are born so, I mean with inclination to it, though both may be heightened by discourse and practice

'He that hopes to be a good angler must not only bring an inquiring, searching observing wit, but he must bring a large measure of hope and patience.' *The Compleat Angler* or The contemplative Man's Recreation. Being a discourse of FISH and FISHING, not unworthy the perusal of most Anglers. Simon Peter said, I go a-fishing; and they said, we also will go with thee. John 21.3. London, printed for Rich. Marriot, in St Dunstans Churchyard, Fleet Street 1653.' Izaak Walton.'

'To Sir Anthony Vandyck for divers pictures, viz. our own royal portraiture; another of the French King's brother, another of the Prince of Orange ... One great piece of our royal self, consort and children, £100. £444 for nine pictures of our royal self ... and most dearest consort, the Queen made and by our command delivered unto our right trusty and well-beloved cousin and counsellor, the Lord Viscount Wentworth, our deputy of Ireland.'

'To Sir Peter Rubens, Knight, £1000, for certain pictures from him sold unto us.' 1630s. Royal accounts paid to Vandyke and Rubens.

'The King's Majesty, in armour, upon a White Horse in a great large Carved frame ... At one of the ends of this Gallery ... a portrait of the king, armed and on horseback, by the Chevalier Van Dyck. And without exaggeration ... he has so skilfully brought him to life with his brush, that if our eyes alone were to be believed they would boldly assert that the king was alive in this portrait.' On Van Dyck's equestrian portrait of Charles I.

'One Mr Vaughan of ye Exchequer office did relieve him {William Dobson} out of Prison, and thereupon he made his picture.' Richard Symonds *Notes*

'He {Pembroke} exceedingly loved Painting and Building ... and was the great Patron of Sir Anthony van Dyck and had most of his paintings.' Philip Herbert, Earl of Pembroke, of Wilton.

24

THE NEW WORLD

'A Map of NEW ENGLAND being the first that was ever here cut ... The figures which are joined with the names of places are to distinguish such as have been assaulted by Indians from others. Scale of forty miles.' c. 1620.

'We whose names are underwritten, the loyal subjects of our dread Sovereign, Lord King James ... having undertaken, for the glory of God and advancement of the Christian faith and honour of our King and Country, a voyage to plant the first colony in the northern parts of Virginia, do by these presents solemnly and mutually ... covenant and combine ourselves together into a civil body politic for our better ordering and preservation ...

'In witness whereof we have hereunder subscribed our names at Cape Cod, the eleventh of November ... Anno Domini 1620.
John CARVER, Isaac ALLERTON, William BRADFORD, William BREWSTER, Edward WINSLOW, Miles STANDISH {& others}.'

'The harvest being gotten in, our Governor sent four men on fowling, that so we might after a more special manner rejoice together, after we had gathered the fruit of our labours. They killed as much fowl as, with a little help beside, served the Company almost a week ... many of the Indians coming amongst us, amongst the rest their greatest king, Massasoit, with some ninety men, whom for three days we entertained and feasted.'
1621 Autumn. Edward Winslow.
The first Thanksgiving.

'... fresh cod in summer ... our bay is full of lobsters ... we can take hogshead of eels {and} mussels ... the earth sendeth forth naturally very good sallet herbs ... grapes, white and red and very sweet and strong, strawberries, gooseberries, rasps etc. plums of three sorts, with black and red being almost as good as a damson, abundance of roses, white, red and damask, very sweet indeed. The country wanteth only industrious men to employ.'
1621 *Mourt's Relation*

'The Generall Historie of Virginia, New-england and the summer Isles with the names of the adventurers, Planters and Governors from their first beginning An.1584 to this present 1624 ... also the Maps ... their Commodities, people, Government, Customs and Religion yet known. Divided into six books by Captain John Smith, sometimes Governor in those Countries, and Admiral of New England. London 1624.'

'My most sweet husband ... your obedient wife, Margaret Winthrop. {PS} I send you a turkey and some cheese. I did dine at Groton Hall yesterday. We did wish you there, I could not be merry without thee.' 1628. Letter from Suffolk to Winthrop in London.

'From aboard the *Arbella* riding at Cowes, March 22, 1629 ... only four ships ready, and some two or three Hollanders ... in all about 700 persons, 2400 cows and about sixty horses.'
'My Love, My Joy, My Faithful One ...'
Letters from John Winthop to his wife.

'After their long voyage many troubled with the scurvy, and some of them died.' 1630. Captain Edward Johnson

'Letter to Brother Downing.' 1630, from Charlestown. Winthrop's brother-in-law, father of George Downing.

'I came into this country, where I found a new world and new manners, at which my heart rose.' 1630, Salem. Anne Dudley, wife of Simon Bradstreet.

'I had eight birds hatch'd in the nest
Four cocks there were, and
hens the rest.
I nurs'd them up with pain and care,
For cost nor labour did I spare.
Till at the last they felt their wing
Mounted the trees, and
learned to sing.'
Anne Bradstreet, from *The Tenth Muse lately sprung up in America*, c.1630/40, published in London 1650.

'The like joy and manifestations of love had never been seen before in New England. A great marvel that so much people and such store of provision gathered together at so few hours' warning.' 1631 Nov, Boston. Governor Winthrop on the arrival of his family after 10 week voyage in the *Lion*.

'William Hutchinson .. .of weak parts, and wholly guided by his wife.'
'All the faithful embraced her conference, and blessed God for her fruitful discourses.' Rev.Cotton of Lincolnshire.
'The American Jezebel ... {but} a woman very helpful in time of childbirth and other occasions of bodily disease.' The Hutchinsons sailed for Boston in 1634 when 'our teacher {minister} came to New England'.

'The ground {of the Pequod Indians of Rhode Island} seemeth to be far worse than the ground of the Massachusetts, being light, sandy and rocky, yet they have good corn without fish; after the first two years, they let one field rest each year, and that keep their ground continually in heart.'

'The disorders of the mother country were the safeguard of the infant liberties of New England.' Governor Winthrop. Charles I had threatened to revoke the Massachusetts charter.

'£12 for passage and apparel (for three servants} ...
'Bring up with him a feather bed, blankets and three pair of sheets. Although many households in Virginia are so well provided as to entertain a stranger with all things necessary for the belly, yet few or none are better provided for the back than will serve their own turn ...
{Take corn} lest their should happen a scarcity in the country, through the covetousness of the planters that strive to plant much tobacco and little corn

... bought flour, the fowling pieces, the strong waters and grocery wares.' 1634. Emigration agent's advice to Lady Verney for Tom's voyage.

'Casks, and barrels, shot and muskets, goods, provisions and servants with the charges do amount to £117.13s 6d.' 1634. Additional expenses.

'... {I} would go anywhere, to the West Indies or some unknown place ... rather than lead this hellish life I will take a rope and make an end of myself and then neither father, mother, brother nor sister nor any friends else shall take any more care of me.' 1638. Tom Verney next tried 'Barbathos'.

'I have obtained a 100 acres of land ... send you a true relation of the country. The best and healthfullest in all the western islands ... oranges, lemons, limes, plantins, potatoes, pine-apples, guaves and many more, pepper, cinnamon, ginger ... potatoes which is very nourishing and comfortable, it is the best provision we have both for our selves and servants - potatoes boyled and mobby to drink, which is only potatoes boyled and press'd till the juice {run}, after three hours this is a good drink ...

'Landcrabs, certain months of the year be so thick in the highways, have them bite through our shoes... like our seacrabs {but] most are poysonous.

'New requests might perhaps daunt you, but £200 will pay all.' 1639 Feb. Tom Verney to his father at Claydon. By 1641 he had returned, penniless.

'... never a day passes but she {my wife} is forced to rise at break of day or before, she cannot lay for want of breath, and when she is up, she cannot light a pipe of tobacco, but it must be lighted for her; and until she has taken two or three pipes, for want of breath she is not able to stir, and she has never a maid ... I have none but a small Indian boy about thirteen years of age to help me.' 1640s, New England. Major James Cudworth.

'The winter's frosts being extracted from the Earth, they fall to tearing up roots and bushes with their hoes, even such men as scarce ever set hand to labour before, men of good birth and breeding, but coming through the strength of Christ readily rush through all difficulties.

'After they have found a place of abode they burrow themselves in the earth for their first shelter, under some hillside, casting the earth aloft upon timber; they make a smoky fire against the earth at the highest side and thus these poor servants of Christ provide shelter for themselves.' 1654. Edward Johnson *Wonder Working Providence of Sion's Saviour in New England*

'For pottage and puddings and custards and pies
Our pumpkins and parsnips are common supplied.
We have pumpkin at morning and pumpkin at noon,
If it were not for pumpkin we should all be undone.'
Contemp. verse. New England.

25

RESTORATION 1660

Charles II met the Sealed Knot, or Council Entrusted, at Mons who were planning an uprising but 'the business so publicly discussed of here, there being scarce a lackey, serving-man or woman, which could not say more by much than I knew.' 1654. Capt. Mewes.

'Till it be understood, what is
under Monk's hood
The Citizens putt in their hornes,
Until the ten days are out,
the Speaker haz the Gowt
And the Rump,
They sitt upon Thornes.'
1660, before the Restoration.

'Heard that in Cheapside there had been but a little before a gibbet set up and the picture of Huson {Colonel Hewson} hung upon it in the middle of the street.' 25 Jan. Pepys *Diary*

'Hewson {a cobbler by trade, but a stout man and very good commander; but in regard of his former employment, they {apprentices} threw at him old shoes and slippers, and turnip tops and brickbats, stones and tiles.
'At this time there came forth almost every day, jeering books, one was called Colonel Hewson's Confession.' *Rugge's Diurnal*

'... within seven days for the filling up of their House, and when filled to sit no longer that the 6th May but then to give place to a full and free Parliament.' 1660, February. Monk to the Rump Parliament.

'In Cheapside there was a great many bonfires, and Bow bells and all the bells in all the churches as we went home were a-ringing ...
'There being fourteen {bonfires} between St Dunstans and Temple Bar, and at Strand Bridge I could at one time tell thirty one fires ... and all along burning and roasting, and drinking for rumps. There being rumps tied upon sticks and carried up and down.
'The butchers at the Maypole in the Strand rang a peal with their knives when the were going to sacrifice the rump ... it was past imagination, both the greatness and the suddenness of it.' 11 Feb. Pepys.

'The Rump Parliament, so called as retaining some few rotten members of the other, being dissolved for joy whereof were many thousands of rumps roasted publicly in the streets at the bonfires this night, with ringing of bells and universal jubilee.'
11 Feb. Evelyn.

'Within seven days for the filling up of their House, and when filled to sit no longer that the 6th May but then to give place to a full and free Parliament.' Feb. Monk to Parliament.

'The House had made Monk General of all the Forces in England, Scotland and Ireland.' Pepys.

'The City of London have put out a Declaration wherein they do disclaim their owning any other government but that of King, Lords and Commons.

'... more bonfires than ever, and ringing of bells and drinking of the King's health ...

'Everybody seems to be very joyful in the business ...our seamen, as many as had any money or credit for drink, did do nothing else this evening.'
2 May. Pepys.

'At length, by wonderful impulse of fate,
The people call him back to
help the State.
And what is more, they send him
money too,
And clothe him all from head
to foot anew.'   Andrew Marvell.

'The King with the two dukes and Queen of Bohemia, Princess Royal and Prince of Orange come on board ...

'After dinner the King and Duke altered the name of some of the ships: the Nazeby into *Royal Charles*; the Speaker the *Mary*; the Dunbar the *Henry*; Lambert the *Henrietta* '23 May. Scheveningen, Holland. Pepys.

'Divers maidens presented a petition to the Lord Mayor of London to grant leave and liberty to meet His Majesty on the day of his passing through the city; and that their petition might be granted that they will all be clad in white waistcoats and crimson petti-coats, and other ornaments of triumph and rejoicing.'
Rugge's Diurnal

'...above 20,000 horse and foot, bran-dishing their swords and shouting with inexpressible joy; the ways strawed with flowers, the bells ringing, the streets hung with tapestry, fountains running with wine ... they were seven hours in passing the city, even from two in the afternoon till nine at night.

'I stood in the Strand, and beheld it, and blessed God. And all this was done without one drop of blood shed, and by that very army which rebelled against him; but it was the Lord's doing for such a Restoration was never mentioned in any history, ancient or modern ... nor so joyful a day, and so bright, ever seen in this Nation.
30 May. Evelyn.

'... and the Earl of Manchester, Speaker of the House of Lords, the King adjusted his business so well, that in this nick of time, he had sent over again Sir John Greenville with a commission to Monk to be Captain-Generall of all the forces of England, Scotland and Ireland.' Warwick.

'You have given up your {Monk's} opportunities to do your country service, for a feather in your cap and a little trifling honour ... your title {Duke of Albemarle} will be mentioned as a reproach to yourself, and after your son has had it a little while it will go out in a snuff.

'As for me, I have buried the Good Old Cause, and am now going to bury myself.' Edward Bowles, before retir-ing to Yorkshire as Fairfax's chaplain. Monk's son died childless in 1688.

Retribution

'The Letter {Charles II's} to the Houses had a Declaration enclosed in it, and so had that to the Commons. It promised an act of Oblivion and generall Pardon, in point of religion, such a liberty to tender consciences, who disturbed not the peace of the kingdom, as should be agreed on by Parliament ...
'The Journals are fetch't, and those Acts and Orders razed out which were inconsistent with the Kingly government.' Warwick.

'... though he had no part in the death of the King, {he} was against questioning those who had been concerned in making an example which would be useful to posterity, and profitable to future kings.' Algernon Percy, Earl of Northumberland.

'Sir Allen Apsley too, who, with all the kindest zeal of friendship that can be imagined, endeavoured to bring off the colonel {Hutchinson}, and used some artifice in engaging his friends for him ... Although the colonel was cleared both for life and estate in the House of Commons, yet he not answering the court expectations in public recantations and dissembled repentance, and applause of their cruelty to his fellows, the chancellor was cruelly exasperated against him, and there were very great endeavours to have rased {omitted} him out of the act of oblivion.'
Lucy Hutchinson. Apsley, a Royalist officer, was Lucy's brother.

'I went out to Charing Cross to see Major-General Harrison hanged, drawn and quartered; he looking as cheerful as any man could do in that condition. He was presently cut down, and his head and heart shown to the people at which there was great shouts of joy.' 1660 13 Oct. Pepys.

'The Regicides who sat on the life of our late King, were brought to trial in the Old Bailey before a Commission of Oyer and Terminer.
'Axtell, Carew, Clements, Hacker, Hewson and Peters were executed.
'Scot, Scroope, Cook and Jones suffered for reward of their iniquities at Charing Cross, in sight of the place where they put to death their natural Prince, in the presence of the King his son, whom they also sought to kill. I saw not their execution, but met their quarters mangled and cut and reeking as they were brought from the gallows in baskets on the hurdle. Oh, the miraculous providence of God!' 1660 11/14/17 Oct. Evelyn.

'Where is your Good Old Cause now?' jeered the mob.
'Here in my bosom, and I shall seal it with my blood. I go to suffer upon the account of the most glorious cause that ever was in the world ... By God, I will go through this death and He will make it easy for me.' Thomas Harrison.

'This morning Mr Carew was hanged and quartered at Charing Cross, but his quarters, by a great favour, not to be hanged up.' 15 Oct. Pepys.

'This day it was expected that Colonel Hacker and Axtell should die, I went to Newgate, but found they were reprieved until tomorrow.

'This morning my dining room was finished with green serge hanging and gilt leather, which is very handsome. This morning Hacker and Axtell were hanged and quartered, as the rest are.' 18/19 Oct. Pepys.

'This day were the carcasses of those arch rebels Cromwell, Bradshaw the Judge, and Ireton, son-in-law to the Usurper, dragged out of their superb tombs in Westminster among the Kings, to Tyburn, and hanged on the gallows there from 9 in the morning till 6 at night and then buried under that fatal and ignominious monument in a deep pit; thousands of people who had seen them in all their pride being spectators.'
1661 30 Jan. Evelyn.

'This morning news that Sir G. Downing, like a perfidious rogue, though the action is good and of service to the King, yet he cannot with a good conscience do it, hath taken Okey, Corbet and Barkstead at Delft in Holland, and sent them home in the *Blackamore.*

'... a speech he {Downing} made to the Lords States of Holland, telling them to their faces that he observed that he was not received with the respect and observance now, that he was when he came from the traitor and rebell Cromwell, by whom, I am sure, he got all he hath in the world - and they know it too.' 1662 12 Mar. Pepys.

'At the corner shop, a draper's, I stood and did see Barkstead, Okey and Corbet drawn towards the gallows at Tyburn; and there they were hanged and quartered.

'They all looked very cheerful, but I hear they all die defending what they did to the King to be just, which is very strange. In the evening did get a beaver {hat}, an old one but very good one, of Sir W.Batten, for which I must give him something.' 19 April. Pepys.

'Some of the Sheriff's officers when Okey came to the cart said of him that he was a lusty, stout, brave man as ever fought in England.' Contemp. report. Colonel Okey commanded the dragoons of the New Model Army.

'The colonel's wife and children got a boat and followed him to Gravesend ... he came to the castle {Sandown}, a lamentable old ruined place ...

'As soon as the news came to Owthorpe {Notts}, the colonel's {Hutchinson} two eldest sons and all his household servants went up to London with his horses, and made ready a hearse, tricked with escutcheons and six horses in mourning, with a mourning coach ... because Mrs Hutchinson herself was not come to fetch {the body} they were forced at an intolerable expense to keep all this equipage at Deal.' 1664 Sept. Lucy Hutchinson. In 1663 her husband had been arrested on doubtful evidence of conspiracy. He was imprisoned, untried, under harsh conditions at Sandown where he died of fever within a year.

26

POSTSCRIPT

These extracts from personal letters between husbands and wives cast a revealing light on the very private individuals behind the public figures - the lasst thre speke fer themselfs.

'Sweet Harte,
It is long since I writ unto you, for I am here in such a trouble as gives me little or no respite ...

I know at the worst his Majesty will pardon all, without hurting my fortune, and then we shall be happy by God's grace. Therefore, comfort yourself, for I trust these clouds will away, and that we shall have fair weather afterwards. Your loving husband,
Strafford.

'... wherever they are {Anne and Arabella} my Prayers shall attend them ... their poor Father is ignorant in what belongs women, and other ways God knows distracted and so wanting unto them in all save loving them.

'These are the last lines that you are to receive from a father that tenderly loves you ...

'Never suffer the thought of Revenge to enter your Heart. And God Almighty of His infinite Goodness bless you and your Children's children, perfect you in every good work and give you right understanding in all things Amen.'
{Strafford}
Tower of London   1641 May.

'Dear heart,
I love thee above all earthly things, my contentment is inseparably joined with thine ... I hope and pray that after a few months we may meet again with comfort, and that in the mean time God may give us both strength to endure vexations, if many more be in store for us.'
Charles I to Henrietta Maria

'I am giving the strongest proof of love that I can give; I am hazarding my life {going to France}, that I may not incommode your affairs. Adieu, my dear heart. If I die, believe that you will lose a person who has never been other than entirely yours, and who by her affection has deserved that you should not forget her.'
{Henriette Marie}
Falmouth.   1644 July.
The couple never met again.

'Dear Heart,
I have not yet heard from you since your coming to London, but heard you were safely arrived there. I have endured some hardships since I parted with you, being forced to march and watch night and day this frosty and snowy weather ...

Remember my humble service to all my honourable and noble sisters and Moll {their daughter}. So, dear heart, farewell. Your most affectionate husband,
Thomas Fairfax.'
Yorkshire.   1644 Jan.

'My dearest,

I wonder you should blame me for writing no oftener, when I have sent three for one, I cannot but think they are miscarried {to Scotland} ... But when I do write I seldom have any satisfactory answer ... truly my life is but half a life in your absence ...

I would you would think to write sometimes to your dear friend, my lord chief-justice ... truly, my dear, it might be to as much purpose as others, writing sometimes a letter to the president, and sometimes to the speaker. Indeed, my dear, you cannot think the wrong you do yourself in the want of a letter, though but seldom.

I pray think of, and so rest yours in all faithfulness,

Eliz. Cromwell.'   1650.

My dearest,

I have not leisure to write much, but I could chide thee, that in many of thy letters thou writest to me that I should not be unmindful of thee and thy little ones. Truly, if I love you not too well, I think I err not on the other hand much. Thou art dearer to me than any creature; let that suffice ...

'I assure thee, I grow an old man, and feel infirmities of age marvellously stealing upon me ... my love to the dear little ones, I pray grace for them. Thank them for their letters; let me have them often ... I am weary and rest thine ... Present my duty to my mother, my love to all the family. Still pray for thine,

Oliver Cromwell.
Scotland.   1650.

My dear,

Retain a sober patient spirit within thee which I am confident thou shalt see shall be of more force to recover thee, than all thy keen metal hath been; I hope God is doing a work upon thee and me too, as shall make us study ourselves more than we have done.'

Elizabeth Lilburne.   1655.

*

Spelling was always cavalier

'... figered sattines ... the golde color damask, not that i have any present use of it, but truly tis so very chepe i will by it ... for the backes of cheres, the rest i entende for cortines ... chuse me out a lase that hath but littell silver in itt, and not above a spangell.'
St Albans.   Lady Sussex. 1639 Nov.

'Wee are soe maney frighted peopell; if a dore creeke I take it to be a drom, and am redey to run out of that little valer I have. Poore Sir John Hotham is so afrighted if anything comes but neere him.' Mrs Eure.
Yorkshire.   1642 May.

'I only writ these fu lines tu you as an expresion of the love i ow you, or els i shud a bin sillent for i am in a grt dill of vexsation for pore Oxford ... 12 hondored solgars com ther, and I am afrad that thay will macke a grit masacar of all the books ... Truly i spack this with a soro for we are lick to tast it if threts prove tru, i am in a myty fright.' Cary Gardiner.
Oxford.   1642 Sept.

176

Charles I silver pound
Newark & Pontefract siege shillings

THE SOULDIERS

Pocket Bible :

Containing the most (if not all) those places contained in holy Scripture, which doe shew the qualifications of his inner man, that is a fit Souldier to fight the Lords Batels, both before he fight, in the fight, and after the fight ;

Which Scriptures are reduced to severall heads, and fitly applyed to the Souldiers severall occasions, and so may supply the want of the whole Bible: which a Souldier cannot conveniently carry about him :

And may bee also usefull for any Christian to meditate upon, now in this miserable time of Warre.

Imprimatus,　　Edw. Calamy:

Jos.1,8. This Book of the Law shall not depart out of thy mouth, but thou shalt meditate therein day and night, that thou maist observe to doe according to all that is written therein, for then thou shalt make thy way prosperous, and have good successe.

Printed at *London* by *G.B.* and *R.W.* for *G.C.* 1643.

Aug:3°

Bible issued 1643 to the literate, rather than licentious, soldiery

THE
Witch of the Woodlands:
Or, The
Coblers New Translation;
Written by *L. P.*

Here Robin the Cobler for his former evils,
Was punisht worst then Faustus was with de-
(vils.

London, Printed for *John Stafford*, dwelling at the Signe
of the *George* at *Fleet-bridge*. 1655.

NEWES
FROM
IPSWICH:

Discovering certaine late detestable practices of some dominiering Lordly Prelates, to undermine the established Doctrine and Discipline of our Church, extirpate all Orthodox sincere Preachers and preaching of Gods Word, usher in Popery, Superstition and Idolatry.

Wee de unto the Pastors that destroy and scatter the sheep of my Flocke, saith the Lord. Ieiem. 23. 1.

First printed at Ipswich, and now reprinted for *T. Bates*. 1641.

Title pages of contemporary
'Eye and Ear' witnesses' memoirs

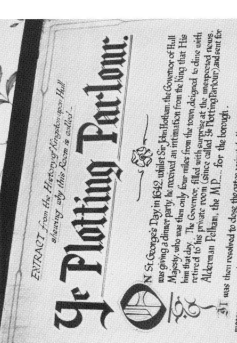

'Ye Olde White Harte',
Silver Street, Kingston upon Hull

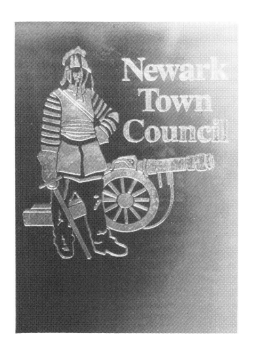

Newark Town Council 1992
pikeman's body armour & helmet

Nantwich pillory, Cheshire
Lobstertail helmet, replica

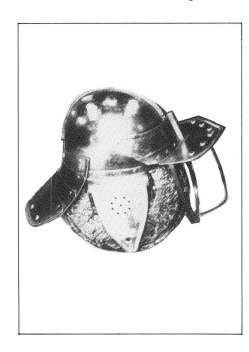

BRIEF BIOGRAPHIES

Men were promoted, knighted or ennobled during the War, but all, except Clarendon, are listed under the names they bore at the outset: Sir Thomas Fairfax, not Lord Fairfax; Sir Jacob Astley, not Lord Astley.

At the Restoration the Cavaliers believed 'all their sufferings were over, and laid in such a stock of such vast hopes as would have been very hard for any success to procure satisfaction.' It was not hard, but impossible, so Charles II was bountiful in the bestowal of honours, but those who had beggared themselves in the Stuart cause found empty titles poor recompense for the long years of poverty and exile. The 1660 'Act of Indemnity and Oblivion' was a further blow, seeming to offer indemnity to most of the King's enemies and oblivion to the majority of his friends.

R = Royalist and **P** = Parliamentarian, from 1642 onwards where these allegiances are clear. Not all MPs constituencies are listed, and major participants are not given thumbnail sketches..

* * *

R. Astley, Sir Jacob 1579-1652
Veteran of continental wars. At raising of Standard at Nottingham. Maj-General of Foot at Edgehill, both Newburys & Naseby. An officer respected and obeyed by Rupert. Surrendered to Brereton at Stow-on-the-Wold '46.

R. Aston, Sir Arthur 1590-1649
Cheshire catholic. '42/43 Col-General Dragoons. Later joined Ormonde in Ireland. Killed at Drogheda, allegedly battered with his own wooden leg.

Baillie, Robert 1599-1662 Scots chaplain, and a negotiator for the Covenanters in Edinburgh and at Westminster.

R. Bankes, Lady Mary Wife of Chief Justice of the Common Pleas, prosecutor of Hampden in the Ship Money trial. '43 defended Corfe Castle for King, but later betrayed by Royalist officer and 'slighted'. Her son, Ralph, built Kingston Lacy at the Restoration.

P. Richard Baxter 1615-91 Chaplain to Coventry garrison, then New Model. *Reliquiae Baxterianae* published 1696

P. Brereton, Sir William 1604-1661 MP Cheshire Commander in Cheshire. Jan '44, with Fairfax defeated Rupert at Nantwich, & prevented the relief of Chester. Active in North West and the Midlands.

P. Brooke, Lord, Robert Greville 1608-1643 MP Warwick Refused the military oath of allegiance at York. '42 Leader with Saye, & Speaker, in Lords, garrisoned Warwick Castle. At Edgehill, killed by sniper at Lichfield 1643.

Burnet, Gilbert 1643-1715 Of Scots descent, bishop after Restoration. *History of his Own Times* publ. 1723.

R. Byron, Sir John 1599-1652 Eldest of seven Cavalier brothers. 1641 Lieutenant of Tower. Powick Bridge, Edgehill, Roundway Down, Newbury. 'the bloody Braggadoccio', defeated at Nantwich, fought at Marston Moor. 1648 led uprising in North Wales.

R. Capel, Arthur 1610-1649 MP Hertfordshire 1645 Uxbridge Peace commissioner. '48 surrendered 'at mercy' at Colchester. Trial by peers, escaped, re-captured and shot.

Charles Stuart, 1600-1649 King of England, Scotland & Ireland 1625-49

Carlisle, Lucy, Countess of 1599-1660 widowed young, 'bold and handsome Lucy Percy', sister of Northumberland. Intriguer, confidante of Queen, alleged mistress of Strafford, then Pym.

P/R Cholmley, Sir Henry 1600-1657 MP Scarborough Parl. Governor Scarborough Castle, then changed sides, 1645 captured, fled to France.

R. Clarendon, Earl of, Edward Hyde 1609-1674 MP Saltash

P. Cromwell, Oliver 1599-1658 MP Huntingdon - Cambridge

R. Derby, 7th Earl of, James Stanley 1606-1651 Defeated at Warrington, took Preston. With Rupert led assault & sack of Bolton. After Marston Moor fled to hereditary fief of Isle of Man. '51 Worcester, aided King's escape, but captured, tried, and shot at Bolton.

R. Derby, Countess of, Charlotte de la Tremouille 1599-1664 Daughter Duc de Thouars, a relative of Rupert. '44 withstood siege of Lathom House, 'better man' of the Derby pair.'

P. Desborough, John 1608-1680 MP Cambridgeshire 'The grim giant Desbrowe', Cromwell's brother-in-law. '45 Langport seconded Bethel's charge. Maj-Gen. at Worcester. General at Sea during Commonwealth. Opposed Richard Cromwell. Implicated in plot to kill Charles II and imprisoned.

P. Dewes, Sir Simonds 1602-1650 MP Sudbury 1639 High Sheriff of Suffolk. Recorded Parliamentary debates, wrote Anglo-Saxon dictionary.

R. Digby, George, Lord 1612-1677 MP Dorset

P/R Downing, George 1623-1684 MP Edinburgh Graduate of Harvard. Cromwell's scoutmaster in Scotland, then envoy in Holland. 1661 bought Charles II's favour by betraying colleagues, Okey, Corbet and Barkstead, then living in Delft. Downing Street.'

P. Essex, 3rd Earl of,
Robin Devereux, 1591-1646

P. Fairfax, Sir Thomas 1612-1671
3rd Baron Fairfax, MP Yorkshire

Fairfax, Anne d.1665
A 'Vere of the Fighting Veres' and zealous presbyterian. Probably the 'masked lady' who intervened in Westminster Hall at King's Trial. Mary Fairfax m. 2nd Duke of Buckingham.

R. Falkland, Lord, Lucius Carey
1610-1643 MP Newport

P. Fiennes, Nathaniel 1608-1669
MP Banbury Fought at Edgehill, then Governor of Bristol. '43 accused of 'improperly surrendering' Bristol, after Rupert's similar surrender in '45, charge of cowardice against him expunged. Son of Lord Saye and Sele.

P. Fleetwood, Charles d.1692
MP Marlborough

P. Gell, Sir John 1593-1671
Sheriff of Derbyshire and Governor of Derby. 'Ungodly officer' of Parliament but effective in Midlands. '43 at Lichfield, Hopton Heath. Suspected of treachery after Naseby. '50 Imprisoned for plotting against Commonwealth

R. Godolphin, Sidney 1610-1643
MP Helston Friend of Clarendon and Falkland at Great Tew. With Hopton in West, killed at Chagford. First of 'Charles' Wain' to fall - others, **Sir Bevil Grenvile**, 1596-1643 MP for Cornwall; **Sir Nicholas Slanning**, 1606-1643, MP Plympton; **Sir John Trevanion**, 1613-1643 MP Lostwithiel; all killed in 1643.

P. Goodwin, Arthur 1593-1643
MP Buckinghamshire Colonel of Foot at Edgehill. His regiment formed guard of honour at Hampden's funeral.

R. Goring, George 1608-1657
MP Wycombe

Hampden, John 1594-1643
MP Buckinghamshire

P. Harley, Lady Brilliana 1600-1643
Third wife of Sir Robert Harley, MP for Radnor. 1643 held out for Parliament at Brampton Castle, but died during the siege. *Letters* published 1854.

Harvey, William 1578-1657
Student of Padua, Cambridge, Oxford. Physician to James I. 1628 Frankfurt, published theory of circulation of blood, in English 1653. With Charles I at Edgehill, and made warden of Merton, Oxford. 1652 statue erected by Royal College of Physicians.

P. Harrison, Thomas 1606-1660
MP Wendover Carried the news of Marston Moor to Parliament. Colonel, then General of Horse. Escorted Charles I from Hurst Castle to trial, signed death warrant. At Worcester. '53 attended Cromwell at dissolving Parliament but later opposed him. Fifth Monarchist leader. Impressed all by his courage at his own execution.

P. Haselrig, Sir Arthur, MP Leicester
d. 1660 (Haslerig, Hazelrigg, Hesilrigge)

R. Henrietta Maria 1606-1669
D. of Henry of Navarre, Henri IV

P. Holles, Denzil 1599-1680
MP Dorchester

R. Hopton, Sir Ralph 1598-1652
MP Wells In 1618 Elizabeth of
Bohemia escaped from Prague riding
pillion behind him. Presenter of Grand
Remonstrance to King, then royalist
general. At Bradock Down, Stratton,
Lansdown, Cheriton, Torrington. 1646
surrendered at Truro, died in exile at
Bruges. A close friend of Waller and
respected on all sides.

P/R. Hotham, Sir John, MP Beverley
- York Sheriff of Yorkshire under
Strafford. 1642 April, as Governor of
Hull shut gates against King. 1643
regained town of Scarborough for
Parliament, but Cholmley still held
Castle. Suspected of treachery and
arrested with his son. 1645 both court-
martialled and shot.

P/R. Hotham, John MP Scarborough
Fought in Fairfax's Yorkshire cam-
paigns. '43 suspected of contact with
court, and imprisoned at Nottingham.
Escaped to join father.

P. Hutchinson, John 1615-1664
MP Nottinghamshire Governor of
Nottingham, held castle throughout
War. Signed King's death warrant,
served Commonwealth until '53, then

MP again in '59 and backed Monk.
Exempted as regicide, but imprisoned
1663 and died in Sandown Castle.

P. Hutchinson, Lucy 1620-1669
Born in Tower when her father Sir
Allen Apsley, was Lieutenant. Married
1638, spent war in Nottingham. Tried
to save the colonel in '63, wrote the
*Memories of the Life of Colonel Hutch-
inson* for their sons. Published 1806.

P. Ireton, Henry 1611-1651
MP Appleby

R. King, James. Lord Eythin
1589-1652

P. Lambert, John 1619-1683
MP Pontefract

**R. Langdale, Sir Marmaduke 1598-
1661** Yorkshire catholic. Commanded
Northern Horse Marston Moor, Naseby,
captured after Preston. Escaped
abroad, served with Venetian forces.

**R. Laud, William, Archbishop of
Canterbury 1573 -1645**

P. Lenthall, William 1591-1662
MP Oxfordshire. The Speaker.

P/R. Leslie, David d. 1682 Scot,
long Swedish service. Second in
command under Leven, Marston Moor.
Defeated Montrose Philiphaugh 1645.
Commanded Scots against Cromwell at
Dunbar, and Worcester, where cap-
tured and imprisoned in Tower.
Created Baron Newark at Restoration.

P/R. Leven, Earl of, Alexander Leslie 1589-1661

P. Lilburne, John 1614-1657

P. Lilburne, Colonel Robert 1613-1665 MP East Riding

R. Lisle, Sir George d.1648

R. Lucas, Sir Charles d.1648
Scots War 1639/40. Served with Rupert, captured Marston Moor and exchanged. Lt-General of Horse, captured '46 Stow on the Wold, set free on parole. '48 uprising with Lisle in Kent and Essex, shot after storm of Colchester under the 'Rules of War'.
Sister, Margaret, married Newcastle, in exile as second wife.

P. Ludlow, Edmund 1617-1692 MP Wiltshire Edgehill. Lt-General in Ireland. Rejected Lord Protector. Fled as regicide 1660, returned under William III but escaped again to Switzerland. *Memoirs* publ. 1698.

P. Manchester, Earl of, Edward Montagu 1602-1671 MP Huntingdon

P. Henry Marten, 1602-1680 MP Berkshire Governor of Reading, and Aylesbury, besieged Donnington. Against peace talks, signed death warrant. Fell out with Cromwell, and at Restoration his skilful defence led only to life imprisonment. A sharp, witty thorn in the flesh of all.

R. Maurice, Prince 1620-1652

Mayerne, Theodore Turquet 1573-1655 Swiss. Medical theories condemned by Paris College of Physicians, Paris. 1611 physician to Queen Anne, later to Henrietta Maria and royal family. Fashionable London practice, made chemical and physical experiments, remedies for plague. Left volumes of notes, in British Museum.

P. Meldrum, Sir John c.1590-1645 Scot. Served 30 years in Ireland and continent. 1635 patent for erecting lighthouses. At Edgehill, raised siege of Hull 1643, out-manoeuvred at siege of Newark by Rupert, forfeited all his guns and ammunition. Killed in scaling attack on Scarborough Castle.

R/P. Monk, George 1608-1670

R. Montrose, James Graham, Earl/ Marquis 1612-1650

R. Newcastle, Earl/Marquis/Duke of, William Cavendish 1592-1676

R. Nicholas, Edward 1593-1669 MP Winchelsea, Dover
1625 Secretary to Admiralty. From 1641 Secretary of State, London then Oxford, and to Charles II in exile. Returned and pensioned off 1660. *Nicholas Papers* published 1886.

P. Okey, John d.1662 Colonel of Dragoons in New Model, Naseby. 1645 captured at Bristol. Signed death warrant, command in Scotland. '59 backed Lambert, fled to Holland. Betrayed by Downing, executed as regicide.

R. Ormonde, Marquis of, James Butler 1610-1688

P. Pennington, Isaac 1587-1660
MP London Replaced Gurney as Lord Mayor 1642/43. Officer in Honourable Artillery Company, leader of City's opposition during war. Cousin to Royalist Admiral Sir John Pennington.

P. Peter, Hugh 1598-1660
1635 minister in Salem, Mass, and a founder of Connecticut, negotiator between Dutch and English colonists. 1641 returned to England, Independent New Model chaplain. Preached in favour of King's execution, and was himself executed as a regicide. Wrote a historical *Relation* of his experiences of battles and sieges.

P. Rushworth, John 1612-1690
Lincoln's Inn. Shorthand writer and later Clerk to the Commons, messenger between Parliament and King. Military secretary to Fairfax and New Model. 1650 Secretary to Cromwell. Died in a debtor's prison. 8 volumes of his *Historical Collections* published 1721.

P. St John, Oliver 1598--1673
MP Totnes
Cromwell's cousin, and Lord Saye and Hampden's defence lawyer in the Ship Money case, drafted Strafford's attainder. Active politician throughout War. Backed army against Parliament 1647, took no part in King's trial but active under the Commonwealth. (A different Oliver St John, also an MP, was killed at Edgehill)

P. Saye and Sele, Lord, William Fiennes 1582-1662
Providence Island, Connecticut, New Hampshire investments. Against King's policies from 1625, Broughton Castle meeting place of opposition, nick-named 'Old Subtlety.' Raised regiment of Bluecoats and four troops of horse before Edgehill. 1642 member Committee of Safety, of Westminster Assembly 1643. Pushed through Self-Denying Ordinance in Lords. Held high office after Restoration. All four Fiennes sons fought for Parliament.

P. Selden, John 1584-1654
MP Oxford University.

P. Sexby, Edward d.1658
1643 in Cromwell's regiment. 1647 leading Agitator in dispute between the army and Parliament, clashed with Ireton in Putney Debates, spokesman and pamphleteer with Lilburne and the Levellers. Colonel under Commonwealth, 1657 plotted assassination of Cromwell, published *Killing no Murder'*. Died in the Tower.

P. Skippon, Philip c.1590 -1660
MP Barnstaple Sergeant-Maj-General
'Daddy Skippon'. 1642 commander London Trained Bands. Sgt-Major General of Foot Edgehill, relief of Gloucester, both Newburys, Naseby. Marshall General in Ireland 1647, London Militia 1648. Cromwell's Council of State, Major-General of London district 1656, House of Lords 1657. Published a soldier's book of devotions *The Christian Centurion*

**R. Slingsby, Sir Henry 1602-1658
MP Knaresborough**
Scots War. Officer in Yorkshire under Newcastle, at Naseby, and surrender of Newark 1646. Misguided loyalty led him into a plot against Commonwealth, arrested and executed on Tower Hill. Complete *Diary* published 1836.

P. Sprigge, Joshua 1618-1684
Secretary to Fairfax, later Bursar of All Souls, Oxford. *Anglia Rediviva*, on Fairfax's military exploits, dedicated to Lenthall, Speaker of the Commons.

R. Strafford, Earl of, Thomas Wentworth MP Yorkshire 1593-1641

**P. Strode, William 1599-1645
MP Beeralston** One Five Members

**P. Thurloe, John 1616-1668
MP Ely - Cambridge University**
Lincoln's Inn, in the service of Oliver St John. 1652 Secretary to Council of State, 'Cromwell's spie-master',in charge of intelligence and posts. Supported Richard Cromwell, arrested, but later acquitted at Restoration. 7 volumes *Correspondence* publ. 1742.

R. Turner, Sir James 1615-1686
In service of Sweden, returned to serve with Scots. Fought at Preston and Worcester. *Pallas Armata* publ. 1683.

P. Vane, Sir Harry 1613-62 MP Hull

**R. Verney, Sir Edmund 1590-1642
MP Buckingham** & **P. Verney, Ralph
MP Aylesbury 1613-1696**

**P. Venn, John 1586-1650
MP London**
City alderman, colleague of Pennington and active in opposition to King's policies before and during War.

**P. Waller, Sir William 1597-1668
MP Andover**

**R. Warwick, Sir Philip 1609-83
MP Radnor**
Father organist of Chapel Royal and Westminster Abbey. Student of Oxford and Gray's Inn. Attended Parliament at Oxford, sent on various missions, negotiated surrender of Oxford 1646. Secretary to King, negotiations at Hampton Court and Newport. 1649 compounded with Commonwealth for estate. Knighted at Restoration. *Memoirs of the Reign of King Charles I, with a Continuation to the Happy Restoration* published 1701'

P. Warwick, Earl of, Robert Rich 1587-1658

**R. Winchester, Marquis of,
John Paulet 1598-1675**
One of richest men in England. Garrisoned Basing House in Hampshire for the King. Stormed and sacked Oct '45, when Inigo Jones and Wenceslaus Hollar among those 'strip'd and rob'd'.

**P. Whitelocke, Bulstrode 1605-1675
MP Great Marlow**

**R. Wilmot, Henry 1612-1658
MP Tamworth** Charles II's companion in his escape after Worcester

ON SITE

Civil War Information Service
The Commandery, Sidbury
Worcester WR1 2HU

English Civil War Society
70 Hailgate, Howden,
North Humberside DN14 7ST

The Cromwell Association
476 Skipton Rd, Utley
Weighley, West Yorks BD20 6DT

The Sealed Knot
1 Rock Street, Croscombe
Wells, Somerset BA5 3QT

Royal Armouries
Tower of London EC3 4AB

National Army Museum - London
Royal Hospital Rd, Chelsea SW3 4HT

National Portrait Gallery
St Martin's Place,
Trafalgar Sq. WC2H OHE

Museum of London
London Wall EC2Y 5HN

National Maritime Museum
Greenwich SE10 9NF

English Heritage
429 Oxford St, London W1R 2HD

The National Trust
36 Queen Anne's Gate SW1H 9AS

English Tourist Board- London
Thames Tower, Black's Road W6 9EL

Welsh Tourist Board - Cardiff
Cadw - Welsh Historic Monuments
Brunel House, 2 Fitzalan Road
Cardiff CF2 1UY

London Tourist Board
26 Grosvenor Gardens, SW1W ODU

Cornwall Tourist Board
59 Lemon St, Truro TR1 2SY

East Midlands Tourist Board
Exchequergate, Lincoln LN2 1PZ

Heart of England Tourist Board
Larkhill, Worcester WR5 2EF

North West Tourist Board
Swan Meadow Rd, Wigan WN3 5BB

Scottish Tourist Board - Edinburgh
23 Ravelston Terrace, EH4 2QP

South East Tourist Board
1 Warwick Park, Tunbridge Wells
Kent TN2 5TU

Southern Tourist Board
40 Chamberlayne Rd, Eastleigh
Hampshire SO5 5JH

Thames & Chilterns Tourist Board
Church Grn, Witney, Oxon OX8 6DZ

West Country Tourist Board
6 St David's Hill, Exeter EX4 4SY

Bristol City Council
14 Narrow Quay, Bristol BS1 4QA

Yorkshire/HumbersideTouristBoard
312 Tadcaster Rd, York YO2 2HF

Coventry Tourism & Conference Desk
Tower Block, Much Park St,
Coventry CV1 2PY

Hull Museums & Art Galleries
83 Alfred Gelder St, Hull HU1 3EP

York Castle Museum   YO1 1RY
York City Art Gallery YO1 2EW

Alnwick Castle
Northumberland NE66 1NQ

Admiral Blake Museum
Bridgewater, Somerset TA6

Basing House
Basingstoke, Hants RG24 OHB

Belvoir Castle
Grantham, Lincs NG32 1PD

Bickleigh Castle
Tiverton, Devon EX16 8RP

Broughton Castle
Banbury, Oxon OX15 5EB

Castle Museum Nottingham NG1

Chepstow Castle (Cadw) Gwent

Colchester & Essex Museum
Ryegate Rd, Colchester CO1

Corineum Museum Cirencester

Cromwell Museum
Market Sq. Huntingdon PE18 6NS

Edgehill Battle Museum - Oxon
Farnborough Hall, Banbury OX17 1DU

Foregate Museum Worcester WR1

Gloucester Folk Museum
Westgate St, Gloucester GL1 2PG

Harris Museum
Market Sq. Preston, Lancs.

Holdeny House Holdenby, Northants

King Charles Tower, Chester
Grosvenor Museum, Chester CH1 2DD

Leeds Castle
Maidstone, Kent ME17 1PL

Lincoln City & County Museum
Broadgate, Lincoln LN2 1HQ

Litchfield, St Mary Centre
Market Square, Litchfield WS13 6LG

Maidstone Museum Kent
St Faith's St, Maidstone ME

Museum of Farnham - Surrey
38 West St, Farnham GU9 7DX

Museum of Oxford
St Aldate's. Oxford OX1 1DZ

Nantwich Museum Cheshire
Pillory St, Nantwich CW5 5LY

Naseby Battle & Farm Museum
Naseby, Market Harborough, Northants

Newarke Houses Museum
The Newarke, Leicester LE2 7BY

Newark Museum Notts
Appletongate, Newark NG24 1JY

Newbury District Museum
Newbury, Berks RG14 5AS

Philpot Museum
Bridge St, Lyme Regis, Dorset

Pontefract Castle West Yorks

Powderham Castle
Kenton, Devon EX6 8JQ

Raby Castle
Staindrop, Darlington DL2 3AH

Raglan Castle (Cadw) Gwent

Rockingham Castle - Northants
Market Harborough, LE16 8TH

Royal Albert Museum
Queen St, Exeter EX4 3RV

Royal Cornwall Museum
River St, Truro TR1 2SJ

Sudeley Castle
Winchcombe, Gloucester GL54 5J

Sulgrave Manor
Near Banbury, Oxon OX17 2SD

Warrington Museum Cheshire
Bold St, Warrington WA1 1JG

Warwick Castle Warwick CV34 4QU

English Heritage

Barnard Castle Co. Durham

Beeston Castle Cheshire

Berkhamsted Castle Herts

Bevil Grenville's Monument
Lansdown Hill, Nr Bath

Bolsover Castle
Nr. Chesterfield, Derbyshire

Boscobel House & Royal Oak
Tong, Wolverhampton, Shropshire

Carisbrooke Castle
Newport, Isle of Wight

Carlisle Castle Cumbria

Chester Castle Phoenix Tower

Clifford's Tower York

Dartmouth Castle Devon

Deal Castle Kent

Dover Castle Kent

Goodrich Castle
Nr. Ross-on-Wye, Hereford

Helmsley Castle North Yorks.

Hurst Castle
Nr. Lymington, Hampshire

Launceston Castle Cornwall

Old Wardour Castle
Tisbury, Wiltshire

Pendennis Castle
Falmouth, Cornwall

Penrith Castle Cumbria

Portland Castle Dorset

Restormel Castle
Lostwithiel, Cornwall

Rochester Castle Kent

Scarborough Castle North Yorks

Sherborne Old Castle Dorset

National Trust

Chirk Castle
Chirk, Clwyd

Corfe Castle
Wareham, Dorset

Powis Castle
Welshpool, Powys
*

Royal Mail Stamps
76 Turnmill St, London EC1M 5NS

B A Seaby Ltd
7 Davies Street, London W1Y 1LL

Sotheby's
34-35 New Bond St, W1A 2AA

*

Guild of Guide Lecturers
2 Bridge St, London SW1A 2JR

City of London Guide
Anna Milford, Kent Edge, Crockham
Hill, Edenbridge, Kent TRN8 6TA

*

The Commandery
Worcester in the Civil War.

THE COMMANDERY, home of the Royalist Wylde family in the 'loyal city', was Charles II's headquarters's during the Battle of Worcester in 1651, and now contains an exciting museum entirely dedicated to the English Civil War.

In the first skirmish, 23 September 1642, Prince Rupert's cavalry won its spurs at Powick Bridge within sight of the city walls. The last battle, 3 September 1651, saw the final defeat of the Royalists' by Cromwell, and the King a hunted fugitive.

The **CIVIL WAR TRAIL** leads from the Commandery to Fort Royal, the Cathedral, St Helen's and King Charles' House.

Open all Year
Special events - re-enactments - living history - wargames - video presentation - armour - portraits - Young Cavaliers club

THE COMMANDERY
Sidbury, Worcester WR1 2HU
0905 355071
Part of Worcester City Council

'We bring the Past to life in aid of the Future'

Founded in 1968 to promote interest in the study of the English Civil war, the Sealed Knot is firmly established as a national institution. The original **SEALED KNOT** was a Royalist secret society founded during the Commonwealth with the aim of restoring Charles II to his throne. Today it is a non-political registered charity and welcomes new members.

With over 3,000 enthusiastic amateur troops at its command, it is the largest and most experienced historical re-enactment society in Europe. Spectacular re-creations of battles, sieges and skirmishes, parades and drill displays of the **English Civil War** have raised over £1m for charity.

The **SEALED KNOT** could draw large crowds to your event with all the colour and pageantry of 17th Century warfare: uniformed and armed infantry, cavalry and dragoons, firearms, cannon, banners, baggage trains and camp followers. Promoters must guarantee a fee related to the size of the event and provide sufficient land and other campsite facilitites.

THE SEALED KNOT

The Agitant General N A J Bacon
Rock Bottom, 1 Rock Street, Croscombe,
Wells, Somerset BA5 3QT   0749 342202

English Civil War Society

The King's Army   **The Roundhead Association**

The **ENGLISH CIVIL WAR SOCIETY** exists to educate, research and raise interest in a fascinating period of British history, and in doing has raised thousands of pounds for local and national charitable causes. We are a treasure-chest of expertise for those seeking information, and are a highly-creditable lobby in areas where our heritage is threatened - one campaign saved the Littlecote House armoury for the nation.

The Society co-ordinates annual battle re-enactments, *Living History* displays and *Demonstrations of Drill*. Volunteers from the King's Army and the Roundhead Association have fought it out in films and TV serials, including *By the Sword Divided*.

The King's Army holds an annual Whitehall march in January, the anniversary of the death of Charles I.

The Society publishes material of interest to teachers, students and members of the public who share our interest in the period. For information on membership of either Army, or the Friends of the English Civil War Society, and of publications, send a large sae to:

70 Hailgate, Howden, N. Humberside DN14 7ST

0430 430695

THE ENGLISH TOURIST BOARD

*Major events and special exhibitions are being
staged across the country to mark the
350th Anniversary of the English Civil War*

Contact local Tourist Information Centres for details

English ⌗ Heritage

Historic Buildings & Monuments Commission for England

Step back in time at an English Heritage Special Event or Civil War presentation to bring this decisive era of history alive. Many of our 350 historic properties played significant and strategic roles during this turbulent and bloody period.

Ashby de la Zouch, Barnard, Beeston, Bolsover, Deal, Donnington, Carisbrooke, Carlisle, Chester, Colchester, Goodrich, Helmsley, Hurst, Launceston, Restormel, Scarborough, Pendennis, Penrith, Portland, Rochester and **Sherborne** castles are among those in our care besieged, stormed, captured, recaptured or 'slighted' during the War.

For a free Events Diary and details of membership:

ENGLISH HERITAGE

Special Events Unit, Keysign House
429 Oxford Street, London WIR 2HD

071 973 3457

NATIONAL PORTRAIT GALLERY

The National Portrait Gallery houses one of the finest collections of early 17th century portraits. Within the Gallery, just off Trafalgar Square, many of those involved in the Civil War are represented: *Charles I* and *Oliver Cromwell*, *Strafford* and *Laud*, *Prince Rupert* and *Thomas Fairfax*, as well as those associated with them in the armies, in Parliament and in the country, during this period.

To commemorate this 350th anniversary, the National Portrait Gallery has published a postcard pack *Charles I and the Civil War* containing twelve of the Gallery's significant portraits. These include Charles I by *Gerrit van Honthorst 1628*; Lord George Stuart by *Anthony van Dyck*; Oliver Cromwell by *Samuel Cooper 1649* and Elizabeth Claypole by *John Michael Wright 1658*.

Available from the NPG bookshop, or by mail order from the Publications Dept. Price £2.50 + p&p

NATIONAL PORTRAIT GALLERY
St Martin's Place, London WC2H OHE

071 306 0055

NATIONAL ARMY MUSEUM
CHELSEA

Packed with colour, history and drama the galleries of the National Army Museum tell the soldier's story in peace and war. How they lived, worked and fought from Tudor times to the present day.

The treasures on display include weapons, medals, paintings, uniforms and silver. Videos, models, reconstructions and a host of unusual personal relics bring the soldier's story vividly to life.

Open seven days a week 10am - 5.30pm
Closed 24-26 December, 1 January, Good Friday, May Public Holiday, admission free

The National Army Museum
Royal Hospital Road,
Chelsea,
London SW3 4HT
Tel 071 730 0717

NATIONAL MARITIME MUSEUM
THE QUEEN'S HOUSE

Built on the site of the old palace of Placentia, birthplace of Henry VIII and Elizabeth I, Inigo Jones' Palladian masterpiece was designed in 1616 for Anne of Denmark, wife of James I. It became Henrietta Maria's 'House of Delights' in the 1630s, and she returned to Greenwich as Queen Dowager in 1660.

1990 saw completion of the restoration to its 17th century glory, with every effort made 'to achieve historical accuracy'.

The royal apartments contain a unique collection of Stuart portraits by Mytens, Van Dyck, Dobson, Lely and others, including James I, Charles I, Prince Henry, Elizabeth of Bohemia, Henrietta Maria, Prince Rupert and James II.
The ground floor maritime display includes seascapes of the Dutch School, navigational instruments and ships' models.

THE NATIONAL MARITIME MUSEUM
Greenwich, London SE10 9NF
081 858 4422

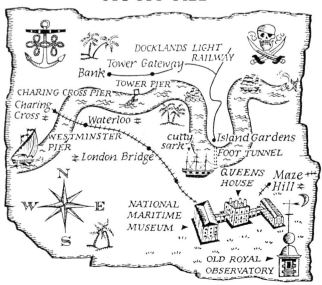

ROYAL ARMOURIES

'On the March   1642-1651'

TRAVELLING EXHIBITION OF ARMS & ARMOUR
shown for the first time outside London
sponsored by **THE TIMES**

HULL: April/May - COVENTRY: June/July
NOTTINGHAM: 1 Aug - 20 Sept - WORCESTER: 26 Sept - 3 Jan 1993
CIRENCESTER: 9 Jan - 28 March 1993

The Royal Armouries is the national museum of arms and armour and Britain's oldest museum.   Its internationally renowned collection developed from the arsenal of medieval kings, and during the Civil War the Tower was the Parlimentarian's key arsenal and stronghold.

Through the arms and armour of kings, commanders and ordinary soldiers, the exhibition will present the realities and reveal the myths of the conflict of Cavaliers and Roundheads.

A facsimile edition of **The Times**, as it might have appeared in December, 1642 and a definitive wallchart are on sale at the exhibition venues.

Permanent collection

HM TOWER OF LONDON EC3N 4AB
071 480 6358

BROUGHTON CASTLE Banbury Oxfordshire

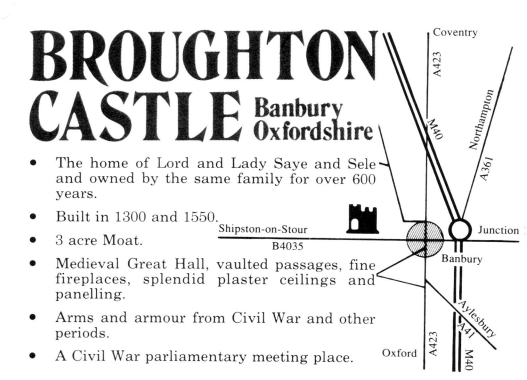

- The home of Lord and Lady Saye and Sele and owned by the same family for over 600 years.

- Built in 1300 and 1550.

- 3 acre Moat.

- Medieval Great Hall, vaulted passages, fine fireplaces, splendid plaster ceilings and panelling.

- Arms and armour from Civil War and other periods.

- A Civil War parliamentary meeting place.

Map labels: Coventry, A423, Northampton, M40, A361, Shipston-on-Stour, B4035, Junction, Banbury, Aylesbury, A41, A423, M40, Oxford

BROUGHTON CASTLE

William Fiennes, the eighth baron was created first Viscount Saye and Sele in 1624. Known as 'Old Subtlety' he played host to Pym, Hampden, and others in the years leading up to the Long Parliament, and one of his four soldier sons was Colonel Nathaniel Fiennes. Charles I in 1639 reproached Lord Saye as 'averse to all my proceedings', and Clarendon found him 'a man of great parts and the highest ambition.'

Gardens and park - tea room and shop - free car park.

Open: mid-May - mid-September 2.00-5.00pm
Wednesdays & Sundays. Also Thursdays in July-August.

BROUGHTON CASTLE
Banbury 0295 262624/812027

NOTTINGHAMSHIRE IN THE CIVIL WAR

Nottinghamshire's heritage is integral to the Civil War and its outbreak 350 years ago.

On 22 August 1642, Charles I raised his Royal Standard outside Nottingham Castle, thus marking the start of the Civil War. For nine tumultuous years the people and places of this key county played a major role in the conflict.

Follow the *Nottinghamshire and the Civil War Trail* through charming countryside studded with reminders of the conflict to the town-scapes of **Nottingham, Newark** and **Southwell**, cornerstones of the English Civil War.

Discover beautiful, historic Nottinghamshire and choose where to stay from a range of quality accommodation packages.

For a free Nottinghamshire Visitor Information Pack, and the *Nottinghamshire and the Civil War* leaflet, please contact:

The County Tourism Office
Trent Bridge House, Fox Road, West Bridgford,
Nottingham NG2 6BJ

0602 774422

Nottinghamshire **County Council**
Leisure Services/Tourism

SULGRAVE Manor

THE HOME OF GEORGE WASHINGTON'S ANCESTORS

Sulgrave Manor appears in Domesday Book, and as a religious property in 1539 was surrendered to Henry VIII who sold it to Lawrence Washington, builder of the present Tudor manor.

The Washington's were royalists, no republicanism yet, and Colonel Henry Washington fought at Edgehill, led his dragoons at the storming of Bristol in 1643, and in the attack on Stockport during the Marston Moor campaign. An uncle was governor of Oxford, and his cousin, Colonel John Washington, sailed to Virginia in 1656 to found the American branch.

Special events - cavalry demonstrations - re-enactments living history - and the annual **Siege of Sulgrave 1644**

OPEN: 1 March - 31 December.
Closed January - open February by appointment.

The Colonial Dames of America have generously endowed the Manor House and co-operate with the Board in its upkeep.

Sulgrave, Nr. Banbury, Oxon OX17 2SD 029576 0205

Edgehill Battle Museum

WEAPONS

ARMOUR

STOCKS

PILLORY

GIFTS

BOOKS

SOUVENIRS

MUSIC

MAPS

UNIFORMS

DIORAMAS

MODELS

CAVALRY

PIKEMEN

MUSKETEERS

DRAGOONS

GUNNERS

CAMP FOLLOWERS

Edgehill Battle Museum.
The Estate Yard
Farnborough Hall, Farnborough,
Banbury.
Oxfordshire OX17 1DU
Telephone: (0295) 89593
Evenings (0926) 313677

Office/Weekdays (0926) 332213

Open Wednesday and Saturday
afternoons April to September inclusive.

2pm to 6pm

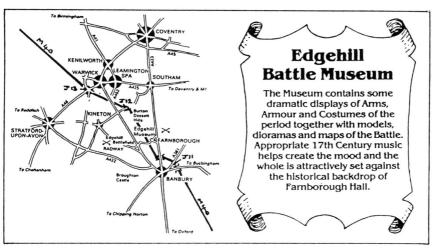

Edgehill Battle Museum

The Museum contains some
dramatic displays of Arms,
Armour and Costumes of the
period together with models,
dioramas and maps of the Battle.
Appropriate 17th Century music
helps create the mood and the
whole is attractively set against
the historical backdrop of
Farnborough Hall.

*Battlefield Tours of Edgehill and Audio Visual presentations
for groups by prior arrangement.
Tel: (0926) 313677 (evenings) or (0926) 332213 (weekdays)*

Northamptonshire
Rose of the Shires

'BY THE SWORD DIVIDED'

Rockingham Castle provided the authentic backdrop for BBC TV's tale of civil strife, *By the Sword Divided* and is just one of the many attractions in the County that are steeped in history, many of them playing a significant role in the Civil War. The 'King's Walk' in the grounds of **Holdenby House** commemorates the time when Charles I was held captive there in 1647 and one of the most decisive battles of the Civil War also took place in Northamptonshire; the **Battle of Naseby** in 1645 signalled the decline of the Royalist cause.

For further information about these historic sites and the many attractions for visitors to Northamptonshire, please telephone or write to:

The Tourism Unit, Northamptonshire Enterprise Agency Limited, Elgin House, Northampton NN1 5AR   Telephone 0604 37401

ROCKINGHAM CASTLE

Arnescote of the BBC TV series *By the Sword Divided*

Built by William the Conqueror and royal fortress for many centuries. Granted to Edward Watson by Henry VIII in 1530 and, apart from a brief period during the Civil War when the Castle was besieged and garrisoned by the Parliamentarians, occupied by his descendants ever since. Norman towers, Tudor Great Hall, Long Gallery, Brewhouse and Bakery

Armour & portrait collections, spiral staircase to Salvin's Flag Tower

12 acres of beautiful grounds - Rose Garden and Wild Garden

Twice winner of the Sandford Award for Heritage Education

homemade cream teas - gift shop

Open Easter Sunday - 30 September, Thursdays & Sundays, Bank Holiday Mondays and Tuesdays following. Tuesdays in August only. 1.30 - 5.30pm. Groups at other times by appointment

ROCKINGHAM CASTLE

on A6003, 2 miles north of Corby, Northants
0536 770240

York Visitor and Conference Bureau

York was King Charles' key city in the North, but was besieged and taken by Parliament after Marston Moor in 1644. Thanks to Sir Thomas Fairfax, a proud Yorkshireman, little damage was done to the Minster or York's historic buildings and medieval churches.

Walk the **Walls**, visit the **King's Manor, St William's College**, once the King's printing press, **Clifford's Tower, Guildhall**, the **Castle Museum**, the **Yorkshire Museum** - and incomparable **York Minster**.

YORK CITY ART GALLERY's internationally important collection dates from 1350 to the present day; it also has a unique collection of paintings, prints and drawings with specific York and Yorkshire connections. Among the portraits relating to the Fairfax family, are **Ferdinando, second Lord Fairfax** by *Edward Bower*, and a lead bust of his son, **Sir Thomas Fairfax**.

Details of places to visit & accommodation from:

YORK VISITOR & CONFERENCE BUREAU
The Travel Office, 6 Rougier Street York YO1 IJA
0904 620557

WARWICK CASTLE
The finest mediaeval castle in England

Britain's most visited stately home, soaring above the Avon, is set in over sixty acres of beautiful grounds which include the famed rose garden - and the haunted Watergate Tower.

Robert Greville, second Baron Brooke, garrisoned Warwick Castle for the Parliament at the outbreak of the Civil War and his regiment of Purplecoats fought at Edgehill. Brooke was killed at the siege of Lichfield in 1643, shot in the head by a sniper from the cathedral tower, and his armour is preserved in the Castle, along with Cromwell's death mask.

A new tour was added to the attractions in 1992 to commemorate the Castle's involvement in the Civil War. Advance booking is required, and it is available all the year round *except* school half terms and Bank Holiday weekends.

Warwick Castle, Warwickshire CV34 4QU

0926 495421

Officers and Regiments of the Royalist Army

VOLUME 4
S - Z

Stuart Reid

ENGLISH CIVIL WAR
Notes & Queries

PARTIZAN PRESS

SCOTS ARMIES
OF THE 17ᵗʰ CENTURY
1. THE ARMY OF THE
COVENANT
1639-51

STUART
REID

1: ENGLISH FOOT

Stuart Peachey & Les Prince